Cringe

Bruce Sinclair

Copyright © 2015 Bruce Sinclair

All rights reserved.

ISBN-13: 978-1516971725

ISBN-10: 1516971728

DEDICATION

To Jacqui, Sarah and Adam – serenity, courage and wisdom.

CONTENTS

Acknowledgments	i
Chapter 1	1
Chapter 2	9
Chapter 3	13
Chapter 4	19
Chapter 5	26
Chapter 6	33
Chapter 7	43
Chapter 8	48
Chapter 9	56
Chapter 10	60
Chapter 11	63
Chapter 12	72
Chapter 13	77
Chapter 14	80
Chapter 15	86
Chapter 16	92
Chapter 17	96
Chapter 18	100
Chapter 19	107
Chapter 20	113

Bruce Sinclair

Chapter 21	119
Chapter 22	128
Chapter 23	133
Chapter 24	141
Chapter 25	147
Chapter 26	150
Chapter 27	157
Chapter 28	165
Chapter 29	173
Chapter 30	178
Chapter 31	185
Epilogue	197

ACKNOWLEDGMENTS

Thanks to librarians the world over, physical and virtual, for their guidance, rigorous cataloguing expertise and advice which facilitated the research for this novel. Though The Morocco Manuscripts are fictional they contain extant historical documents or adaptations thereof. The sources of these include: Project Gutenburg, particularly: *Captain Cook's Journal During the First Voyage Round the World*, parts of which formed the basis for Francis Austen's log entries; *A Complete Account of the Settlement at Port Jackson* and *A Narrative of the Expedition to Botany Bay* by Watkin Tench were plundered to write the letters from him; *The Diary and Letters of Madame D'Arblay* provided the details on Fanny Burney and the extract on her thoughts concerning Talleyrand. Thanks to Brian Southam for his article *Jane Austen's Sailor brothers* for providing historical detail and from which I lifted the text of Francis' biographical extract and letter on pages 83 and 84, available at: http://www.jasna.org/persuasions/printed/number25/southam.pdf. Many thanks to Jenny Talia for permission to use her lyric *Should I Fuck on First Dates*. The real Tora Hymen continues to perform this in bars along Oxford Street in Sydney.

Finally, many thanks to the following for much needed encouragement, thoughts and advice on early drafts of this work: Ann Fazey, Osian Barnes, Jackie Evans, Peter Marshall, Alan Graham, Louise Disley, Libby Porteous, Michael Cook and especially to Alice Grundy, David Henley, Sam Van and the other writers who met monthly upstairs at Gleebooks, without whom I would never have started this work.

CHAPTER ONE

Six feet four in stocking feet, Harvey Dominic Premnas was a magnificent sight on a Friday night. As he enjoyed the play of ideas in literature; the unexpected juxtaposition that jarred insight, so he sought to bring this to his manner of dress. Though tonight he was facing a dilemma. Should he go for uber-surban Sydney or slut military? He heard the strike of steel stilettos ringing down the wet corridor and caught a whiff of urine and something else. He turned to see Tora standing in the dressing room doorway.

'Still deciding? Go for the blue, it matches your eyes,' she said.

So that is how he arrived at tonight's ensemble. A 1960's Royal Australian Air Force officer's tunic, cinched at the waist, with matching peaked cap, the air force blue set off fetchingly by a carnelian toxic red, bobbed wig. To enhance his Olympian frame he wore satin-top stockings and suspenders, cami-knicker briefs, and a pair of thigh length, black leather stirrup boots. He was in Heaven. He struck a vampish pose in the full length mirror and picking up a riding crop, cracked it against the boots. Ride 'em cowboy.

It was his last night in Sydney before leaving for the UK and, expecting that he'd have to tone it down for the Brits, he was determined that tonight's should be an exceptional showing. Though he planned to pack this particular ensemble for a night's clubbing at *Trans-mission* in London, he thought that rural Yorkshire might be less tolerant. He didn't expect the locals at The Ferret and Trouser Leg in Cragg would greet him with the same wave of whistled admiration he regularly received upon parading onto the stage at The Stonewall Hotel, where he was hosting tonight's show with Tora Hymen and Carmen Geddit headlining. It might also get in the way of being taken seriously. So the ensemble would stay in the bottom of the suitcase until London and he resolved to behave in the sober manner he expected was necessary to impress the uptight rural Brits.

He had been awarded a visiting fellowship at Laudanum Grange International Research Centre to work on his PhD: *'Wise Children and Foolish Fathers: the Learian Gaze'*, a rattle bag and inter-textual mash up of Angela Carter, Jane Austen and Shakespeare. Though there was a respectable pedigree of gender bending in literature; *Orlando* and *Twelfth Night* sprung to mind, to be presented with six feet ten of towering transvestite was probably not the best way to establish yourself as a serious scholar on your first international outing. So the academic staff at Laudanum Grange would be left in the dark regarding this particular passion.

'History is remembered, the future is here', reads the slogan above the porticoed entrance to The Stonewall Hotel, one of the few buildings to retain its original neo-classical frontage on Sydney's Oxford Street. It refers to the riot in the Stonewall Bar, Lower Manhattan, in the early hours of June 28, 1969, the day after Judy Garland's funeral. Police, practiced in hassling homosexuals, had raided the bar and the patrons' resistance was viewed as the touchstone for the militant gay rights movement. For Harvey Premnas, the future was no longer here, but set to arrive with him in England in twenty-four hours' time.

He was sat on a beer keg in the poky dressing room behind the stage. It held a crammed, bountiful display of neon-candy wigs, pots of foundation goo, musical instruments, makeup, racks of dresses and assorted costumes. The house band had arrived and they were all waiting to go on. He read some of the new graffiti:

Drink, feck, arse, girls.
Eat, drink and do Mary, for Tamara's all mine.
When Eddie Izzard is naked is he still a transvestite?

As he sat and pondered the last of these he felt a tap on his shoulder. He turned and started upon finding Peter's flaccid penis there.

'Arrgh, Christ mate.'

'Aw, gan on, ya kna ya wan'it,' Peter said, laughing.

Harvey Premnas jumped up and away from him. Not upset, just startled. Peter was the overweight bass player in the house band and it was not unusual for him to carry on in this way. He had a wide repertoire of indecent acts: grabbing your crotch from behind; tripping you back against his outstretched leg, falling on you and tickling you senseless; lunging and trying to stick his long tongue in your mouth. The strength that he had developed in his forearms and hands through bass playing meant that it was like being attacked by a randy gorilla. Harvey Premnas explained this behaviour as the actions of a man in denial. So sexually hampered by his upbringing in Newcastle, in the North of England, that he continued to deny he was gay even when it was least necessary to do so; engaging in this sexual rough-and-tumble to show that he was so comfortable in his sexuality, he could only be a hetero-macho man. When in fact, he was trying to pass by pretending he was not trying to pass, and in so doing, obtaining some small frisson of sexual satisfaction. Harvey Premnas played along with this charade because, despite disliking the behaviour, he was very fond of Peter and it was done with some humour. On this occasion he had silently mugged 'watch this' to the rest of the band as he tip toed toward Harvey's back, unzipping his banana yellow jump suit and pulling out his member.

'Alreet, alreet, gan canny hinny,' he said, laughing, redressing himself. 'Ya kna I divn't kna what yees're all upity aboot, I'd have thought you'd like a plonka on yer shoulder.'

When Harvey Premnas had first met Peter he had failed to understand most of what he said, assuming that he was speaking one of the Scandinavian languages rather than English. However, with the constant exposure ensured through sharing an apartment, and the help of *Geordie Shore*, with Peter translating, he had become familiar with the accent. The above translated as: 'OK, calm down. I do not know what the fuss is about. I would have thought you would appreciate a cock on your shoulder.' Once, having been inspired by meeting Peter, and in a vain attempt to stimulate some appreciation of his scholarly prowess, he had read up on the socio-phonological roots of Geordie and tried to enlighten Peter:

'It belongs to the non-rhotic accent group, excluding the sound /r/ from the syllable coda before a consonant or prosodic break.'

Peter squinted and frowned at him. 'Non-rhotic eh? Bloody eerotic more like, wha' wi aal them vikin's invadin', rapin' ahn pillagin an all that.'

Harvey Premnas sighed, however, he had to acknowledge some accuracy in Peter's analysis. There was historical and linguistic evidence of the association, with the phrase 'gan hyem', easily understood as meaning 'go home' in Norwegian.

With the band at their places on stage Harvey Premnas arrived at the mike and, affecting an arch camp delivery, said:

'Good evening. Well, as you all know, tonight is my last for some time. I'm off to England tomorrow.'

Shave and a hair-cut   two bits

, played by an Alembic bass.

'Thank you Peter,' he said turning and smiling. 'So, with England expecting, let's give a big hand for Tora Hymen to do her duty, singing, *Should I fuck on first dates?*, Tora Hymen ladies and gents.'

Clapping he moved to the side as Tora, Tiffany-blue foot high beehive, Karen Millen sequined, little black dress and black, peep toed,

11cm heels, sashays through the red curtains.

Teeth and smiles, she waves and blows kisses as the band play a medium paced tango with a Greek feel, mandolin and doo-wop backing vocals.

'I'd just hit my teens, I was still pretty green, About boys and the ways of the world, All the questions and doubts, Trying to figure it out, Just what were the rules for the girl?' Tora, resplendent, all Liza Minelli Cabaret, gestures the suggestive lyric. Delineating her décolletage with poise in her fingers. Scratches her head quizzically, spreads her arms and shrugs her shoulders. She moves into a 1950s, lizard lounge, smoochy-cooch shuffle across the stage. *'There's a boy in me class, Who got the courage to ask, Would I go to the school dance with him? I blushed and said yes, Then what I did next, Was call up and ask all me friends.'* Hands on hips, shimmies her breasts and holds a thumb and finger phone to her ear.

'Should we touch on first dates? And does that mean he likes me? Should we go to first base? Whatever that might be. And is it OK, To slip me hand in his pocket? 'Cos I never felt...., A willy before.................. Or will he ask me to stop it?'

'It didn't take long, To learn what's going on, And just what makes a man tick, 'Cos when it comes to girls, They see the world, Through the eye of their dick.' Points to her mid-temple, nodding. Ticks her finger at the audience. Points to her eye, then to the end of a large, imaginary penis. *'So at the end of the night, When it's time to decide, Do I go home, or go home with him, It's all up to me, So what will it be? Will we both lose or both have a win?'* The band is relaxed, running through a comfortable groove. Tora turns, batts two inch lashes, winks, and draws a line toward the chorus.

'Should I fuck on first dates? Should I stay 'til the morning? Will I remember his name? Was I just drunk and horny? Would I see him again, If he says he likes me? If he only rates...., Less than an eight............Not fucking likely!' Raises her middle finger, spoken as an outback ocker ranger asked if the queen would visit.

The drums cut and the music slows to half time. A Hammond organ swirl is released from the Celestian speakers. *'So when I'm old and I'm grey, And I've seen better days, And my tits and arse start headin' south, And the men in me life, Are in worse state than I'm in, Plagued by the droop and the gout.'* Angelic vocals soar. Spoken more plaintively; reminiscing. Salad days; transvestite youth, not forgotten but longing, a memory for the flesh. *'Well I'd like to think that some of me bits, Will still work as good as they do now,'* She points to the significant proximities. *'So when the men come a calling, Or get wheeled to me door, I'll let 'em in an' then help 'em out.'* Throws a fuck off air-wank as if from a car window then wipes deposits from the corners of her mouth. The music slows further as it slopes toward the chorus.

'Should I suck on first dates? Might not be here tomorra,' Shakes her head sadly.

'Should I spit it out? Or just gargle and swalla?' Lets the space of her memory

play about a past now gone, with a body less able yet desires still raging. '*If he still gets it up, Aw then I'll do the rest, I'll dim down the lights, And take out me teeth, And gob him to death.* Mimes toothless gums and a deep throated fellatio.

To applause, spins, throws a pose and with arms raised and wrists akimbo, she turns and leaves the stage.

'Ah don't geddit,' said Peter polishing down his expensive Alembic bass guitar. 'Ah don't get why you'd wanna gan all that way to Old Blighty to get a butchers at some old boooks. Ahn ya kna, it'll feel like winter there. It'll be all cold 'n' gloomy, lucky if ya get more than fourteen degrees. Ahn there's the rain, ya kna about the rain divn't yas? More rain than you're expected to have in a month, in two days. Why, I divn't kna why you'd gan for that.'

Harvey Premnas pulled off the carnelian red wig revealing short black hair and placed it on a polystyrene head, whittled to a close likeness of Tony Abbott wearing lip stick. Looking down smiling, he put his hands on his knees and shook his head. 'Ah Peter, Peter, I'm not going for bad weather mate, I'm going for the books and collections.'

'Why, that's something else I divn't get. You gan all that way, twenty four hoors cramped on a smelly plane, all for old booooks, when you could simply walk down the street ahn by a new one at Dymocks. Ahn there's the money. You'd save cash that way too.'

He placed the bass in its case and snapped the lid closed.

Harvey Premnas, peeled off the oversized eyelashes, clumped with mascara. 'It's not the same Peter, yeah I could buy a copy of *Sense and Sensibility*, or whatever here, but there I get to study the actual manuscript, see what was crossed out, the marginalia,'

A shadowed wrinkle crossed Peter's brow.

'Notes in the margins,' Peter nodded. 'I'll get to read Austen's correspondence too. In her letters I'll be able to look for first hand evidence about how she felt about her father, not just someone else's opinion. And the collections at Laudanum Grange are world class, they've got items that no one else has, and some of it hasn't even been studied properly yet, especially the Morocco Manuscripts. So that gives me an edge, that's the thing about a PhD, it has to be original, you need an edge.'

'Wass tha Morocco Manuscripts?'

'A couple of years ago Deirdre La Faye, a renowned Austen scholar, was doing some research at The National Library of Morocco. Nobody's quite sure how, but a couple of Austen's letters to her older brother Francis, he was in the navy, found their way there. The dates suggest most likely when he was in the Med in 1805 picking up provisions from North Africa. Anyhow, so Deirdre La Faye searches the catalogue and calls up these letters from the stacks. The librarian can't find them, searches all over, not there. You can imagine, this is baad news,'

Peter nodded. 'Aye, though ah aalways thought nee news was good news. Carry on.'

'No. A national library loosing important documents. Bad news. So, as the librarian's searching around she sees a leather folder slipped down between the stack and the wall. Well battered. Stained and crushed up by the stack being rolled back and forth against it. She pulls it out. It's got no ID card on it, but they're just loose anyway, so it could have fallen off. She looks inside. Sees "Francis William Austen, Captain" signed on one of the manuscripts, so figures, well maybe these are the letters and they just got shoved in with some other stuff. Takes it up for Deirdre La Faye to look at. Explains that she's not sure if this is what she want's 'cos the card's missing. Deirdre starts to look through the folder and, well, the rest is history. She's come across previously unknown papers, letters, notes and manuscripts belonging to Francis Austen, somehow lost, but which apparently include a detailed account of daily life growing up in the rectory at Steventon at the same time as his sister Jane,' said Harvey Premnas.

'Sounds a bit Indiana Jones to me, holy grail, woooooo,' acting out a ghostly pose, 'watch oot for the Nazis.'

'No Peter, seriously mate, it's really exciting. Accounts of family life in the Austen household are very sparse, there's not much known about it. And though she uncovered it, Deirdre La Faye wasn't able to study the documents because they were in such poor condition, really fragile, some of them fallen apart. They've only recently been restored and conserved by Laudanum Grange. I'll be among the first to look at them and they might reveal new details about her relationship with her father and mother.'

'Fathas an' muthas, it's aalways fathas and muthas.'

It was upon reading of the *Francis Austen Morocco Manuscripts* and speculation on their content, that Harvey Premnas had finally formulated his PhD thesis.

For some time he'd pondered the micro-political, economic and emotional relationships of the Austen household. Her father was the rector at Steventon, not particularly well paid even in more pious times, with the money stretched thinner by the need to feed the large Austen brood. When her father died things got worse, with her mother and sisters saved financially by her brother Edward. He gave them a cottage on the Chawton estate that he had inherited from his adopted but childless parents, Thomas and Catherine Knight.

This is the cottage at the centre of the Austen industry today. Turned into a museum, tourists can ogle the desk where *Pride and Prejudice* was written and buy an Austen action figure. However, what you don't get, is that whilst today it appears as a quaint, well maintained and brightly decorated country cottage, in an expensive Des-Res part of Hampshire, in Austen's time it was a leaky, cold, peasant's hovel, in the middle of nowhere, with the road outside ankle deep in horse shit. You'd have thought that six well off brothers could have clubbed together and provided their two sisters and mother with something a little better. This had puzzled Harvey Premnas and he had wondered whether the answer lay somewhere with their now deceased father. The traditional accounts all pointed to a close, nurturing and creative bond with her father. Had these been sanitised? Edited to make the father appear more palatable? Would the patriarchal conventions of the time have indulged a public record where the venerated positions of father and rector appeared deeply flawed? These accounts were in stark contrast to the father figures in Austen's novels, who were invariably weak, flawed and unreliable. Was Austen's father more like these? Harvey Premnas knew that she had felt unhappy when her father had moved the family to Bath, wouldn't this resentment not be resonant somewhere in her writing? The son who was perhaps best positioned to help them in 1805, when her father died, was Henry, a wealthy London banker and businessman. Yet he doesn't, and goes on to become a failed banker. The brother, George, is thought to have been retarded and the other, James, appears as a melancholic, jealous of his sister's literary prowess. Also, wouldn't the close, creative, nurturing bonds stressed in the popular accounts have been present for the brothers too? If so, wouldn't this have led them to rally round in adversity? Imprudent finances, mental instability, depression, jealousy, inability to care for their siblings and mother, where were the antecedents to these?

For Harvey Premnas the accepted accounts felt a little too pat, one dimensional, lacking the short comings and saddened illusions that can grow upon coming to understand a parent's flawed humanity. He too had had a close relationship with his father, but it hadn't stopped them coming to blows on occasions, particularly when he had encountered Harvey's creative relationship with his mother's wardrobe. In Kalgoorlie, a town where men were men and so were most of the women, there wasn't a lot of space for the artistic soul to come to terms with its expression; a misjudged interest in make-up or an appreciative gaze at a Gucci handbag, was enough to arouse suspicions of perversion and the attentions of tongues which had harried some out of town, and some out of life. Harvey had seen occasional inklings in his father that mining and the narrow town hadn't always been things that he'd clung to out of desperation, but then like the heat and close proximity of opinions that stilled life, he'd let them seep like a beaten pulse through the family home. When Harvey had heard that the Morocco Manuscripts contained hither to unknown accounts of Austen family life, he'd thought that maybe, as escaping Kalgoorlie had released him, so this could be the key to unlocking his other puzzle, his edge.

He had also theorised along more psychoanalytical routes, trying to trace the ethereal evidence of an unconscious influence in the work of other writers, believing their creativity led to a particularly sensitive ability to attune with the tensions in Austen's writing. He conceived that the strains between her literary rendition of fatherhood, the supposed creative nurturing bond of her own father, and the nature of her brothers, had actually been picked up, reflected and refracted in the writing of more contemporary authors; that unconsciously these inconsistencies had set up resonance in the writing of later writers who had read Austen. One writer in particular that he intended to focus on was Angela Carter. In works like *The Magic Toy Shop*, *The Bloody Chamber* and *Wise Children*, a number of unreliable and threatening fathers featured. It was Harvey Premnas's hunch that Carter had intuitively known that Austen was reflecting more of the reality of her life in her work; that Austen actually grew up in an overly repressed, controlling, dysfunctional and patriarchal household, which was trying to pass the test of respectability by presenting the opposite to the world; and that Carter's writing and reimagined faery tales were also ways of allowing Austen's repression, with the reality of her life only echoed in her writing, to live again through a vicarious and sisterly endeavour. That somehow Carter had known. Studying The Morocco Manuscripts would be an important part of moving toward a proof, or otherwise, of this conjecture.

CHAPTER TWO

Pamela Larrup marched up the steep gravel drive that ran up to the porch of Laudanum Grange International Study Centre. It was a grey, rainy Monday in late June with a cold blustery wind driving the drizzle across the ling grass moors. She had slept in and though she was not late there was something in her stride that suggested annoyance. Somehow the sense of order in the world had been disrupted and it was tilting at her in an accusing manner. She was straining to carry her duffle bag which held the seventy applications for the visiting fellowship program. She paused, grabbed the scruff of the bag and hauled it higher up her shoulder. She intended to dispatch the applications by mid-morning, culling them to the dozen or so she would be prepared to discuss with Rick Callow, the centre's CEO, Rachel Unthank, Professor of Comparative Literature at Northrop University and Giles Skeffington, the librarian. Rick would do as he was told, however she could not say the same about Unthank, who sometimes held to faddy and unsubstantiated opinions that she thought better left unsaid.

    She had on occasion replayed conversations she had had with Unthank, cutting and editing them in a manner that left her superior sense of the literary canon triumph. Unthank's passing literary fads were no match for the timeless art of punctuation and sentence analysis, which were the craft that would launch her reputation across the academic community, securing her tenure at a more serious place than Laudanum Grange. To her mystification Unthank appeared unable to resist picking up these fads. They seemed to hold the same appeal for her as wide eyed homeless kittens. She imagined the strays mewling up at Unthank as she grabbed the wrought iron handle of the oak front door, twisted sharply and heaved it open.

The top floor of Laudanum Grange housed the office spaces that had been converted from the former servants' quarters and had the neutral air of a smart hotel. Inoffensive beige walls and dried flower arrangements. Pamela Larrup was sat at her desk with her back to the window looking out across the well-tended lawns and formal beds of the grounds which were surrounded by a small wooded area and a high stone wall, then out to the sombre cloud scape above the Yorkshire Moors.

The building had been converted to a library, museum and study centre as one of the projects of an eccentric Irish millionaire and now housed a growing collection of eighteenth century rare books and special collections including original works and paraphernalia belonging to Jane Austen, Walter Scott and Maria Edgeworth. Recently it had been taken over and subsumed by Northrop University's English Department. Architecturally it was a mess. The seventeenth century manorial hall had seen a number of gauche additions as the family that owned it had prospered and grown, only to slowly degenerate once the aristocracy had given way to industry and business. With the recent addition of the Grimalkin Library and Museum, a glass and steel tower that appeared to have lost its sense of balance, hanging in a postmodern slump against the manor hall, the building had become a bleak statement to monstrosity.

Pamela Larrup had first seen the house in a magazine article about the growing stock of minor stately homes and grand houses that had outlived their occupant's ability to maintain them. Some of these had been saved by TV executives creating variations on property makeover programs; sending overbearing and strident celebrities as business developers to slap around and ridicule the hapless heirs. Pamela Larrup enjoyed a secret vicarious thrill at the faux jeopardy injected by the celebrities; bringing the minor aristocratic dolts to their senses just in time with an injection of cold business sense. More order. She had become particularly interested when she had read that Laudanum Grange was to be restored and conserved prior to housing a number of international collections, with an ambition to become the pre-eminent centre for the study of Jane Austen's work. She had visited the place shortly after it opened in 2008 and had been charmed by the different levels, switch backs and architectural stutters as you passed from one building to the later additions. It seemed to her the epitome of an English grand house; quirky, with surprises that to her suggested wit. A perfect building to house a Jane Austen collection. She had been appointed as Director of Research a year later and now, having been in post for four years, she considered that there was little more the place could offer her.

She was quickly scanning the fellowship applications, allocating them to a maybe pile or the bin. One of them in particular made her scoff, *"Wise children and foolish fathers: The Learian gaze"*. It placed the writer Angela Carter, a so called 'feminist', who she believed wrote fairy tales of all things, in the same academic company as Jane Austen. As a serious scholar of Austen's writing style, her PhD had been '*Pride and Punctuation: Dashes, Semicolons, and Inverted Commas: Austenian Punctuation Conventions and Their Meaning*', she could see little merit in the proposed research schedule. It was also from an Australian at the University of Sydney. Not a city she cared for. She had been there once and it had condemned itself by its own uncivilised behaviour.

She had stayed one night, stopping over on her way to deliver a paper at the Jane Austen Society of New Zealand's Wellington conference. She recalled the hotel she had stayed in, 'Rent room by hour', on a hand written sign beside the door. Good, cheap. She had always appreciated a bargain. Daughter of a minister of The Kirk in Berwick-upon Tweed, she had been brought up to appreciate a finely wrought balance sheet. Time and the home exchequer were two things she measured with the dour patience of a priest. The overnight stop-over in Sydney had been the highly reasonable price to pay for a very cheap flight. Comfort and ease were something she was quite willing to forgo, although she had allowed herself the guilty indulgence of a cheap bed for the night.

She had got off the train at King's Cross station. Jet lagged, sweating, labouring under the weight of an unwieldy back pack, she bustled along the busy humid street, overtaking rackety looking groups of skinny old men in shorts and flip-flops. It had started to rain and the neon lights smudged across her vision. She pulled her large floppy hat closer onto her head. A tall woman in high heels and a tight fitting dress approached her from under a shop awning.

'Pussy darling?'

She shook her head and bustled on. Cats? Cats. Loafers of the animal world, mewling, ungrateful, and why anyone out here would think she looked like a person with an interest in adding a cat to her baggage was beyond her. Further down the street she was approached by another woman.

'Would ya like a lady?'

'What?' With a moment's pause it dawned on her that cats were not the subject on offer. 'Wha...what do you think you are doing?' she said, in a mildly outraged border Scots brogue. 'I am a respectable scholar and a woman, this is disgusting.' She stomped off down the street to the hotel.

'Phew,' she said, arriving at the check in red faced. 'It's very hot and humid, are your rooms air conditioned?' she asked the man at the counter.

'No.'

Glancing down at her heavy walking boots and smiling he said, 'You should wear thongs like us, let the air in.'

Her eyes widened as she bristled to her full height of five feet two. 'I think that is none of your business.'

Though she did prefer the security of Marks and Spencers knickers to, what could only be, the discomfort of a wanton thong, she was not about to enter a conversation on the matter; a subject entirely unsuited to decent manners. That this minion assumed she was not wearing a thong and felt able to broach the matter, clearly indicated that the vulgarity of their convict past had still to be bred out of Australians.

The proposal in front of her confirmed this. Its author had clearly overreached himself. First, he had asked for access to The Francis Austen Morocco Manuscripts. As she had already readjusted her own research schedule to give the documents the appropriate early consideration necessary, this was a little presumptive, and as she was planning to study the much more important and timeless matter of punctuation style, making a comparative analysis of Francis Austen's with his sister's, her work would rightly take precedence over anything as faddy as this Australian's proposal. Second, he undoubtedly lacked the cultural sophistication to benefit from the nuanced use of the collections she expected. Fairy tales and Jane Austen? Really? One was one of the finest writers ever to compose in English, whose punctuation style, grammar and sentence formation she had analysed in minute detail, she composed herself whilst she considered the effects of a well-placed comma, a subject worthy of serious study. The other? Well, best left where it was intended. The nursery. She binned Harvey's proposal.

CHAPTER THREE

Rick Callow was suspicious of those who knew too much. It seemed to be a ruse that too many people used in place of forming the type of authentic connection that was the epitome of his management style. It got in the way of that true communication that he so prized. Not for him the bamboozling overreach, arcane depths and academic terminology of specialisms that seemed to go beyond anything worthy of understanding. No, for him to be seen to know such stuff would be to become the subject of his own suspicion and, he had an inkling, could be his undoing. So he had cultivated a manner of speech that made it clear that he knew nothing and could not be called upon in the matter. In this way he negotiated the tiny interactions that intruded on his way of making sure that he was not accountable for anything he was responsible for.

He had perfected a way of talking that made the air between you seem to slowly petrify; the sounds cloying in a manner that made you wish to digest your own brain; turning boredom into a weapon of self-annihilation. With this he was able to blunder through the day sure that people would agree with him simply to end the pain of sharing his company. It was also useful for cutting down his workload, meaning he need make no written record of anything he had agreed to do, since, realising that it had not been done, people would do it for themselves, wishing to avoid the degradation of another encounter. In this way he had been able to persuade himself that to know nothing, and to be able to talk about it, was an expression of his guile and superior management skills.

He liked to think that he dressed smartly, in the fashion and frugally. Today he was wearing a silver-grey, polyester suit with tan suede shoes and he had just given himself a haircut, what black hair that was left resembling an unhappy mushroom. What made this suit even more first-rate was that he had obtained it for free. He bobbed noisily about Laudanum Grange, his small feet making as much noise as possible on the flagstone corridors.

'BOGOF,' he said, pleased, as he appeared in various office doorways, showing off the front of the suit jacket to display its quality. He then skipped and waltzed away down the corridor. Having once taken dancing lessons on a Butlins holiday he enjoyed the figment that he might just be invited to perform on Strictly Ballroom one day.

He was sitting at his desk in his office, the beige walls blank, with a book case that was neatly filled with leather bound classics by eighteenth and nineteenth century authors beside the window. Giles, the librarian, was due to arrive at any moment, so he turned on his computer and tried to look busy. There was a knock on the door.

'Come in. Ahh Giles, Giles, come in, come in, just working up that idea you had for promoting the collection, what was it again?' Nodding at the blank screen not visible from Giles Skeffington's vantage point.

'Writing a newsletter for previous visiting fellows?'

'Newsletter, that's it, yeess, excellent idea, just the ticket.'

'I wanted to talk to you about security. I still can't find the first edition of *Sense and Sensibility*, I'm convinced it's been taken. I think we should ensure that the cameras in the reading rooms are actually recording, so we can check back when something like this happens,' expecting he would regret it, he asked, 'What do you think?'

'Yeess,' this could cost money and would require effort. 'Aha, now, you know I think security is something, clearly important; we should take the opportunity afforded by your very good question to think about aspiring to improve the security, although as aspirations are all very well, they also need to be ensured and encased, ahha, yes and then, and then, we ought to consider some of the synergies, moving the business practices in line with our aspirations towards a more holistic vision, that captures our aspirational security aims in a strategic manner in alignment with the planned and calculated efficiencies that could emerge through an overall corporate purpose that is neither too long in the short term, nor too short in the long term...aha, yeess, and that also could.........'

As Giles Skeffington listened he began to feel light headed, as though his body were starting to drift towards the ceiling; becoming unattached from what he was certain, moments ago, was reality. He could hear the sound that was coming from Rick Callow's mouth, indeed there were words, but they increasingly ceased to lock onto anything meaningful, they had started to become only the sound of words, and to engage with their pitch and yaw left one becoming a mind adrift. Rick Callow's face added to the effect, for though he was smiling, his features were set like a carved, smooth polished, African mask, the immobility providing no aid to interpretation. Giles Skeffington was aware that the sane thing to do, would be to ask Rick Callow what he meant, but somehow the sound and his smile anesthetized, leaving you struggling to initiate the will to act, which you knew you could, and yet as you considered trying, became lost, as you continually followed the habit of trying to make sense from the sound.

He let his gaze be taken by the titles on the book case beside the window. He had been interviewed by Rick Callow in this office several years ago and the range of titles had provided him with his gambit.

'That's an impressive collection, are they all your personal copies or do they belong to the library?'

'Ah yes, all mine, I like to make sure I understand all the important writers of the era that surrounds our work here', Rick Callow had replied. He had been impressed at the time. It was only after he had been appointed, alone in the office one day, that he had pulled a copy of *Persuasion* off the shelf, to find that it was an empty book cover for display purposes, as were all the others.

Giles Skeffington blinked back to consciousness as he realised that the sound had stopped. He walked back to his office. Why had he bothered? It was always the same. Blather. Vague promises. Plans and agreements to do things which, as far as he could see, were never even started. Particularly if it involved spending money. And he really was becoming very concerned about the security of the collections. He was convinced other items had previously gone missing. Sometimes he would find these mis-shelved later, but sometimes he wouldn't. He recalled the growing sense of uncertain dread that had overcome him a couple of months ago whilst carefully turning the pages of the 1507 Wytfliet atlas.

He was looking for the map that showed California as a peninsula for the first time. Having turned and re-turned some pages back and forth it began to dawn on him that it was missing. An impression confirmed upon finding the sharp edge of the missing page cut tightly against the opened gutter. However, he couldn't be certain that it had been removed whilst at Laudanum Grange as there was no record of how the atlas had arrived in the collections, nor what its state had been. When he'd raised this with Rick Callow he'd been persuaded that unless he could prove it, there was nothing more he could do, with Rick being particularly concerned about any publicity scaring off future donors. Which he'd argued was surely just another reason why they should spend some money on improving security. All to little avail.

He reached his office door and paused. Maybe it was time to get out, move on. His was a rarefied field. By their nature rare books and special collection libraries were limited in number, Laudanum Grange being unusual as a recently created organisation, and rare books librarians? Well, they too helped ensure there were scanty career prospects. They didn't tend to move about much, some becoming ensconced for years, like brothers in a monastic order, tucked away, custodians of a world to be protected from change. This meant that, short of dying in post, it was only when they retired that positions tended to become available.

Giles Skeffington was a scarce commodity in this world. Unlike some, he did not believe that rarity and speciality were to be ensured by placing a protecting arm around collections; keeping them not just safe, but a secret from the world; arcane knowledge, not to be wasted on the uninitiated. He thought that there should be change. That a rare books library should be a living, breathing entity; metaphorical dust blown from the shelves and the light of action lit out from the collections. No longer should the words, 'rare', 'books' and 'library', suggest lone scholars in the staid, closeted atmosphere of a shut up room. He had wanted to use social media to promote the library, digitise some of the most significant items in the collections, post them on the internet, taking them out to the world. He had not been able to do any of this of course. His ideas having been either talked into oblivion by Rick Callow or slapped down by Pamela Larrup's bullwhip tongue. He was supposed to be on an equal footing with her in the Laudanum Grange hierarchy, however, because Rick Callow was spineless and easily overawed by arguments which threatened insensible thunder rather than the cool light of reason, it was her views, launched with no consideration of how the organisation could prosper, that held the place poised in the aspic gaze of a still life painting.

'Giles.' The harsh bark of Pamela Larrup started him from his reverie. 'I have put a sign on the common room door saying it is out of bounds this afternoon, we need it to discuss the fellowship applications. Can you let any readers know that they will have to go for their break elsewhere.'

Something bridled and Giles Skeffington took a short intake of breath. Did she understand the meaning of 'common room'? Though she had her own office, easily big enough to accommodate the small numbers normally involved, she would frequently commandeer the common room for her meetings. Any visitors wishing to make a cup of tea, deemed an irritant, clearly 'common' and quickly dispensed with minimal civility, like naughty children found in the grown-ups parlour. Lord knows, let's not make anyone feel welcome. It's the dining table that probably does it. More formal ceremony for her self-importance. Her at the head of the table. Though she would probably be better suited to a dais, judge's wig and gavel, donning the black cap and dispensing judgement and order down upon us all.

The common room was pleasantly appointed making the most of the flat light entering through its large, lead mullioned windows. It contained a leather Chesterfield sofa and armchairs, light refreshment facilities and a large dining table with ten chairs. Pamela Larrup moved to sit at the head of the table, with Professor Rachel Unthank and Rick Callow pulling out chairs on her left and Giles Skeffington to her right.

'Right, let us set out the terms of engagement,' said Pamela Larrup, taking control as the others sat down.

Rick Callow turned to the rest of them, nodding, indicating "let's sit, it's OK, let her do it".

'Firstly, we are looking to whittle down the applications to four. To save us all some time here is one that I prepared earlier.'

She passed out copies of a list with twelve names and the titles of their proposals. Professor Rachel Unthank settled her reading glasses half way down her nose. After considering the list she peered over them at Pamela Larrup, her hand on the loose leaf file holding her copy of the seventy applications.

'What criteria did you apply?'

'Sorry?'

'When you were whittling how did you decide which ones to shortlist?'

There was a pause whilst Professor Rachel Unthank waited for a reply which did not come, Pamela Larrup looking at her quizzically.

'It's just that there are some missing from this list that I would like to discuss and, whilst I appreciate your efforts in trying to save us time, I don't think we'd agreed on this, had we?'

Professor Rachel Unthank looked to Rick Callow and Giles Skeffington. Pamela Larrup blinked. Kittens, mewling, not to be resisted. Not only faddy, she was going to insist on protocol today as well. She had come across this before with Unthank. Completely unnecessary. Fools who would be bureaucrats, placing barriers in the way of efficiency. And a further irritant, she could see this was going to become an excuse for a long winded unfolding of Unthank's podgy ego. Well past its prime. A space to parade the mewling of the latest bunch of waifs and strays she had rescued from the contemporary dustbin of a journal she edited. Rather than getting on with the task of simply picking the successful applicants, a task to which Unthank was largely superfluous since it was not Unthank, but herself, Pamela Larrup, who would be working with them, there was going to be discussion. She could see it coming and wrinkled her nose.

'No, we hadn't agreed on any hard and fast pre-selection,' said Giles Skeffington, 'not one that meant we wouldn't be able to have some initial say.'

'Good, then can we agree that we each put forward the proposals that we would like considered, see if there's any common ground?' said Professor Rachel Unthank.

Rick Callow looked nervously toward Pamela Larrup. Would he have to intervene, say something? This may require a decision and maybe that would be something that he could think about. He shifted in his chair.

'Well, I think it's only fair on all the applicants,' said Giles Skeffington.

'They've put considerable time and effort into their applications, the majority anyhow, and if any of them realised that we hadn't even discussed the field in an open and fair way, then, if that got out, it could affect our credibility, as an institution, don't you think?'

'I certainly agree,' said Professor Rachel Unthank, looking at Rick Callow, 'Don't you Richard?'

Rick Callow squirmed, catching Pamela Larrup's glare.

'I don't think that we shouldn't have a discussion,' he said wincing slightly, 'just, perhaps, it could be the type of discussion that takes us to a place that has the means to move us to making a decision as a collection of people who have provided some consideration, but without the need to be wholly inclusive, not that being inclusive is a bad thing, but it needs the inclusivity to be exclusive to our need of picking the right proposals for all of us in the face of our, and the institution's, ongoing mission statement.'

Giles Skeffington looked blank. 'So we're having a discussion?' he asked.

'Yes, lets?' said Professor Rachel Unthank, looking at Rick Callow, who nodded his head, smiling through his teeth with a set rictus.

Pamela Larrup sighed. 'Very well, if we must.'

'Good. I would like to start by including the first Australian proposal we have had,' said Professor Rachel Unthank.

CHAPTER FOUR

The blockers in The Screaming Assault Sirens and Babe City Rollers were lined up on the pivot line, with the jammers, Bone Smacked Burney and Tart of Darkness, a few feet behind on the jam line. It was the last jam of the fourth quarter at the University of Wyoming's roller derby. The scores were equal, tempers were frayed and things were getting ugly. Vladimir Naboobkov had been sent to the penalty box for elbowing Wuthering Frights in the face shouting, "You can always count on a murderer to throw fancy elbows." Wuthering Frights, passionate, vengeful and wearing Goth make-up, had slyly tripped Tess of the Derby Wheels who had gone sprawling across the track. Tess felt that Wuthering had despised her from the start for being a pure player, faithfully presenting the best chances for her jammer. Meanwhile, Whoremione Granger, whose motto was 'skate 'til you spew', and who had perfected the dark art of smuggling her jammer through a crowded field with supernatural acuity, had been attracting the attention of Whistler Smother whose lack of sentiment and spare skating style meant she had flattened opponents with consummate ease. The whistle blew and the blockers took off rolling out at a medium pace around the banked wooden track. Two further quick whistle blasts, and Bone Smacked Burney and Tart of Darkness sprinted after them. Tart of Darkness was first to reach the pack of opposing blockers. Looking at the dense mass in front of her, she began to feel uneasy, their horrid backsides looming like an overgrown impenetrable wall, there was something ominous in the primitive way they hung and roiled together. Nothing, nothing could infiltrate such a horde. Bone Smacked Burney took advantage of her disquiet. With delicacy and grace she eased left then right, avoiding the thrusts and parries of hips and backsides with wit and judgement. Suddenly finding herself in the light and air in front of them, she felt surprised and slightly embarrassed by the effortless way she had slipped through to become the lead jammer. "Hell yeah," she whooped, raising her fist.

Clad in slim fitting black jeans, white shirt and a well-tailored black men's suit jacket, the pristine cuffs of her shirt extending over the back of her hands, Fenella Morningstar's petite frame belied the extent of the punishment she could inflict. At times, when seen from behind, she had been mistaken for a small, slightly effeminate man, her flicked shoulder length hair lending an overall impression of Nick Cave in his early Bad Seed days. However, when she turned, the ease of her smile, the well framed features and the light about her eyes, coolly disarmed any questions about her sexuality. When she entered a room, taking neat steps in her black Cuban heeled boots, her urbane poise gave a sense that she had more time than most, somehow able to slow the action such that she could take hold of events and elegantly define their outcome. This was sometimes done with such charm, you failed to notice the switch blade that had been slid into your spine until it was too late. You had been taken down by a class act; a debonair assassin.

Fenella Morningstar, A.K.A. Bone Smacked Burney, had come to Laudanum Grange at her publishers suggestion to write dirty Austen; to do research for an entertainment, *'Persuading Emma: The Missing Shades of Grey.'*

Working on the premise that eighteenth-century writers would suffer the same cuts judged necessary for the market place as contemporary writers, she was looking for evidence of missing scenes in Austen's correspondence; especially scenes of a sexual nature, intending to recreate them. In the event of finding no such evidence, her publisher had encouraged her to use the collections as inspiration and to get creative. It would probably upset a few but she enjoyed enmity, and besides, wrapping the risqué with the sensibilities of Austen, would provide much needed titillation for cardigan wearing primary school teachers everywhere.

She opened the door of the taxi and stepped out into the fresh Autumnal breeze that blew across the car park of The Ferret and Trouser Leg, one of the two pubs in the small village of Cragg that stood either side of the road that led up to the big house. It was a black and white, Tudor, wooden framed building. As the taxi pulled away she looked out across the valley to the moors beyond then turned and looked at the pub's sign; a man's trousered leg with some kind of indistinct furry animal curled around it running out onto his shoe. It was difficult to resolve what the animal looked like as the paint was peeling. What was a ferret anyway, a bit like a beaver or a gopher? And what was the significance of its association with trousers? Had their pelts been used to make them? She turned to look past the row of oaks, across the road to the second pub. This was a heavy, square, red brick building, though with the bricks narrower and laid with a much thinner course of limed mortar than in contemporary buildings. The sign that swung in the breeze read: The Hung, Drawn and Quartered. It showed a man being held by two others who were pulling open his shirt, whilst being approached by another holding a knife, with gallows in the background. Now this *was* something that she knew about and why she had chosen to book a room here rather than at The Ferret and Trouser Leg. She had easily overlooked the use of 'hung' instead of 'hanged' by the sign maker due to the historical association of the building, it being the place that Major-General Thomas Harrison had been found and arrested in 1660 prior to being escorted to London for his trial and execution. One of the first to be found guilty of the regicide of King Charles I.

There was a plaque on the wall. Written in gold on a black background it read:

Saturday 13th October 1660
So to London. I went out to Charing Cross, to see Major-general
Harrison hanged, drawn, and quartered; which was done there, he looking
as cheerful as any man could do in that condition.

She chuckled, that Pepys, picked up her case and walked into the Hung Drawn and Quartered.

After she had dumped her bags in her room she went down to the bar to read, drink, eat and wait for the jet lag collapse. The bar had a low ceiling that was stained nicotine yellow from the days before smoking restrictions. There were a number of long, rough-hewn, tables and benches. On a pillar in the middle of the room was pinned a large array of bank notes from around the world.

'Could I have a martini please.'

The barman moved to the bottles at the back of the bar. 'Red or white?' he said.

Fenella Morningstar paused. 'Sorry?'

'Red or white martini?' Gesturing at two bottles.

She grimaced. 'Bottled martini? No no, don't you mix your martini's here?'

The barman looked confused.

'You must know how to mix a martini? Look, I'll teach you, it's really simple and it'll give you a bit of class. First, y're gonna need gin and French vermouth.'

The barman stood motionless and stared at her. However, as Fenella Morningstar unpacked her explanation with smiling ease, he sighed, began to nod and started to move to follow her instruction.

'We have dry vermouth, but I don't know if it's French,' said the barman.

She looked at the bottle. 'That'll do, now you're gonna need a mixing glass.'

The barman looked blank then reached above the bar and pulled down a mottled glass tankard. 'This do?'

'Yep, that'll do it. Fill it with ice, and you're gonna need another to mix the ingredients.'

He reached for a bottle of Gordon's gin.

'May I?' She gestured towards the bottle, unscrewed the cap and sniffed. 'Mmmm, the juniper's a bit profound, softer would be better. Do you have any others?'

The barman turned and picked up a bottle of Beefeater gin. 'There's this?'

'Perfect,' said Fenella. 'Now, you need two and a half jiggers of gin.'

The barman looked at her. 'A jigger?'

'It's a measure.'

'We have gills?' he said, holding up a brass measuring cup with 1/4 of a gill stamped on the side.

'OK, that looks about half a jigger I'd say, so you're gonna want five of those in the mixing glass and two of the vermouth.'

The barman poured out the measures and tipped them into the glass.

'Now pour it over the ice.'

'And I suppose I shake it,' he said smiling.

'Oh no, that's James Bond ordering a weak cocktail and being snooty about it. No, always mix. If you shake it the ice smashes and melts more, it changes the texture. Always mix.'

The barman did as instructed, the ice clinking as he stirred the oily, creamy liquid.

'Now I don't suppose you have a martini glass?' Fenella Morningstar asked.

The barman looked sorry, holding up a small wine goblet.

'That'll do it,' she smiled, 'fill it with ice,' the barman complied, 'tip it out, and now drain the martini into it. You're gonna need something to hold back the ice.'

The barman apologetically held up a wooden slotted serving spatula and Fenella Morningstar smiled and nodded.

'Now all we need is a sliver of lemon peel.'

'Now that ah can do,' said the barman, as he walked into the kitchen behind the bar, returning with a lemon and potato peeler, which he proceeded to use, peeling a slice from the lemon.

Fenella Morningstar took it from him, wiped it around the inside rim of the glass and dropped it into the liquid. 'And that, caramelises the oils,' she said. 'There a perfectly rural martini, a new classic,' she said smiling, raising the glass to the barman. 'Cheers.'

'You're welcome, my dear.'

She took a long pull on the drink savouring the clean, crisp flavour in the comingling of gin and vermouth, exhaling the finish on her breath. She paid the barman.

'You'll be up in the big house then?' said the barman, as he gave her the change.

'Sorry?'

'Up in the big house, doing some studying?'

'Yeah, I'm visiting to research for a few weeks.'

'There's another of your lot over there,' he said, nodding towards a tall man in a black T-shirt and jeans, sat on a wooden bench reading, a book open on the table.

'American?' said Fenella Morningstar.

' 'appen as like,' said the barman.

She looked across the bar towards the tall man. He was sat at the table to the left of the inglenook fireplace. No fire had been lit but the grate had been laid with newspaper, kindling and logs ready for the first autumn chill. He appeared engrossed in what he was reading so she hadn't intended to interrupt him, but as she crossed the bare oak floor he looked up and smiled.

'G'day.'

So not American. She smiled back. 'The barman said you were another of my lot, I thought he meant American but I guess he meant researching at Laudanum Grange?'

'Yeah, I arrived last night. You?'

'Just this morning. Morningstar, Fenella Morningstar,' holding out her hand.

'Harvey Premnas, I'm studying at Sydney Uni, good to meet you.'

'I'm from Cheyenne, Wyoming.'

'Pull up a pew,' said Harvey, gesturing to the chair opposite.

'Wouldn't want to disturb your reading.'

Harvey Premnas held up his book to show the cover, *Jane Austen, Game Theorist*.

Fenella laughed. 'Seriously?'

'Yep,' he said, nodding, resigned to his penance.

'OK, I suppose you could do with saving,' she said, as she sat opposite.

'See you made a friend there,' nodding toward the barman.

'Yeah, well at least you'll be able to get a proper martini now, even if the bar tools are a bit crude. What brings you here?'

Harvey Premnas talked animatedly about his PhD, emphasising points with languid and graceful movements of his long fingered hands and rangy arms. Fenella Morningstar nodded slowly, sipping her martini occasionally.

'...... so as you can imagine getting a fellowship here, and with free accommodation, fair dinkum,' he said, raising his pint and taking a swig.

Fenella Morningstar smirked. 'Sorry, I didn't think Australians really said that. Fair Dinkum. What does it mean exactly?'

'There are two competing theories. One, that it comes from England where it was used in the seventeenth and eighteenth centuries and "dinkum" meant work. So "fair dinkum" was a fair day's work and pay, so, fair play. The other, which is the one I prefer, is that it's Chinese and was used in the Ozzy gold fields when they'd struck a lode. "Din" and "kum" loosely translates as "true gold" or "good gold", so there ya go.'

'Interesting,' said Fenella Morningstar, 'I just meant, kinda, what does it mean ordinarily, but I get it. Why do you prefer good gold?'

'My home town, Kalgoorlie, it's a gold mining town in WA.

'WA?'

'Western Australia.'

Fenella nodded. 'I'm imagining the Klondike; wild west prospectors, deep rutted muddy streets, thrown up clap-board bars and whore houses.'

'Yeah, it hasn't changed much.'

Fenella laughed.

'No seriously. The only reason the place is there is the gold mine. Before the gold it was just bush. Though that's not strictly true of course. There's always a before in Oz, if you know how to listen. Kalgoorlie means, "place of silky pears". Now it's one of the biggest holes in the world and I couldn't wait to get out.'

'Is that one of your specialties, the meaning of words?'

'No, not really, not officially anyway, I just get attracted to that type of stuff. I like solving puzzles, and I'm not very good at not knowing something, so I'm always on the look out to know stuff, then it just sort of collects until I can find an excuse to tell someone, like you,' he said, smiling. 'What about you, where did you pick up your martini skills?'

'Ah, the value of a misspent youth. When I was in high school I worked as a waitress in a fine dining restaurant which had a reputation for its martinis. I watched the barman, listened, and after hours, putting the place to bed, me and a friend would do a little underage mixing.'

'I see. So what else are you doing here, besides martini instruction?' said Harvey.

'I'm an independent, with an honorary position at The University of Wisconsin. I've written and published a lot on the influence of sexual power in politics. My publisher is keen to push the sex bit. Good for sales,' Harvey Premnas started to nod. 'It's her that's paid for this trip. You see she's encouraging me to widen my subject of interest, to step outside politics and sex. I'm supposed to be trying to find out whether Austen ever tried to write anything dirty. I'd like it really dirty, like Marquis de Sade dirty, but I don't suppose I'll find that, so I'm gonna make it up,' she said, with a slightly distanced look to her eyes.

Harvey's eyes widened. 'Oh,' he said, placing his fingers across his lips, suppressing a smirk, 'I guess that'll ruffle some feathers.'

'Hey yeah, but what about you? You're gonna do the same if you find what you're lookin' for. You're gonna upset a few purists aren't ya?'

'Yeah, suppose I am.'

'To purists and their feathers,' she said, raising her glass.

Harvey nodded and raised his pint towards her martini.

CHAPTER FIVE

The small crowd milling around the reception lounge at Laudanum Grange was largely female, in their fifties and sixties, with a scattering of young male fogies wearing public school ties. The self-aggrandising behaviour of the men was thrown into more irritating relief by their youth. These were the members of the 1813 society, dedicated to celebrating the life and works of Jane Austen. Meeting annually, they were the wealthy and privileged that were courted by an oily Rick Callow for donations.

Giles Skeffington endured such occasions with the self-consciousness of a debtor held in the gaze of his creditors, ever wary that his salary could be sacrificed to an inappropriate frown, or misjudged smile. The unspoken demand to be deferential to a crowd whose disdain seemed to pull at his teeth, set him on edge, so he was looking for the one person with whom he knew he could take some refuge, Major Duncan Sinclair. In his company Giles could relax a little. At least here was a person whose spirit, though not exactly kindred, at least perceived the scene with comparable dismay, and who was prepared to puncture some of the pretence, deflating the egomania with an apparently absentminded pot shot, allowing Giles to snigger up his sleeve.

He had met Major Duncan Sinclair at a similar event at Laudanum Grange's parent organisation, Northrop University. The vice chancellor had just given a speech about the value of donors' gifts in support of liberal education and had introduced the DeLittle investment banker, Meredith Ferryweather, to the podium, explaining she was going to talk about her motivation for creating and funding the Sophie Ferryweather Memorial Scholarship.

'Thank you Vice Chancellor. When Sophie was diagnosed with arthritis in her hip at the age of seven we were horrified. Almost overnight she went from being full of life and playful mischief to a shadow of herself.

She became hobbled as she limped around the garden. Her mood changed too. Whereas previously she was loving and would curl around your leg or settle on your lap, she became very grumpy and would try to claw you when you stroked..'

'I thought it was a child,' boomed Major Duncan Sinclair, sitting next to Giles, in an aside apparently intended as sotto voce.

Giles Skeffington and a few others repressed sniggers.

Apparently unawares, Meredith Ferryweather continued: 'Now after two year's research Carl, who was awarded the scholarship, has developed a ground breaking new technique for allowing us to relieve the type of arthritic pain that Sophie suffered with a hip replacement operation that scales down the technique used on humans and modifies it for cats. So, unlike Sophie, cats everywhere will no longer have to continue suffering. Thank you.'

As she shuffled up her papers, Major Duncan Sinclair raised his arm. 'Meredith, could I ask a question? Only I have a friend who has a cat with a bad hip.'

'Yes?'

'How much does it cost?'

'I'm glad you asked because Carl's technique was originally quite expensive, but his recent modifications have brought it right down to around £25,000.'

Major Duncan Sinclair nodded sagely as Giles Skeffington, shaking, bit the back of his hand.

In the great hall the sofas and arm chairs had been pushed to the side and rows of upright chairs set out. These had slowly filled as the guests had moved from the reception lounge with their drinks, where a lute was playing madrigals. At the far end of the hall a podium had been erected with a lectern in the centre. As the last of the guests settled, Rick Callow stepped onto the podium, his rictus grin surveying the room.

'Yeeesss, ladies and gentlemen, it's so good to see you all here today at our annual gathering of the 1813 society,' he said, in a reassuringly superior tone. 'Yeeess, aah, as you'll have seen from the exhibition in the foyer of our library, we've all been working very hard at putting your donations and bequests to good use. Yeeesss, I myself was researching one of these books and it particularly brought to my mind the reasons why this group is so named as it is, the 1813 group. As in this year we, aahhh, are celebrating two hundred years since the very, very publication of Pride and Prejudice, which is of course Jane Austen's most popular novel. And now thanks to your very, yeess, aahh, very generous gifts we have been able to extend our scholarship this year by buying and conserving all the papers uncovered by the very well renowned Deirdre La Faye in The Francis Austen Morocco

Manuscripts. I know I for one, am greatly looking forward to studying them. Now, I would like to introduce our guest speaker, Professor James Page from Pentalhangar University. As many of you will know Professor Page is a professor of international renown, respected the world over for his insights and contributions to the world of literature and all things booky and renowned for his understandings in his own writing, and about Jane. He's also quite good on the guitar I believe, Professor James Page.'

There was some slightly hesitant applause as a large, loose limbed man, with a mane of silvered hair strode to the lectern, his well-tailored black suit hanging easily about his frame. He held the sides of the lectern confidently and spoke, without notes, in a mid-Atlantic accent, tinged with the deep South of the United States.

'Good afternoon. When I received the invitation to speak today I was a little confused. You see I can only research and teach stuff I love. Stuff that is really good writing. That you can return to again and again, and find that what you thought you had understood, is not only still there, but it has matured and moved, and as you have changed, so it has pivoted in a manner that causes you to converge upon yourself with a new, and perhaps, unexpected intuition. So my research and courses reflect this - Chekov, Roth, Tolstoy, Miller, Mailer, - all the serious writers. You may also notice they are all blokes. Real blokes blokes. Heterosexual blokes. And this was the source of my confusion. You see, I just have yet to find any women writers of the same quality, and that's why I don't teach them on my courses.'

There was a rustle of papers and a squeaking of chair legs on the wooden floor. Giles Skeffington tensed and look towards Rick Callow standing to the left of the podium, his face frozen in what was becoming a fearful smile.

Grinning under his moustache, his eyes shining, Major Duncan Sinclair nudged Giles. 'Watch out, this is going to be fun,' he muttered.

'I tell my students,' Professor Page continued, 'that if you want that, you need to go down the hall to someone else. So you see my confusion. Why would a society, which holds Austen as all hallowed, want me to speak? Anything I may have to say probably won't play too well to the converted. So I phoned Richard, and speaking with him I began to understand. It wasn't that he didn't understand me, to do that you'd have to have read me.'

There was some slightly suppressed tittering. Then, placing the back of his hand to the side of his mouth, in a staged whisper, 'It was that the guy really didn't have a clue. Kept asking me how the guitar was going. Never played one in my life.'

Some of the audience laughed nervously. Giles Skeffington glanced sideways at Major Sinclair whose smile had broadened. This was becoming too delicious. Rick Callow started to sway a little.

'So I told him. I said, "Rick man, listen. I don't know anything about Jane Austen, tried once, couldn't get on with her, so I don't know what you'd expect me to do". Then we talked a bit more. I listened a bit. Got bored.'

He paused, part of the audience laughed a little more. Major Sinclair leaned forward on the edge of his chair grabbing Giles Skeffington's knee, finding it difficult to contain the anticipation of what he believed was about to happen.

'So, I said to him again, "Listen Rick, I really don't know much about Austen", and then Rick said, he said,' as he controlled his laughter, 'he said, "That's OK, nobody will mind, just speak about what you do know." Then I thought, you know what, I'm gonna do it. Cos hey, if this guy is stupid enough to get me up to speak about something I don't rate, to a bunch of people who do, then hey, he deserves the flack.'

Rick Callow, standing at the side of the podium had gone pale, his world reeling. He looked across the audience, a mixture of mildly embarrassed, restrained smiles and frowning, wrinkled brows, many of them turned on him. He widened his frozen rictus and made a decision to panic. From the corner of his eye he spotted the small door that led to the servant's passageway. It would take two steps to reach it. Whilst keeping his gaze fixed on the audience he started to sidle towards it. Something caught against his left foot. The carpet rucked and he tripped sideways into the wall beside the door, his elbow smashing into the fire alarm. A rising, two-tone whoop split across the room and there was general pandemonium. Giles Skeffington jumped up and started to guide people through the corridor and outside. As he passed, Major Duncan Sinclair put his arm round Giles' shoulder and shouted in his ear.

'Masterful, absolutely bloody masterful.'

Having quickly cornered Pamela Larrup and outlined a strategy for damage limitation, she and Giles circled among some of the more outraged members of the 1813 society, explaining the communication mix up between their front office and secretarial staff in the English Literature department at Pentalhangar University. That Rick Callow had not been involved in organising Professor Page's visit as he was far too busy, and they understood how upsetting, and clearly wrong, his views were. Laudanum Grange was terribly sorry for this mix up and there would be a re-scheduled event with a free meal to compensate for their distress. Giles had checked none of this with Rick Callow, who had not been seen since his headlong plunge through the servant's door after setting off the alarm.

When the members of the 1813 society had dispersed Pamela Larrup sought Rick Callow in his office. She was carrying a large sheaf of papers which she hoisted against her bosom as she knocked on the door. There was no reply. She knocked again and was just considering trying the handle when it opened a crack and Rick Callow's eyes appeared in the gap.

'Oh, it's you Pamela.' He ushered her in and peered around the corridor, before closing the door. 'Oh, that was awful, awful. You know he really was wrong, I had read about him. I did that Googling thing, but it must have been a different James Page. The one I read about was a guitarist who loved Jane Austen. I thought it was him I'd invited.'

'Well you will be pleased to know that I think I have contained the situation.'

Pamela Larrup explained the plan she had executed, without mentioning Giles. 'I think you will have to send them each a personal apology, along with the explanation. If we sit down together we could include details of a rescheduled event along with the meal.'

'Oh good thinking Pamela, that was an excellent idea. Ah yees, well done, well done. Though a meal? Do you think that would really be necessary?'

'Some of the members were quite upset Rick, we do need their donations.'

'Yes quite. Perhaps a buffet.'

'I think you would need to go a little further to repair the offense.'

Rick Callow glanced to the side of his desk. 'Yes. I expect you're right Pamela. You think they're alright for the moment?'

'I think so, but you should write to them.'

'Oh yes, exactly, I will. I'll write them an open letter.'

He let out a deep breath and sat back in his chair, the fretful lines of his forehead returning to their more featureless, waxy repose. He would craft them one of his best. A Callow special. Lovely long sentences that would leave them all in no doubt that, though a mistake had been made, it would not be one that would remain unanswered; not for him the dodging of responsibility and the miserly, thin lipped apology. No, his would be fulsome and gushing. Just as he'd suspected, an administrative mix-up had come to his attention, specifically identified amidst the operation of administrative procedures to the effect that it was the system through, in, and of its own conception, that had lacked the transparency to reveal that a mistake was about to be made. Now however, as he was at the apex of the investigation, members of the 1813 Society should be left in no doubt that lines of accountability were being drawn, and these would all lead to somewhere and to someone else, who would be identified as responsible to other positions within the administrative system itself, that would mean, should such a situation occur again, in the future, it would be possible to account for it by reference to those amongst themselves who had organised the system to reveal that the system had indeed transgressed in the first place. Ah yees. Something like that should be just the ticket.'

Pamela Larrup started to shuffle around with the papers on her lap. 'While I am here, have you time for me to run through the fellows who arrive tomorrow?'

'Ah, yes yes, why not eh. Now we've got things under control. Who've we got, anyone interesting?'

She leafed further through the pile and pulled out some stapled sheets which she passed to Rick.

'We have four, three Americans and one Australian.'

'Oh yes. One of our first Ozzies, isn't he? What's his name? Bruce?' he said, chortling.

'Ah, no.'

'Oh that's a shame. I was looking forward to a bit of Ozzy repartee with him, doing that old Python sketch. You know, where everyone's "Bruce, from Woloonga". Never mind, maybe I could get him to sing a bit. You know, "Tie me kangaroo down sport, tie me kangaroo down".'

'Err, no. His name is Harvey,' she scanned down the page, 'Harvey Dominic Premnas, from the University of Sydney, researching for his PhD, and he wants access to The Francis Austen Morocco Manuscripts. That was one of the things I wanted to talk to you about. How is their conservation going?'

'It's done. Giles is picking them up later today.'

'Ah good, I was looking forward to making a start on them.'

'Oh you're using them too, that's good. You can share them with this Harvey chap, show him the ropes eh.'

'Well I will consider that of course, however, my research will have to take precedence.'

Rick nodded fulsomely. 'Of course, of course. Whatever you think best, eh Pamela. Who else have we got?'

'Well there is Ms. Melissa Budai from Columbia University who is doing research for a book on Maria Edgeworth. Quite why we need another of those I do not know.'

Rick Callow nodded knowledgeably.

'We have an Assistant Professor from Williamsburg University and Ms. Imogene Jung studying for a PhD, something to do with the representation and meanings of mad women, from the University of Nebraska.'

'Are there a lot of them there?'

Pamela Larrup looked aside at Rick.

'Mad women?' he clarified.

'No, not from Nebraska. In the novels of Walter Scott.'

'Ahh.'

'Though I would not be surprised if there weren't a few more than is usual there. It's not a place I would choose to study.'

'Quite,' said Rick Callow.

Pamela Larrup gathered her papers and started towards the door.

'Isn't there some independent chappy here too?' Rick Callow asked.

'Yes there is,' said Pamela, pausing in the doorway, 'Miss Fenella Morningstar. She is some kind of writer I believe, although I have not heard of her before, and I'm not sure I want to seek her out either.'

'Where's she coming from?'

Pamela Larrup held her papers to her chest and started to shuffle through them. 'She's based at the University of Wyoming I believe, certainly American. Yes, here it is,' she brandished a sheet of paper. 'She's actually some kind of political writer,' she said, looking as though she had just chewed on a wasp, 'works in the politics department there. Not that you would know it from what she plans to do here.'

'Oh, what's that?'

'Well, let us just say that I'm not impressed, and if I had my way I wouldn't be indulging it, but as Giles is constantly at pains to remind me, we are, "open access," ' she said, affecting an English accent, 'I told Giles that I wished he had checked with me before he accommodated her booking, but it is too late now.'

'Why, what's the problem?'

'Let's just say that her research will involve some moves that Miss Austen would not have approved of, not approved of at all,' she said, shaking her head, walking through the door and out of earshot.

'Oh, dancing eh. Yes, I see the problem,' said Rick Callow, confused.

CHAPTER SIX

Fenella Morningstar and Harvey Premnas met as agreed in the lounge of The Hung, Drawn and Quartered after breakfast the following morning. Harvey was staying further down the road in The Terrace, a block of five, nineteenth century terraced houses that had been bought by Laudanum Grange and knocked through to form an accommodation block for visitors to the centre. During the night he'd heard the arrival of the three remaining visiting fellows around 4.30. However, as they were flying in from the States he didn't expect to see them until much later in the day.

They turned into the drive, the gravel crunching under their feet. The day was bright and cool, with light streaks of cloud lifting the eye high above the red roof of Laudanum Grange.

'Have you met any of the staff yet?' Fenella Morningstar asked.

'Nah, not really. I was given a key for The Terrace by the caretaker, but aside from that, no. I know I'm supposed to be working with the Director of Research, Pamela Larrup, though I'm not quite sure how that works.'

'I've spoken with the librarian, Giles Skeffington, about what I'm gonna need access to and what I'm doing.'

'How'd that go?'

'He seemed fine, even laughed a bit. So I guess he's fairly laid back about the idea.'

'It'll be the hard core Janeites that'll go for you,' said Harvey.

'What do you mean?'

'Ah, you haven't come across the Janeites yet? Mad as a bunch of cut snakes. They are to Austen as Trekkies are to Star Trek. Committed. Very, very committed. They're like a cult, can't really handle irreverent or ironic. Woe betide anyone who crosses them. They'll set out to get'cha.'

Fenella held a wry grin. 'Aw shucks.'

They stepped up into the porch of Laudanum Grange and Harvey Premnas pressed the button marked 'push'. An electric bell rang deep in the house. They stood silently. Harvey looking up at the ceiling as Fenella turned to the view from a small window at her side. They waited. Harvey Premnas turned and looked down the poplar lined drive.

After a minute or so they looked at each other.

Harvey widened his eyes and pursed his lips. 'Again?'

'I guess.'

He pushed the button sounding the distant bell, the house letting the ring echo down long corridors and empty rooms. They waited and looked at each other again.

Fenella Morningstar gestured, I'll have a go. She pressed the button and held it for a count of five then stood back. Some birds were singing and the rustle of a breeze disturbed some dying leaves. The house retained its long silence. Fenella Morningstar tried the wrought iron door handle. It gave, but the door would not budge.

'Locked,' she said. 'Wha'd'ya think?'

'Dunno. They were expecting us weren't they?'

'I received a letter confirming the date and time of my arrival, so yeah.'

They turned, standing side by side in the porch looking down the drive and across the moors. The quiet, mild, Autumnal morning, brought the air cooler to their bodies.

Fenella Morningstar considered the view. The long drive lined by poplar trees, running down to the old millstone grit gate house, gave onto semi-formal grounds surrounded by a wooded area and a high stone wall. Then, rising across the shallow valley beyond, the Yorkshire moors, and on the far horizon there seemed to be some kind of monument. She breathed deeply. It was something she had only ever seen on TV, and though it was annoying to find there was apparently no one home, the unplanned pause in her expectation of the day provided her mind with a reprise that placed the rest of her life at a stilled distance for a moment.

'Let's look around, see if we can see anyone,' she said, setting off down the steps.

They followed a flagstone path around the side of the building. Turning the corner Fenella Morningstar froze mid-stride. 'What the fuck is that?' she declared, standing open mouthed.

'That,' said Harvey Premnas, pausing for emphasis, 'is the library.'

'What, why. I mean, why would someone go an' do that? It's anti-godlin. Don't they have planning laws here?'

'Don't ask me. If it's anything like Sydney, planning usually involves a couple of property developers and a politician cooking up a rort on a millionaire's yacht.'

She was looking at The Grimalkin Library, newly added five years ago.

It was named after the philanthropist, Brendan Grimalkin, who had bought Laudanum Grange for the purpose of establishing the international research centre and included a small, though prestigious, museum. The family money had come from ancestors who, having been gifted land in Ireland by Oliver Cromwell for being particularly brutish at Drogheda and Wexford, used their business acumen in the seventeenth century equivalent of asset stripping; demanding extortionate rents from peasants and evicting them when they couldn't pay. The drunken stumble of concrete and glass propped against the shoulder of the manor house seemed to have inherited something of this, exuding a postmodern scream against ancestral monstrosities. Harvey knew about it as he had been all over the web site when applying for the fellowship. Fenella, however, had obviously assumed something like the sandstone, brick and wooden panelling of an Oxbridge college that the old manor house implied.

'That just looks so wrong, it looks as though it's about to collapse. I don't think I'd feel safe in it.'

'It's state of the art, won international design prizes,' said Harvey Premnas.

'It's a bloody state alright, sheez,' said Fenella Morningstar, standing in repose upon her right leg, hands on her hips.

A figure emerged from the revolving door of the library and walked down the path towards them, doing something that looked like a skip but may have been a trip, half way down.

'I see you're admiring our library,' said Rick Callow. 'You must be some of the new fellows,' he said, extending his hand, 'I'm Richard, but you can call me Rick.'

'G'day, I'm Harvey Premnas, from Sydney,' he said, shaking Rick Callow's hand, then discretely wiping his own on his jeans.

'And you are the delightful .....?' Rick Callow said, turning to Fenella Morningstar, inviting an ingratiated reply with his eyebrows and holding out his hand.

Momentarily transfixed, her pupils contracted as she stared at Rick Callow's hair. Who had done that to him? 'Err, Morningstar, Fenella Morningstar. I'm not one of the fellows, I'm an independent researcher, using your collections for a few weeks.'

'Ah, excellent, excellent, good to have you on board, the more the merrier, eh?' said Rick Callow.

She shook his hand, the greasy, limp grip making her feel slightly queasy. She folded her arms.

'We rang at the front but there was no reply,' explained Harvey Premnas.

'Yes, the reception staff don't arrive until 10.30, part of my rationalisation plan,' said Rick Callow, holding his hands behind his back and swinging forward, 'so I thought I'd be here to let you in.'

'But you weren't,' said Fenella Morningstar, smiling and raising her eyebrows.

'Hm?' said Rick.

'There to let us in, we rang and rang.'

'Oh, I know, but were all here now, eh,' he said, jocularly, leading them down the path and through the revolving door into the library.

As they entered the building Harvey Premnas was taken by the scale of the ambition in the space around him. Regardless of anyone's feeling about the building from the outside, the space inside had been rendered with a sense of the grand statement, providing levity for the mind to range and ideas to play, a testament to delight meant to confound any notion of bunged up, oak panelled stuffiness. Harvey Premnas felt his spirits lift a little. The lack of an answer at the front door, and the unprepossessing encounter with Rick, had made him begin to wonder what he had let himself in for. Now however, he began to feel the whisper of intellectual inspiration emerging in the space around him. He could do business in this place.

The Grimalkin Library and Museum is set on five levels, with the library occupying the ground floor and lower two, and the museum taking up the first and second floors above. Entering on the ground floor, the revolving door is set in a twenty foot wall of glass. The dark veined, marbled lobby includes a small shop and café to the left, whilst the space opposite opens into a triple height atrium, extending from the floor above down to the reading room below, with a glass walled light well cut down from the garden outside.

Standing at the railing on the ground floor, you look down into the reading room and reference library, furnished with long, heavy, burr-maple reading tables, set with stainless steel, angle-poise lamps. The tables are lined on each side with oak chairs featuring the same three-legged sculptural form as those commissioned recently for the Bodleian. As you look across the atrium, a glass wall runs the height of the three stories, giving out to the garden with natural light flooding the reading room below. At the ground floor level, this is etched with the names of patrons and sponsors, and above, much larger and crossing the width of the glass:

> *In books lies the soul of the whole Past Time: the articulate audible voice of the Past, when the body and material substance of it has altogether vanished like a dream.*
> — Thomas Carlyle (1795 - 1881)

Past the café and shop, taking the width of the entrance hall and extending across the rest of the ground floor, there are a number of seven foot, softly lit, display cases, which house exhibitions from the collections.

Harvey and Fenella followed Rick Callow across the marble floor. A neat man appeared coming up the mahogany circular stairs, wearing a finely woven, brown twill jacket, matching waist coat, white shirt and deep red tie.

'Ah Giles good, you're here. These are two of the, ahhh, new fellows. Just arrived. Can I leave them with you to get settled?'

'Yep, fine,' Giles Skeffington nodded, pushing his round framed spectacles above the bridge of his nose.

After the introductions, when Fenella Morningstar had explained that she was not a visiting fellow, he led them down the wooden circular staircase. Fenella let the curve of the cool, steel handrail lead her down.

'This is the lower ground level, the reading room,' said Giles Skeffington, as he stepped from the bottom step onto the mid-beige carpet. It did not feel like a space that was below ground, with the mellow Autumnal sun filtered through the glass of the light well. 'It holds most of the reference collection, academic treatises, analytical, critical works and the likes, and you can use the learning spaces,' Giles pointed to two glassed-in rooms with whiteboards, oval tables and chairs, 'if you want to have any meetings, seminars etcetera. The stacks housing the main collection are below us on lower ground level two. I'll show you how to fill in the call slips in a bit.'

Harvey Premnas and Fenella Morningstar looked around the space, they smiled at each other. It was going to be a real pleasure to work here.

'If you're a visiting fellow we allocate you a seat which is yours for the duration. So you can leave out the materials you're working on. As you're first to arrive you can take your pick,' said Giles Skeffington, waving toward the heavy reading tables, 'and as were not due to be overly busy, I think we can do the same for you,' he said, looking at Fenella Morningstar.

'Thanks, that's good of you,' she said.

After he had shown them how to search the on-line catalogue, fill in call sheets and gone over the conditions of use, Giles Skeffington left them to settle into the library.

Whilst Fenella Morningstar searched the catalogue, Harvey Premnas went up to the ground floor to look at the exhibition.

A sign read:

Great Novels of 1814.
Austen, Burney, Edgeworth, Scott.
Mansfield Park, The Wanderer, Patronage, Waverley.

Presumably to celebrate the bi-centenary. He browsed slowly around the display shelves, stopping occasionally to read the interpretation notes.

He was looking at a first edition of Mary Wollstonecraft, *The Vindication of the Rights of Woman*, "to achieve equality rather than be 'rendered weak and wretched', the culture..." As he read, he felt a presence behind his right shoulder. He turned to see a trim woman in her thirties with crew cut, flame ginger hair. She smiled and nodded.

'Hey there, interesting huh?'

'G'day. Are you another of the visiting fellows?' he asked.

'Arlene Kendrick, from Williamsburg, Virginia,'

When Harvey Premnas introduced himself a flutter of anticipation struck Arlene. So, this was the guy who had got in ahead of her on the Morocco Manuscripts. Not that she was one to bellyache. Fair's fair. Though she hadn't come explicitly to use them, having booked before she was aware that Laudanum Grange had them, to be able to use them would be a boon. Having ascertained that Harvey would be studying them whilst she was here, she'd had a hankering to meet him so she could win him into her attention and maybe he'd let her in on them. If not, then she'd just watch, maybe things'd go all Jonah on him.

Assistant Professor Arlene Kendrick was Head of Bromantic Comparative Studies at Williamsburg University, a recently created course that started with Aristotle's description of friendship as the first prototype; "It is those who desire the good of their friends for the friends' sake that are most truly friends, because each loves the other for what *he* is, and not for any incidental quality." It sought to explore this theme through literature and culture from antiquity to the present, though Arlene Kendrick's speciality was the eighteenth century. It was her diamond eyed insight, tracing the influence of Chapter 94. *A Squeeze of the Hand*, in Melville's *Moby Dick*, where the mariners all squeeze the whale sperm together, that had sealed her reputation as a scholar of Bromantic distinction.

They were sat in the café when Pamela Larrup appeared at the bottom of the circular stair case running down from the museum. She has holding a large print featuring the overwhelming, cavernous mouth of a lion. Inside flames licked about a large pot, horned demons loading it with hapless souls. It reminded Harvey of something by Blake or Bosch. Pamela Larrup threw Harvey and Fenella a lofty glance and hurried past through the revolving door.

Arlene Kendrick leaned forward. 'I think that was Pamela Larrup,' she said.

Harvey Premnas looked towards the still turning door. 'Really? You'd think she'd have said something, she's supposed to be working with us, supervising us or something, though I'm not sure how that works.'

'No, me neither. I suppose she'll know the collections and will be able to guide us.'

'Isn't that what the librarian's for?'

'Yeah, normally. But I've heard she's a bit bossy. A friend of mine was here a couple of years ago. She likes to be in control apparently. Doesn't really think librarians should be let anywhere near us scholars, not unless they've got a PhD in something literary. Thinks they should just stick to shelving.'

'So what does she think a masters in librarianship gives you? Super shushing powers?'

Arlene Kendrick laughed.

Fenella Morningstar emerged from the staircase.

'Hey there, what'cha up to?'

'Fenella, this is Arlene, another visiting fellow,' said Harvey.

Having greeted one another, Fenella said, 'So, what've you got planned for the rest of the day? I've done a little searching, but it's such a nice morning I thought I might take a walk around a bit. Fancy it?'

They left the library, walked down the path and turned the corner in front of the house just as Pamela Larrup descended from the museum, looking towards the empty cafe.

Having delivered the *Mouth of Hell* to the front office, where it was to be collected by a courier, she had returned via her own office, picking up the list of visiting fellows as she did so, coming back through the connecting walkway between the top floor of the house and the second floor of the Grimalkin Museum.

She looked around. Where were they? They were here a moment ago. She looked quickly along the aisles of the exhibition. No. Then went down the spiral stair case to the reading room. She looked around the book cases housing the reference collection. Not here either. Peculiar, where can they have gone? You would have thought they would want to crack on. She flapped the piece of paper with the names and research schedules on it. This was infuriating. She had gone all the way up to her office especially to get this and now they had gone. Well, if they were going to be shiftless then that was their problem, she had better things to do than chase after feckless researchers. It was their look out. She walked back up the circular stairs to the museum, heading back to her office.

She was crossing the floor of the museum, between a case holding some of Jane Austen's slippers and what was reputed to be a pram belonging to the family, when she encountered Giles Skeffington.

'I cannot find them anywhere,' she said.

'Who?'

'The visiting fellows. I went all the way up to my office to get the list so I would know who they were and when I came back they were gone,' she said.

'Oh.'

'Have you seen them?' she said.

'No.'

'Where do you suppose they would go?'

'I've no idea. Maybe they just went for a walk.'

'Why would they do that? They saw me. They must have known I would be back.'

'Maybe they didn't know who you were. Did you talk to them?'

'Well, I just think that it is rude, ill considered. I think I'll have a word with Rick to warn him, let him know what to expect,' she said, striding away from Giles Skeffington.

He watched her back recede through the walkway towards the house. I wonder how Rick will feel about being 'warned'? Hope he doesn't take her too seriously.

Giles Skeffington had been on his way to the stacks to retrieve the first edition of *Persuasion*, amongst other books, ready for a group of undergraduates visiting with Professor Rachel Unthank later that day. After he had retrieved them he left them on a trolley in the reading room and went back to his office. On the way across the walkway he spotted Harvey Premnas, Fenella Morningstar and Arlene Kendrick heading back to the library. He paused, turned and headed back down. Better try to ward off something that could possibly become ugly. The three researchers were looking around the exhibition when he arrived.

'Hello there,' he said, 'I just thought I'd let you know that Pamela Larrup was looking for you. I think she wanted to talk to you about starting your research. I'll let her know your back if you'd like.'

'Yeah, we thought we saw her. You thought it was her didn't you Arlene?' said Harvey, turning.

'I thought it might be her. She looked busy,' said Arlene Kendrick, 'Yeah, let her know were here, we just went out for a stroll. Try to shake off some of the jet lag.'

Giles Skeffington phoned Pamela from the service desk. 'She'll be down in a moment,' he said, returning.

Giles made small talk with them about their trips, packing and the weather, before the tread of determined footsteps turned his gaze nervously towards the stairs.

'Ah, here you are,' said Pamela Larrup, bustling toward them. 'I have your research schedules here,' waving the piece of paper, 'so I thought we would just get down to business.'

'You won't need me then. I'll just go and get started,' said Fenella Morningstar, gesturing toward the circular stairs down to the reading room, moving in that direction.

'And what makes you so special?' barked Pamela Larrup.

'Er. I'm not one of your visiting fellows for a start. So I guess my research schedule isn't on that list. I mean, that's my guess. What would you say?'

Pamela Larrup reddened.

'Oh, yes. No. I didn't know. Sorry. Just assumed'

'That's OK,' said Fenella Morningstar, 'I'm just an independent researcher. So, as I say, I'll just get on.' She walked off in the direction of the circular staircase, letting the cool steel of the handrail run smoothly through her hand as she descended.

Pamela Larrup turned to the others. 'Where are the rest? There should be four of you.'

Harvey Premnas shrugged. 'Dunno,' looking toward Arlene Kendrick.

'We arrived together very early, about 4.30. They're probably still asleep,' she said.

'Well you are both here,' said Pamela Larrup.

'Yeah. But I haven't been to sleep yet. At some point in the day I'm gonna keel over,' said Arlene Kendrick.

'Oh well. You will have to do to start with. Shall we?' She gestured towards a table in the cafe. 'I will deal with you first,' Pamela Larrup said to Harvey, 'I can obviously advise you on the Austen and Shakespeare. However the other one, what is her name?'

'Angela Carter?'

'Yes Carter. I'm afraid you are on your own there.'

On his own? He'd never assumed anything more.

'You will need to call the early writings we have. Austen's juvenilia. And we have some of her correspondence. I would expect you to develop a working outline within the first week and report to me on your progress. I will guide you from there.'

Arlene watched Harvey nodding as Pamela spoke. Though he appeared to show willing, there was something sketchy about his gestures.

'Are the Morocco Manuscripts available yet?' Harvey asked.

Pamela Larrup raised her chain and mashed her lips together.

'They are available, but you should look at the Jane Austen materials first. I would say they are more immediately pertinent to your aims than the Morocco Manuscripts.'

Harvey's eyebrows flashed faintly. 'Mmm. Well yeah. OK.'

'Good. And now you', said Pamela Larrup turning to Arlene Kendrick, 'remind me what you are about?'

Arlene would normally need little invitation to talk about her work. However, the tone of the question took her back to the rural school house and the horn rimmed heckle she had received for handing in a project whose creativity had exceeded her teacher's ability to suspend disbelief, her enthusiasm sent back to dwell on its indulgence.

'Actually, I'm beginning to phase out,' said Arlene Kendrick, 'so if it's all the same, I'm going to crash for a bit. We can talk about it later.'

Pamela Larrup blinked. 'Very well. If you see the others tell them I shall be in my office when they are ready to get started.'

CHAPTER SEVEN

If anyone had asked he would have said he was taking a break. However, what appeared to be the mundane activity of a mild mannered librarian was, for Giles, a statement of resistance in the face of overbearingly conceited meddling.

According to the schedule Pamela Larrup had emailed him, he should have been shelving the books on the returns trollies, including those from the visit of Professor Rachel Unthank and her students. The moment he had read the email he had deleted it with a truculent stab. Not only would those books be needed the following week when the students returned, Pamela's communication had continued with a list of such hectoring detail, that his rising ire had cloistered any good intentions towards the subject of their interference. The books on the trollies were set to remain as a statement of obstinate intent.

So, he was taking a break. Spending time on a pet project, researching the local history of the village of Cragg down the road. In order to provide some balm for his irritation he had turned to cartography. There was something about a map, especially an old map, that made his immediate surroundings recede to the stilled quietude of the shrunken topography.

He was studying a first series 1843 Ordnance Survey map of West Yorkshire, digitised by the British Library. It clearly showed the two pubs, The Ferret and Trouser Leg and The Hung Drawn and Quartered, and the two churches in the village. However, there was another building marked which he was sure was no longer there. He was making a sketch of the relative positions trying to work out what, if anything, was on the location now. Arlene Kendrick came down the circular wooden stairs.

'Hey.'

'Good Morning Arlene, how are you?'

'Good thanks.'

'I've put the books you asked for on your desk.'

'Thanks.'

'How's your outline for Pamela coming?' asked Arlene, as she sat down opposite Harvey.

He looked across to her from under resigned brows, his lips a vexed squiggle. 'I'll have to show willing I suppose.'

'I suppose,' she agreed, 'though I thought you kept your cool pretty well yesterday.'

Harvey looked questioning for a moment before nodding. 'Yep, just a bit patronising. Has she laid it out for you yet?'

'Oh yeah. I was corralled first thing this morning. I'm not sure why I'm bothering to do my own research when it's clear that she could do it so much better.'

Harvey smiled.

'I think it's her own insecurities,' Arlene continued. 'I had a look at her profile on Scholar Universe. She doesn't publish much, and what she does isn't really in the right place. Some of the journals aren't even peer reviewed.'

'That's a bit basic isn't it? If she's got her own research, why's she so interested in micro-managing ours?'

'That's it. She does have her own, but I think she kind o' knows that it's not very good. Controlling other peoples' is a way of dealing with it. Projection. Sorting us out, when really what she needs to do is sort out herself.'

'Yeah, I suppose we need to keep her sweet though,' said Harvey

'Yeah,' said Arlene Kendrick slowly, looking into the distance. 'Maybe.'

Harvey plugged his headphones into his mobile as Arlene settled down to her research on the Austen brothers and their male counter parts.

Building on her readings of the relationships of men at sea in *Moby Dick,* she had developed an interest in the two Austen brothers who had joined the Royal Navy, Francis and Charles. When she had pitched for the fellowship she had used her earlier work as the premise for developing a more historically grounded piece, analysing how long periods at sea may have affected their relationships with other men. News of the conservation of the Francis Austen Morocco Manuscripts had excited her attention and though she'd not been able to get explicit agreement to use them, the first call having gone to Harvey Premnas, she had hoped that once she was on the ground she'd be able to gain access to them. There was plenty more in the collections for the time being.

Both Austen brothers had joined the navy as mid-shipmen at the age of twelve. Twelve. When she was twelve she had been running around her parent's small farm in Virginia, the boundaries of her world defined by the six mile horse ride back and forth to school every day. These brothers had been sailing the globe. That they were out there amongst the dangers and vicissitudes of the worlds' oceans, concerned in skirmishes and conflicts that they could have little understood, was something that, though she could appreciate it intellectually, escaped her empathy.

She put aside the book she had been working with and looked towards Giles on the service desk. He was quite a good looking man. Seemed a little crusty and old fashioned in that British way that made you want to ruffle his hair and disturb his reserve. He looked up, caught her eye and smiled. She managed to give the impression that she had been caught gazing off into a reflective place that was only coincidentally in his eye line, smiled back and returned to her book.

Giles had moved on to cataloguing some of the new acquisitions on one of the three heavily laden book trolleys beside the service desk. He was systematically working his way through them in between retrieving items called by some of the visiting fellows and four other readers who had booked in that morning. He browsed through *A Tour of Scotland* by Thomas Pennant, 1774, prior to cataloguing it, looking at some of the plates, reading about the Admirable Crichton and the murder of the Laird of Innes, when he glanced up again to see Arlene Kendrick looking towards him, slightly flicking her eyes and eye brows to the space above and behind him. He puzzled the gesture for a moment, as from somewhere behind his shoulders, he sensed an aura of displeasure emanate. He turned to see Pamela Larrup regarding him with her arms folded.

'Everything alright Pamela?'

'I want you to put The Morocco Manuscripts on reserve to me for the next three weeks.'

'OK. Would you like me to get them out for you now?'

'No. I will not be using them just yet, but I want them available when I am ready.'

'Well, when will that be?'

'Why, it will be when I am ready. Which I will know later.'

'Well, why don't you let me know then? If I put them on reserve now nobody else will be able to use them. I mean, Harvey Premnas will be needing them soon I would think.'

'Harvey's nowhere near ready for them.' She looked disdainfully towards Harvey, his headphones rendering him oblivious to her comments. 'He has got at least a couple of week's work on the Austen manuscripts yet, and you do know that my research is much further ahead than his?'

'It hardly seems fair to block book them to you when you aren't sure when you're going to need them.'

'My research cannot go ahead without them as I said, so I will be needing them immediately. And while we're on about efficiency, did you get my e-mail?

'Which one?'

'The one that instructed you on how to sort out this mess.' She pointed to the trollies of books.

'Oh yes. I got that.'

'Well, you did not reply.'

'No, I didn't think it needed a reply. I took it as read that you'd know I'd seen it.'

'I think it is clear that you may have seen it, but you have yet to act on it,' she said, nodding to the books on the trollies.

'Those are books yet to be catalogued.'

'Can they not go somewhere else, out of sight?'

'Well, then it would make cataloguing them more time consuming.'

'But it would be tidier. What about those?' she said, pointing to the second trolley.

'They're the books that the fellows have called, but which they aren't using at the moment, though they may return to.'

'Well, once again, it would seem that you are putting your easy life ahead of the neatness and efficiency of the library. And those?' Nodding to the third trolley.

'They're the books that Professor Unthank and her students will need next week.'

'Well there, I rest my case. Why are they cluttering up the place a week ahead of when they will need them?'

Giles reached for a reprieve. 'Look Pamela, it's a bit like you wanting to block book The Morocco Manuscripts. Though they are coming as a group next week, Professor Unthank has told her students that they can drop by individually anytime ahead of their visit to prepare. So they need to be available, just in case.' He crossed his fingers under the desk and quickly moved on. 'So, I'll just block in The Morocco Manuscripts for you then shall I?' he said, clicking on the reservation icon on his computer screen.

'Yes, I see what you mean that does make sense. Yes, book them for me, and see if you can't just tidy some of these a bit.'

'Will do Pamela. Oh and if anyone does ask for The Morocco Manuscripts, I'll get them to check with you, just in case you're not using them.'

'If that would keep you happy, I suppose so, but nobody will need them.' She turned and walked towards the circular stairs.

Giles Skeffington breathed heavily and reserved the documents to her.

After Pamela had gone he looked across to Arlene Kendrick and mockingly wiped his brow, mouthing 'thanks'.

With her elbows on the desk, she raised the palms of her hands, and blinked a suggested 'no problem'. After a moment she went across to him. 'Which part of Scotland is she from?'

'Ah, Berwickshire I believe, border country. Never could decide whether it should be English or Scottish. Why?'

'Aw, nothing really, I was just thinking that if she's a typical Scot then why are you English making such a fuss about keeping them in The Union?'

Giles Skeffington allowed the ghost of a smirk to cross his face before adopting a mock frown. Arlene Kendrick batted her hand at him as she returned to her seat.

'Like, we can't see that she's barking, Giles.'

He let the grin return a little and slipped back into the release he had felt upon executing a Larrup side step a few moments before.

The upcoming referendum in Scotland had not been a subject of conversation between himself and Pamela. Having once made the mistake of commenting on another woeful performance by the Scottish rugby team; pumped up with testosterone fuelled bag pipes prior to the game, only to wilt embarrassingly, passion once again proving no substitute against the bravura of the English, he had learned to avoid the question of their respective national identities. Though sometimes he wished he had a little more of the blatant parade of triumphalism displayed by the English as they ran in try after try. Something to steel against the sense of cowed expectation that emanated from Pamela.

His gaze fell upon a row of Penguin books with orange spines on the shelves above his desk. Graham Greene first editions. His personal copies. *Our Man in Havana*, *Brighton Rock*, *The Man within*. He'd always liked him, reread the lot. Greene's bitter, cynical world lulled him with something like a feeling of security. At least you knew where you stood with that. The moral conflicts, with evil always attendant, weighted against a vigilant struggle to avoid sin, appealed to the sense of the guardian in Giles. Though sin was not something he struggled with since the associated temptations didn't seem to bother him much, the notion that there was a world of better motives was something that he held dear, and which represented itself physically in the collections he cherished. What did bother him, however, was not so much evil, but the strident flutter of doom lurking ever present behind his shoulder. It seemed like a natural state of affairs, in which he'd learned that escape felt persistently amiss, and was something more like what being the English librarian at Laudanum Grange felt like. Always falling toward the end of autumn, waiting for the leaves to fall, with some wintery blast ever threatening to strip them away before they could settle.

CHAPTER EIGHT

In Sydney he would have been running the undergraduate seminar on Latin American fiction this week, marshalling arguments about the relationship between the Romantic realist tradition in Spanish literature and the emergence of magical realism. A debate he had narrated enough times to confidently resolve most viewpoints within the expected parameters. Even though he was obligated to run the seminars as part of his scholarship, he had not expected to be thinking about them in the way he had over the last couple of days. This was something that had increasingly crept into play as the avenues of enquiry in his research were re-directed and diverted into more and more obscure cul-de-sacs, making him wonder whether his time and the cost of the airfare had been worthwhile.

True, some of the manuscripts did have some intriguing annotations that hinted at something, but they were barely a foundation for what he had hoped to build from the furtive promise of The Morocco Manuscripts, which he had still to gain access to.

He was sat with Arlene Kendrick at a large table in the oak beamed bar of the Hung, Drawn and Quartered, using the remains of a slice of bread to mop up the gravy from his evening meal, pie, mash and peas, whilst listening to Fenella explaining to Arlene:

'I'm supposed to be writing some scurrilous Austen sex scenes that my publisher thinks will sell, but I've let myself get distracted.'

'Why's that?' asked Arlene.

'I'm not really that interested. I went along with it to keep her happy until I can present her with something more substantial.'

'Like what?'

'I'm not sure. Most of my work involves power, politics and sex. Contemporary stuff mostly. Though I've written stuff on Machiavelli as well as Thatcher, and a book on the relationship between fagging in public schools and Whitehall mandarins. I've been thinking of trying to do something similar with historical literary figures instead of political figures.

That's one of the reasons I went along with my publisher when she suggested coming here. See what I could dig up.'

'I would've thought there's something there,' said Arlene, 'I've come across mention of them in the journals of the men at sea I'm studying. And the close relationships certainly spilled into politics on land. I'm not specifically interested in literary figures, but they are there.'

'Homosexual relationships?' asked Fenella.

'Sometimes, and certainly latent. Have you come across anything like that in the Morocco Manuscripts Harvey?'

'Can't tell yet. I've still not been allowed to see them.'

'Oh?' said Arlene.

'I know. I've reached a point where I really need to see them but when I put in the call slip Giles told me I needed to talk to Pamela about it. Apparently she's put dibs on them.'

'So she's using them?' said Fenella.

'Not that I'm aware of, but she seems to have some hold over Giles. He said he couldn't issue them without her agreement. I'm going to talk to her tomorrow.'

'If there was anything, would you expect evidence of homosexuality?' asked Fenella.

'Don't know,' said Harvey, 'I know they contain personal documents, and some people think Francis deliberately lost them, so who knows?'

'Maybe letters from Jane admitting to being a lesbian?' Fenella said archly.

Harvey Laughed. 'I doubt it. Though she was very devoted to Cassandra, her sister.'

'She couldn't have been a lesbian anyhow,' said Arlene.

'Why not?' said Fenella.

'Didn't exist.'

Fenella looked sceptical. 'Oh, yeah.'

'Well legally anyhow,' said Arlene'

'What do you mean?'

'Well homosexuality wasn't illegal until the Victorian era. Queen Victoria signed the bill that made it a crime but she wouldn't sign the bill outlawing lesbianism because she refused to believe it existed. So women couldn't be convicted of being a lesbian.'

Harvey nodded.

'Get outta here,' said Fenella, 'so the action only exists if the law says so,' she mused. 'What was the punishment?'

'Jail.'

'That makes sense, there's never been any homosexuality there,' said Fenella.

'The Australians favoured a more permanent solution,' said Harvey.

'What's that?' Fenella asked.

'Cannibalism. Arthur Philip, the commander of the first fleet and first governor, when they were formulating the first laws, he wanted to send anyone guilty of sodomy to New Zealand to be eaten by the natives.'

Fenella laughed.

'That's outrageous,' said Arlene, 'just shows how attitudes change.'

'I don't know, there's some who'd still prefer that option,' said Harvey.

'Seriously Harvey, what expectations do you have of the manuscripts?' asked Fenella.

'I'd be interested to know if there's anything on who paid him, and how much?' said Arlene.

'Why's that?' asked Harvey.

'Just something I came across which sounded odd. Apparently the East India Company paid him a small fortune in the early 1800s. I couldn't find out what it was for. I'd be interested if there was any mention of it.'

'I'll keep a look out. That's if I ever get the things. However, I have been keeping myself busy. Composing a little ditty,' said Harvey, handing out sheets of photocopied A4 paper with what looked like a poem on it. 'I came across Captain Grose's, *A Classical Dictionary of the Vulgar Tongue* today...'

'Oh, I do like that,' said Arlene.

'What is it?' asked Fenella.

'A dirty eighteenth century dictionary,' said Arlene.

'Just my thing,' said Fenella.

Harvey continued. 'I've written something for an eighteenth century Tom Waits. If you will prepare yourselves I will enlighten and entertain you with *The Ballad of Bastardly Jack Gullion and Jerry Sneal the ruffler*.'

Harvey composed himself, cleared his throat and reading from the sheet in front of him a mocking, gravelled Tom Waits emerged into the room.

'I was out walkin' one night down by Millers Point, when an old whisky sailor, bent and burstin' from the tide wrenching his life, time a crumbling through his skin, waved me to his doorway saying, "Hey fella can you spare a dime for a man that's all washed up and run out of line? If you can, I can tell you the old, old tale, how Jerry the ruffler lost his clothes to a nail." So I flicked him a nickel, he cracked his salt lips and grinned, and this is the tale that he sang for my sins.

Cringe

The Ballad of Bastardly Jack Gullion and Jerry Sneal the ruffler.

Listen well my young friends and let me bounce you a tale,
Of a bastardly Gullion who did buck on his bail,
A bruiser he was, a bully cock too,
Fomenting them quarrels, just to rob all your loot.

A ruffler he chanced, a cribbage-faced cove,
Drank balderdash tea, lived on old Clutchcunt Road,
He would lend out his arse and shit through his ribs,
If it meant he could tickle ye and filch all your nibs.

Now the ruffler he squints like an old bag of nails,
When he's boxing the Jesuit and bashing his tail,
When really his need is to butter a bun,
To make to a coffee house of an old woman's cunt.

So bastardly Gullion goes to Old doxy Nell,
Not chicken breasted, sports her blubber well,
A wench whose cunt would bite her own arse,
She'll see him a grin agog to catch his own fart.

So the beast has been made, Jerry's done his best,
Turned arse to arse, they are taking their rest,
When bastardly Gullion, a cock pimp a gander,
Comes 'cross the scene with old Bawdy Randler.

Says Gullion, 'Now come, the cull has rum rigging,
Let's ding him and mill him, and pike while he's frigging',
So the flat cock and Gullion run smobble his clothes,
Hide out with St. Giles Breed to make a scapegallows.

Old Jerry on waking was all sparrow-mouthed,
In buff with his lobcock swinging low to the ground,
'I'll roast the dab, I'll ring a peal to his ears,
He'll polish the King's Iron for this I do fear'.

Now up 'fore the beak Bawdy Randler blew the gab,
And did plead that her belly was full with a lad,
Old Gullion was grim and did look quite gulled,
'til he greased off the gaoler to play the bob culled.

Now 'tween Gog and Magog old Gullion does hold,
That no sleeveless errand will run from him cold,
He spies on the lowly whose conscience he keeps,
At ease with the Almighty, frets not in his sleep.

'That's priceless,' said Arlene, 'a very worthy act of procrastination.'

Harvey Premnas surveyed his audience with a pleased smile and folded the sheet of paper.

They stepped out into the doorway of The Hung, Drawn and Quartered. The cold made them pause to wrap their coats tighter about themselves. The smell of wood smoke gave the cold air a heavier sense of autumn settling in the moonless night. They could see the lights of the Ferret and Trouser Leg across the road and shining through the stained glass of the church next door.

Arlene Kendrick turned on a torch, playing the beam across the branches of the trees when it momentarily caught the moon stone glare of a pair of eyes.

'What was that?' exclaimed Fenella.

Arlene tracked the beam slowly back and caught the turning head of an owl, 'I thought it was a possum,' Fenella said.

'Don't think they have possums here,' said Harvey Premnas.

'No? But they do have ferrets,' said Arlene, shining the torch light onto the pub sign opposite.

'Should we go for night cap?' asked Fenella.

'Not for me, said Harvey, 'I've got some things I need to do back at The Terrace. You two go on if you want.'

'Why I do think that would be the best of ideas Fenella,' said Arlene.

'You won't be wanting one o' them fancy gins again, will you?' said the barman to Fenella.

'No, a whisky please.'

'Make that two,' said Arlene. 'What's your fancy gin?'

'I showed them how to mix a proper martini.'

'Ahh. Very exotic.'

The drinks arrived. They continued to stand at the bar, Fenella with her boot on the foot rail.

'I wasn't expecting to meet someone like you here. I mean, mostly I meet other literature types an' historians when I come on these things, not contemporary politics writers,' said Arlene.

'No, I suppose it is a bit unusual. I'm fairly new to the world of eighteenth century studies, well the literature anyway.'

'I don't think you'll find much about Austen's sex life, not unless there's something in the Morocco Manuscripts.'

'No. Me neither.'

'How come politics and sex?'

'Well it started with my master's thesis on Mrs. Thatcher. It led to a book about how she used the sexual peccadilloes of some of her ministers to manipulate them.'

'Kind'a sexual strategising.'

'Yeah.'

'Couldn't you apply the same thing to Austen?'

'Go on.'

'The way that different characters double think their tactics depending on how they think another is thinking? Isn't that the same kind of thing?' said Arlene.

'I suppose it is. Trying to work out which strategy would lead to the best pay off. But in a fictional world, the micro-politics of it.'

'Yeah, I think that's one of the things that keeps Austen appealing. Putting voice to the thoughts we exploit about others. We use it all the time.'

'Unless you're completely clueless. Though even then I suppose that would work. You behave different if you think someone's clueless,' said Fenella. She drained her glass. 'They have very small measures here.'

'Why, don't they just. Another?'

'Why Arlene, I think that would be just dandy,' said Fenella, affecting a southern twang, 'but let's make it a double eh?'

They ordered another whisky each.

'I was reading *Castle Rackrent* today by Maria Edgeworth?' said Fenella.

'Yeah I know it.'

'I was reading the part where Sir Kit Rackrent marries a "Jewish" for her money, then serves her sausages and bacon at every meal. I understand why she'd be upset enough to throw herself in her room. But I wasn't convinced about Sir Kit locking her in for seven years. That just doesn't ring right, surely someone would have known?'

'But isn't that what Edgeworth wanted you to think? I mean Thady Quirk, he's meant to be one of the first examples of the unreliable narrator.'

'Oh I see,' said Fenella Morningstar, nodding slowly.

'And because Rackrent is the lord of the manor, though people knew, or suspected what he'd done, they never challenged him because of his position. So the locals are kind of complicit in an act of moral madness.'

'I suppose acts of madness in a consistently mad world would seem normal if that's all you've ever experienced.'

'And it's those in power who set the boundaries for what's mad and what's not, it's them that define the world. For Edgeworth, that's Rackrent.'

'Like Queen Victoria and lesbians,' said Fenella, taking a sip of whisky.

'Leshbian eh,' a slurred, gravelled voice said from behind her.

Fenella turned to see a large, bulky man with deep set, flattened features and a brick red tan.

'Ah didn't know Queen Victoria was a lesbian, she kept that quiet di'n'tsh',' he paused and looked into the space above the two women, his head swaying a little as he seemed to consider something. 'Ah jus got back from Majorca,' he said, the beer slopping around in his glass.

'That's nice,' said Arlene.

'Yeah, weren't any lesbians there, not then. Must've gone.'

'Really, how do you know?' said Fenella.

He looked down and pulled his eyes into focus on them. "Ow'd ah know wot? The lesbians? 'cos ah know a lesbian when ah sees one. But...but, you wouldn't think old Vicky was one,' he said, gesticulating a finger at them. 'Naw. Anyhows, 'ow do you know she was a lesbian. You lesbians are you?'

'Could be,' said Fenella. She felt a poke in her side and turned to see Arlene giving a small shake of her head. Fenella indulged a roguish grin. 'What du ya think?'

The man regarded them for a long moment, his head hunkered back into the heft of his neck. 'If you wasn't then you wouldn't be askin', an' if yer was then yu wouldn't be talkin' to me, so ah reckon you are, but you are the type of lesbians that like a man.'

'Ah, very perceptive,' said Fenella.

'Fenella,' said Arlene, between shushed teeth.

'Ah ah. Ah know. Ah got some pictshus of leshbians, they're all good, ha, ah can show you.'

'You know, I think we're OK,' said Arlene, draining her glass and placing it on the bar.

'Ah, come on ladies, you know you want to. Ah tell yer wot, 'ere, ah got one here, you take a butchers.'

Fenella's mischievous grin started to dissipate.

He reached into his jacket pocket, pulled out a large, over stuffed wallet and started fumbling around in it.

'Let's go,' said Arlene, grabbing Fenella's elbow.

Fenella paused a moment. 'Yeah,' she said, allowing Arlene's steer to take her towards the door.

'Gor it,' said the man, looking up to see the two women heading for the door. ' 'Ere, ladies don't be like that. Come 'ere, ah got the pitsha,' he said, waving a grubby looking photograph and lurching after them.

Arlene hunted through her bag for the torch as the two of them stumbled outside, the door closing behind them. She turned it on as the door opened again, the frame filled with a bear like silhouette.

'Come on,' said Arlene, setting off briskly, though weaving slightly. Fenella caught up with her and linked elbows. The man held himself upright with the door frame then set off after them. Arlene and Fenella looked behind them and quickened their pace. 'Let's get back to The Terrace,' said Arlene.

'Ladies, ladies. Come on ladies.'

CHAPTER NINE

Harvey Premnas returned to his study bedroom in The Terrace. He sat down at the built in desk under the window, opened his lap top and sent an e-mail to Pamela Larrup asking to meet with her tomorrow to discuss the progress of his research. He deliberately didn't mention The Morocco Manuscripts. He walked to the window and looked out at the darkness. His room faced South East and looked down the steep valley across Brink Wood and Spa Wood, down to Cragg Brook, then up over Deacon Hill and out across the moors beyond. He only knew of this because of the view in daylight, discerning the outline of the woods now by the winking lights of farm houses and cottages spread across the dark pane of the window, with the road in the valley defined by the glitter of street lights and the occasional tracer of a car's headlights. What was the time difference to Sydney? Eight p.m. here, nine hours behind, so it would be 5 a.m. Tuesday there. Everybody would be asleep. He was here for another three weeks. He should plan to go out and do some sightseeing. Next weekend. He turned from the window. It was too early to go to bed. He wasn't really tired enough anyhow. He looked to the built in wardrobe and pictured the Australian Royal Air Force tunic hanging there, recalling the feel of the material brushing against the top of his legs. He opened the wardrobe door and looked at the jacket. He had bought it at one of the vintage clothes shops on King Street down the road from the university. It was made of coarse wool with a winged air force ensign over the left hand breast pocket. He turned to the window and drew the curtains. Why not?

It took him ten minutes to layout the jacket, cap, wig, stockings and suspenders, and briefs, divest himself of his mundane, everyday clothing and, taking his time, to address the ensemble to his frame. With the boots, wig and cap on he was now six feet ten of towering tranny. He hadn't bothered with the full make-up, boobs and tucks, he had them in his case but that would take too long. Just a quick fix. He placed his i-pod in the dock of the portable player, flicked through the screen, turned the volume up and selected a track. He stood in front of the mirrored door of the wardrobe, preened for a moment, then turned his back and assumed the position. Hands on hips, shoulders proud, lips poised in a dangerous pout. He pressed play.

Fenella and Arlene arrived breathlessly at the front door of The Terrace. They could hear the sounds of lumbering Cragg man, lurching across the middle of the road behind them as they turned the corner away from him.

'Come on, we can get in before he sees us,' said Arlene, trying to balance the torch whilst looking for her key, 'here, hold this,' she said, passing the torch to Fenella. She started to jumble through the litter in her bag as drunken protestations approached closer around the corner.

'Where is it? Everything's jabbled up. Trust us to get lumbered with a faunching drunk. Ah ha.' said Arlene, producing the key and letting them into the row of cottages.

Fenella closed the door quickly, slowing it and letting the lock close quietly. They stood still and listened. Heavy footsteps lumbered outside, crunching grit into the tarmac. They came still, stepping around, then set off again, getting quieter as they moved away.

'I think he's gone,' whispered Arlene, locking her eyes on Fenella and slowing her breathe. The moment stretched, freeing some relief between them. The pulse in Arlene's ears began to slow. Two beats longer and she could let go.

A piercing, terrified scream came from upstairs, followed by a loud blast of music. They both jumped and there was a triumphant, slurred shout from outside. The iron gate of The Terrace banged open and a heavy lurch of footsteps advanced towards the front door.

'Now what?' said Arlene.

'Let's get Harvey,' said Fenella, looking up the stairs in the direction of the music.

'No, wait,' said Arlene, trying to listen. She caught the sound of footsteps on the path outside that seemed to pause in the air for a moment before a jumbled detonation of thuds hit the door and a large body slumped to its foot, followed by a drunken moan and laughter.

'Ah ha ha ha, here's Billy.'

Arlene put her finger to her lips whilst loud stabs of music burst down the stairs. Fenella gestured towards the sound. What's the point. Arlene flapped her hands at her. I don't know.

'I know you're in there ladies, come on. I can take some picshuers if you like.'

There was a clump of hefty paws walking a heavy weight up the door, before a rattle and clicker in the lock as different keys were tried.

'Come on. Ah like yer music ladies, you gonna dance fer me?'

'Can he get in?' Whispered Fenella.

'I don't think so. I don't know,' said Arlene.

The loose handle continued to clatter as the lock was tried and re-tried, keys scratching off the metal housing.

Arlene gave up on silence behind the door. 'Listen, you need to go,' she shouted. The sound of the keys stopped and the volume of the music dropped.

'Why, wotcha wan' me to get?'

'We don't want you to get anything. If you don't go we'll call someone.'

'Ass alrigh', ah'll get someone. Ah'll getta friend, a foursome.'

Arlene startled at Fenella. 'This is your fault,' she hissed.

'My fault?'

'You shouldn't have encouraged him.'

'I wasn't, I didn't, I didn't mean to. It doesn't matter, it's him who's the problem.'

'You're right, you're right.'

'Ahm phoning my friend, he'll come. Ear. Ear, Charlie, Charlie? It'sh Billy. Listen. Listen mate.'

'If you don't go we'll call the police.'

'It's alrigh' Charlie's gor a uniform, you gor a uniform ain't cha Charlie, yeah they want yu to wear yer uniform....the girls...couple a lookers. Gonna do lesbian stuff fer us, yeah, yu uniform, kinky tarts. He's gonna wear 'is unifrom girls, yer alright.'

Fenella looked to Arlene. 'Let's get Harvey.'

Arlene nodded as they both started towards the stairs.

Harvey Premnas pictured the scene. Brad and Janet soaking wet in the hallway of a spooky mansion, having been let in by the butler, Riff Raff, their preppy voices nervously trying to extract themselves after witnessing a decrepit assortment of rackety souls dancing *The Time Warp* again. A bass guitar started. Da-dum dum dum dum, da-dum dum dum dum. He started to bring his left heel down on beats two and four as the caged lift he visualised himself in started to descend. Janet's eyes widened as Harvey's cloaked back appeared in Tim Curry's body. He span to face her in his mirror, his face under lit. "Arrrghhhhhhhhhhhhhhh!," she screamed, accompanied by a burst of guitars and cymbals as Harvey Premnas turned into his performance of Tim Curry's, Dr. Frank-N-Furter, singing *Sweet Transvestite.*

Lip syncing with his best Bloomsbury pout curled onto his vowels, he widened his eyes in time with the horn stabs and arched his eyebrows at

Brad and Janet looking on from behind the mirror. He strutted on the spot and rolled his shoulders into the stride, turned and skipped down the aisle formed by the admiring former Time Warpers, leading up to a small stage which he mounted. He span to face Brad and Janet again and became lost in his performance.

He vogued, smouldered, struck Schwarzenegger poses, slouched his pelvis into the beat, vamped with Freddie Mercury intensity, raising a quizzical eyebrow to Brad's camera eye, as he circled his arms like the pistons of a steam train and stepped into a New York Travolta hustle.

He reached the final chorus and started to sing out loud. 'I'm a PhD transvestite …..from inter-textual..Australia..ah ha ha.' The music built louder. 'Hit it, hit it. Just a doctoral candidate...with a trans-textual.. postulate..ah hay hay.' He spread his arms Christ like and threw back his head.

Knock knock. Knock. A knock!

There was another knock on the door, then again.

'Harvey, are you in there,' Arlene shouted, panting. The door started to open and Arlene Kendrick's head appeared around the frame. Her eyes widened as they were taken a foot higher than where she expected Harvey's head to be. She let go of the handle, placing her hand over her mouth, whilst the still opening door revealed Fenella Morningstar similarly transfixed, though with a growing smile of approval.

Harvey stood frozen as the final chords faded.

'It's not what it looks like,' he said.

'It looks like you're a fucking drag queen Harvey,' said Fenella Morningstar.

Harvey paused, and dropping his outstretched arms to his sides, realised denial would only result in the search for more disconcerting truths, which at this moment eluded him.

'OK, it is what it looks like.'

Billy Crouchmoor dropped his keys on the path. 'Blast 'n' buggered up bastards.' He crouched down to pick them up, rising on one knee as the slow golden light from the opening front door spread in front of him. He looked up to see a huge figure of some kind of avenging angel silhouetted in the doorway. The sound of a riding crop cracked against leather.

'Can I help yu buddy?'

'What the fuck...'

CHAPTER TEN

'So how do you do the boobs?' Fenella Morningstar asked.
'Well, you can use balloons filled with dissolved gelatine'
'You mean, like jello?' said Arlene Kendrick.
'Yep, exactly. Only problem is you can spring a leak.'
'I'd imagine,' said Arlene.
'So, if you want to do it on the cheap, something like pantyhose filled with rice or bird seed. That jiggles quite nicely. Downside is, if you get sweaty then you start to smell like boiling rice or bird seed. So you need a lot of perfume when you're dancing. The best is silicone stick-ons. Lots of places do them for women who've had mastectomies, and then if you've got a low cut top you can use make-up to create highlights and shadow that enhances the effect.'

'So you actually do shows back in Sydney?' asked Fenella.
'Yes I do.'
'I'd love to see one, we don't get a lot of that type of thing in Wyoming. Don't suppose they have many around here either.'
'Naw, I very much doubt that. You'd really have to go to London, or maybe Manchester.'

There was a pause long enough for Fenella to start to frame questions which she wasn't sure whether to ask. She looked to Arlene who was looking at her hands, flat on top of the kitchen table.

Arlene raised her head, caught Fenella's look and spluttered: 'Well I'll be sneetered. And I thought meeting Fenella was odd enough. I never thought I'd be meeting a full on Sydney drag queen. Why have you..., I'm not sure I know what the words are, why have you got you're 'costume', is that what you call it? Why have you got it with you?'

'I was going to go clubbing in London with a friend, international scholar *and* international transvestite.'

The conversation dropped again. This time Harvey broke the silence.
'You want to know why and whether I'm gay.'

They both laughed and let go of their restraint.

'Yes, yeah.'

'I've been attracted to women's clothing for as long as I can remember. Used to dress up in my mum's stuff when she was out. My dad found out, he wasn't too pleased. It was a bit much for a Kalgoorlie miner. Not what real ozzy men are about. But for me, it was a kind of release at first. A floaty dress just seemed so much more practical in the heat. I began to think about it more seriously about the same time I got into literature. You'd be analysing these novels for meaning and subtext, exploring motivation and responses to characters, both in their fictional world and the real world of the author, and then you'd be looking at how the language itself came to speak of these experiences in new ways, create an artful redrawing and reinterpretation of that world that folded back and reflected on itself. It was such a contrast to the smothering heat and expectations of Kalgoorlie. Grow up, get drunk, follow the footy, get drunk, become a miner, walk to the edge of town, look out at all that space and wonder where you could go with it. I wasn't expected to go to university. Nobody I knew had. But this world in books... it just seemed to release me from those expectations. Then came the women's clothes. They seemed to be the same kinda thing, a way of expressing something that wasn't supposed to be said, but which made me rethink how I fitted in with what was expected of me. There seemed to be so much more choice for women. I know that's ironic. Opportunities and expectations for women in Kalgoorlie were even more restricted than those of men. But their clothes, beautiful clothes. Patterns, colours, styles, the variety, and the makeup. It was just so creative. You could change the way your face looked, become more alluring, mysterious, even to yourself. I remember the first time I made myself up, it was pretty crude, but the transformation made me look at myself as someone who could be something else. Thinking about going to Uni in a big city also got me thinking like that. It just seemed that someone had spent so much more time and thought on women's clothes. It didn't seem fair. And then you'd be reading about repression in something like Tess of the D'Ubervilles. I really appreciated a sense of freedom when I dressed up as Claire. It was like my own creative world, a kind of sartorial expression of the ideas I was looking at in literature. And like literature, it could be so artful. You really had to think consciously about how you were presenting yourself, in the same way that you had to think about how an author presents a character and what this signifies and means. So much more interesting than just throwing on a pair of shorts and a tee shirt. I guess I was jealous of the artful potential of women's clothes. So I started dressing up. And no, I'm not gay.'

As he talked the two women listened with rapt attention. Their heads nodding from time to time. With Fenella mouthing, 'Claire', at Arlene at one point.

'Now I'm really confused,' said Arlene, 'I thought you had to be gay.'

'A common misconception. Most drag queens are. But for a few of us it's just about an artistic expression.'

'So it's not like a political thing?' asked Fenella.

'Not for me, but it can be. It depends on the performer. Because the audience are in on it, how can they not be? Because they've come to see a drag show, then it can allow a performer to say and do things that ordinarily people wouldn't tolerate. Some girls take the whole, "you know, that I know, that you know, that I'm not a woman," that knowing charade, and deliberately use it to subvert conventions. Take a real in-your-face attitude, slag off and humiliate the men in the audience. Who sit there and take it in a way they normally wouldn't. In an odd way they're momentarily more powerful as veiled men, as a female impersonator, than any male executive or banker watching. Though it's momentary and illusory of course. Come Monday they're back at work fucking us over and screwing up the economy as usual, ready for the next financial crisis.'

'I suppose you'd like us to keep quiet about.... Claire?' Arlene said.

'Normally I wouldn't mind,' said Harvey, 'but I think some people might find it difficult. I can't imagine what Pamela would think.'

Fenella guffawed.

'It might be easier not to mention it.'

CHAPTER ELEVEN

Rick Callow was waiting by Pamela Larrup's closed office door, clutching his hands in front of his chest and bobbing slightly on the balls of his feet. He turned and walked into his own office opposite, paced around it and walked back to Pamela Larrup's closed door. He raised his hand to knock on it, paused and pulled back, dropping his arm. He went back to his own office, paused again in the middle of the room, then decided to make a decision. He went down the corridor, descended the winding flights of creaking and tilted stairs and down to the reception office behind the entrance porch. In the office sat two ladies, each working at computers, either side of a broad oak Partner's desk. They looked up and smiled widely.

'Bonjour, bonjour Rick,' they chimed together.

They were not French and looked as though they may have been sisters, appearing easily familiar in one another's presence. They were finely clothed, both wearing blouses, one Paisley, the other cream silk, and cardigans, and they each wore glasses. One had cherry red full framed spectacles, the other half-moon, tortoiseshell reading glasses, which caused her to raise her head and look down as she worked on the computer. They wore make-up which appeared a little too perfectly applied, suggesting they may have once worked on the cosmetics counter of a chic department store. The whiff of Channel No.5 about the office further encouraged the impression.

After their greeting they continued to look at Rick Callow, appearing to expect some request which was taking just a little too long to come, all the while holding wide toothy smiles with no twitch of reassurance or amusement.

'Ah, yees I wanted to ask, well really just to say that, if there are any calls for me from James Broadbent, could you just say that I'm not here today. It's not that I'm not, of course, but I know he's going to ask me some questions you see, and ahh, yees, I don't quite have the answers yet. That is the answers that would be most useful, and well, it would be better if, when he does ask me those questions, that I do have the answers. So you see, if I've had the time to do the research that is really required to provide him with the answers he needs, then I could give him the proper answers more properly, and I need just a little more time to do that. Do you think you would be able, I mean if it's alright, and it's not as though it's doing anything wrong, just making sure we have the time for me to do the research. Is that OK?'

The two ladies looked at him. 'We, we, yes of course Rick, we can do that can't we,' said one, looking over her glasses at the other who was smiling and nodding.

'Oh yes, we can do that,' said the other, 'because, we know what you're doing. We can do that.'

'What do you mean, "know what I'm doing"?' said Rick Callow.

'Why, researching,' said one of the ladies, looking him straight in the eye.

'Researching, of course,' said the other.

'Oh yes, of course, I know. So, yees, thank you for that then ladies. I'll leave you to your work,' he gave them his widest smile, 'keep it up, the good work. And I'll just, ahh yees, I'll just go and get on with that research then. Remember, James Broadbent. Not here,' he said, shaking his head and waving his hand. The two ladies smiled at one another as he left the office.

'So, James Broadbent,' said one.

'The auditor,' said the other, as both of them nodded.

Fenella Morningstar had awoken that morning with a sense that the day was full of promise. Optimism in the air. The type of day when her consciousness, previously haunted by an answer just beyond view, would pull back to reveal a vision of such sweeping clarity, that she could easily reach into the panorama, wave her hand above the canyons and watch the answer come trotting out of the ravines like a spirited Palomino. The feeling was great. If only there was some kind of project it could be put to.

The weather was unusual for Yorkshire's West Riding. It was balmy, positively warm. It reminded her of the weather in Cheyenne in April. Very dry, no humidity. Not hot, but warm. The landlord at breakfast had said it was an Indian summer. She didn't think he was being ironic.

This feeling of buoyancy held some familiarity for Fenella. It had come previously half way through her masters thesis. Then again, a third of her way through her biography of Niccolo Machiavelli, with the revelation that the political strategising in *The Prince* stacked up at least as well, if not better, if it was refracted through the consideration of Florentine sexual culture and the possibility that Machiavelli was gay.

First of all, there was the smile. The paintings reminded her of nothing less than a simpering Julian Clary. Discovering Machiavelli had been arrested for sodomy, she became convinced that *The Prince* was actually intended as a camp comedy, to be taken ironically, rather than as a playbook for aspiring despots, and that reading him with an effete mince made so much more sense.

"There are only individual egos crazy for love."

"The first method for estimating a ruler is to look at the men around them."

"It is a double pleasure to deceive the deceiver."

Her re-casting of him as a pioneer for gay politics received mixed reviews. Though it sold well, the more conservative political theorists argued it was irreverent, misconceived and demeaning to the project of serious political theory. Criticism that she had answered in spades through the pages of academic journals, diverting any serious damage to her scholarly reputation. The extent to which the criticism bothered her had further receded as *Prince Charming and the Machiavellian Camp* had foreshadowed the popularity of her later books. In *Yes Masochist* and *Thatcher Dominatrix* she had ploughed a seamy furrow to feed public fascination with the association between the sexual psyche and politics. In casting around for a new project, *'Persuading Emma: The Missing Shades of Grey'*, was her response to her publishers insistent suggestion that she capitalise further on her earlier work, by writing something which played even more overtly to public appetites for sexual revelations of the famous; taking the popularity for celebrity gossip and giving its prurience the air of something slightly more elevated, by adorning actual or potential sex scenes, with the gown of academia.

Though she was somewhat resistant to this initially, the prospect of playing fast and loose with such an esteemed figure as Jane Austen had appealed to her sense of irreverence. A feeling that was given greater impetus in the face of her publisher's offer to pay for the flight to the UK to see if she could ground the project in some serious analysis of Austen's papers. The prospect of a cheap holiday and the opportunity of studying at Laudanum had been enough for her not to bother her publisher with the expectation that there was probably little to find.

She rang the bell in the porch of Laudanum Grange and waited. She had been about to ring again when footsteps approached and the door opened.

'Bonjour Fenella, Comment allez-vous?' said one of the ladies from the front office.

'I'm fine thanks, I just want to check my mail,' she said, walking across the threshold.

'Bien,' as she led the way into the front office where her sister was sitting at one of the computers set back-to-back across the wide desk. At least Fenella assumed they were sisters, and why do they do that? Why the French when they clearly weren't? This had brought her up sharp at first and she had thought of asking about it, but as it seemed to be accepted with such ease by everyone, it felt a bit like asking why you're breathing, so she hadn't.

She was standing at the row of pigeon holes with her back to the sisters, sorting through her mail, when the bell rang again.

'The bell,' said one of the sisters.

'We, the bell,' replied the other.

They looked at one another.

Fenella Morningstar paused in her sorting, turning slightly to provide a discrete angle.

'I should think one of us should go.'

'I should think that would be the case. For one of us.'

They continued to look directly at one another, as though some telepathic communication were taking place.

'If you go, then I would be waiting. Upon your return I would still be here.'

'That is usually the case. You still there.'

'Then that settles it, I'll go,' said the sister with the half-moon reading glasses, smiling in a fixed manner and slipping the glasses off her nose as she stood, letting them hang on the chain around her neck. She returned leading a man in his mid-twenties, carrying a jacket in one hand and wheeling a large suitcase behind him.

'This is Gustav Crum,' she said to her sister.

'Gustav Crum, bonjour Gustav Crum,' said the other.

'Ah hello, I am here to meet with the Dr. Pamela Larrup. I am her new research assistant. I have come from Denmark.'

'Ah we know.'

'Yes, we know.'

'We have been expecting you.'

'Yes, expecting you to come.'

'And now that you are here, we should make sure you know where to go.'

'Yes, so one of us should call Pamela, let her know that Gustav is here.'

'Yes, one of us should.'

They looked at each other.

Fenella Morningstar glanced from the sisters to Gustav Crum stood in the middle of the room with his back to her, then back again to the sisters.

'When one calls, the other listens.'

'That's usually so. Listens and checks, just in case.'

They looked at one another.

'Then that's settled, I'll call her,' said the sister with the cherry red glasses, picking up the phone and pressing the button.

Gustav Crum looked about the office and at the woman stood at the pigeon holes. He pulled back his shoulders and rolled them against the tension from dragging his suitcase up the drive. As the muscles released he felt the familiar ease of certainty return that had been confirmed upon the news of his appointment as Dr. Larrup's research assistant. His newly minted PhD would definitely bring much needed cache and historical context to the project of eighteenth century studies. How they had got along without an expert in early manuscripts puzzled him. The study of manuscripts that pre-dated the overly regarded codex, was a necessity that any serious research library ought to provide. However, his appointment indicated they had clearly come to their senses and he was looking forward to telling them.

That Gustav Crum was convinced in this, belied the aura through which his interview answers had been received. It was not so much that these had pleased Pamela Larrup, but that in the glow of her imagination they emanated from an Adonis, albeit one that took a certain ascetic upbringing to fully appreciate. He was exceptionally thin, his clothes hanging distant from his frame, and his shoulders slumped apologetically towards the expectation of a pigeon chest. His skin had the look of a fine mineral, like talc or chalk, that appeared as though one might be able to rub an impression of your thumb into it, whilst his goatee aspired to something Walter Raleigh might have worn. However, its wispy growth struggled to stay in shape, revealing a receding and papery chin; an inversion of the Hapsburg lip he had inherited from some stridently inbred association with Danish royalty. The bulbous and lobed forehead that crowned his features meant, to Pamela Larrup's eye, he had an air of graceful, ethereal intelligence that she found beguiling; as though he was not quite solid enough for this world, and would benefit from being grounded by the fulsome sturm of her unwieldy hips.

'Bien,' said the sister putting down the phone. 'Fenella, this is Gustav Crum, from Denmark.'

'Yes, I gathered, nice to meet you,' she said, extending her hand.

He shifted his jacket across to the other hand and shook hers. 'Yes, Doctor Gustav Crum, it is nice to meet me,' he said, in heavily accented English.

'Fenella is a visitor here, researching,' said the half-moon sister.

'And what is it that the research is about?' asked Gustav Crum.

'I'm doing some stuff on Jane Austen.'

'Ah Jane Austen, she is too young for me.'

'Yu think?'

'I studied the older manuscripts for my PhD at Oxford. Where did you study?'

'Er, the University of Wyoming, I'm based there too.'

'Wyoming? I have been to Harvard. It is a long way from Harvard.'

'Some way.'

'You are a professor there?'

'No, I'm an independent, but I have a kinda honorary position there.'

'Ah, it is a pity.'

'What is?'

'Your position, it is a pity position.'

Fenella Morningstar regarded him for a moment. 'Are you going to be here long Gustav?'

'Yes, I will be here for the six months. I am working with Dr. Larrup. After Oxford I am forward looking also to explore more of the British, some more of their local traditions.'

The sound of Pamela Larrup's stride echoed ahead of her into the room.

'Ah. Hello Gustav, nice to meet you again, ready for the fray?' said Pamela Larrup.

'Yes, I am ready for the fray Doctor Larrup.'

'Please, you can call me Pamela. Now let's get to it, this way.'

She led Gustav Crum out of the office.

'Goodbye,' he said, nodding formally at the sisters then at Fenella Morningstar.

There was a quiet, productive focus to the scene in the reading room. Arlene Kendrick and Harvey Premnas were working at one of the large reading tables. The rustle of pages, a shush of pencils on paper, and the occasional creak of a chair leg, accompanied the hollow whisper of the air conditioning and the hum of minds running through scrupulous deliberations.

Giles Skeffington was working through the backlog of cataloguing that was piled on the trollies beside his desk. After some time he got up and went up to the café, joined shortly afterwards by the two visiting fellows.

As Arlene left her seat she pulled a cardboard file bulging with sheets of paper from the bottom of a pile in front of her. At the top of the circular staircase she dropped the file and some of the papers fell out. She cursed and gathered them, failing to notice one sheet that had drifted into the lee of the adjoining staircase running up to the museum.

The smell of fresh coffee drifted amidst the fellow's conversation as Pamela Larrup and Gustav Crum entered the library through the revolving door.

'Good Morning,' she nodded at the fellows as she and Gustav walked towards the stairs up to the Grimalkin Museum. She paused at their foot to pick up the piece of paper there and started to read. She lowered it and looked around. Then raised it again and continued reading. Gustav Crum waited with interest. When she had finished, she lowered it again and looked sternly towards Arlene, Harvey and Giles Skeffington in the café.

'Giles, could I have a word?'

She gestured towards the corner of one of the cases in the exhibition space.

'Excuse me,' he said, rising and walking to meet her. She led Giles round the corner out of view of the fellows, with Gustav following.

'I have just found this on the floor,' she said, handing him the piece of paper.

Giles Skeffington read the sheet, trying and failing to stifle smiles as he did so, with Gustav Crum craning around his shoulder. Something about the language seemed familiar to Giles, though he couldn't quite place it. 'Well, it is a little fruity,' he said.

'What is a ruffler?' asked Gustav Crum.

'I think it's some kind of criminal,' Giles Skeffington replied, 'like you get pick pockets and muggers nowadays.'

'What do you think we should do?' Pamela Larrup said, under her breath.

'What do you mean?' said Giles.

'And what is a Clutchcunt?' asked Gustav Crum, loudly.

In the café, Harvey's attention twitched.

Giles looked to Pamela, who turning said, 'It is not a polite word Gustav, not polite at all.'

'Oh, I see.' said Gustav Crum. 'It is a swearing word then?'

'Yes it is Gustav. What do you think we should do Giles?'

'I'm not sure we should do anything.'

'Somebody over there wrote this filth,' she said, tilting her head in the direction of Harvey and Arlene.

'Well yes, maybe, but what does it matter?'

'It matters because it is an abuse of the trust we place in them to make fruitful and purposeful use of their time here. If someone is writing this sort of thing,' she said brandishing the poem, 'then they can hardly be considered to be doing that, and we should really have given their place to someone more deserving. It will have to be raised.'

'It may not have even been one of the fellows. It could have been anyone who's used the library recently. Besides, it's clearly meant to be a joke,' said Giles.

'In very poor taste if so. It wouldn't surprise me if it was the work of Miss Morningstar. We will have to challenge this and find out, it simply cannot be ignored. I will have to know,' she said, walking toward the seated fellows.

Giles Skeffington watched her close in on the researchers. Oh dear. What had seemed to be a day poised on the cusp of fruitful purpose, was about to descend into the acrimonious welter of someone's petulant indignation.

'I am sorry to interrupt you but a most urgent matter has been brought to my attention which must be cleared up immediately.'

Arlene and Harvey stopped talking and looked to Pamela Larrup.

'I found this on the floor over there.'

Arlene took a deep breath and her eyes widened with an inadvertent look towards Harvey.

'Ah, yes, that's mine,' said Harvey.

'So you admit to writing it?'

'Yeah, but it's hardly a criminal act.'

'The language is filth and not what I would expect from a scholar's use of the collections here.'

'I agree. It is filth, but that's only because I found the language in your collections.'

'In our collections?'

An intimate sense of knowing broke more immediately on Giles Skeffington, 'Oh, Oh, he's right Pamela, I thought I recognised it,' he said, joining them. 'It's all taken from Grose's, *A Classical Dictionary of the Vulgar Tongue*, 1796 I believe. It's on the open shelves downstairs.'

Pamela Larrup bridled.

'I'm sorry if it's offended you Pamela,' said Harvey, 'but it wasn't meant for public consumption. It was just a bit of fun, keeping me entertained while I waited to speak to you about The Morocco Manuscripts. I sent an e-mail arranging to see you so I could talk to you about it. I really can't get on without them.'

'I see.'

'Yeah, I've reached a real impasse and I was getting really restless. I knew I'd need to talk to you but you hadn't replied. So I was wondering around the library when I came across the vulgar dictionary. And, as I said. I was just playing around. Sorry for any offense.'

'Very well. Tell me what you have done.'

'I'll see you later,' said Giles, walking away to the safety of the reading room. Having seen Pamela face looming certainty before, this conversation was not one he wished to be present at when it ended. He had quickly appreciated how adroit and perceptive Harvey was, methodically expediting his review of the materials. In calling Harvey to account, Giles could only see Pamela trying to frustrate the ineluctable progress of a mind which could easily festoon her path with all manner of papers, theses, manuscripts and ideas, so as to create a veritable skid pan out of the marble floor of the café. He could almost see the documents slipping from under Pamela's feet as she sought to arrest her drag towards an inescapable conclusion. He knew from experience that if she'd been alone with Harvey, any reasoned opposition would have quickly given way to a fractious collapse and his dismissal. However, whilst in private her sustained tirades could end in a trouncing rout, to do so with an audience was to lay herself open to questions about her sanity, an insight which even she was aware of. No, it would not be a pretty sight. Pamela realising, with growing inevitability, that her will to hold the world in ransom to her ego, was not sufficient to extort the rational endeavours of a thoroughly prepared mind. Giles could imagine the exasperation of her plight eroding a purpose that must have once felt as solid as the ground now slipping away beneath her. Though there was something delicious in the thought of this, he didn't want to see it. This ran the risk of becoming victim to a beast whose self-importance had become so maimed, it could bear little witness. He'd learned to be scarce on such occasions.

'I had intended to study them myself,' said Pamela, her cheeks flushing and looking from Harvey to Arlene then back. 'I suppose you do need them.'

'Can you let Giles know?' asked Harvey.

'Yes, yes. I can do that.'

'And once again, I'm really sorry about any offense from that.' Harvey said, nodding at *The Ballad of Bastardly Jack Gullion* lying on the table.

Pamela nodded curtly. 'Come Gustav,' she said, retreating up the circular stairs to her office.

CHAPTER TWELVE

A distraction was needed. Something to take his mind off the confusion with those numbers and spreadsheets. He would, of course, sort these out, but there was no real urgency. It could wait for a day when the need for these things was such that he could find someone else to do it for him. Maybe he could ask Pamela to do it again? She had done it the last time, or at least she'd seemed to. What was needed now, was the thing that really required his immediate attention. Not the nitty bitty niggle pick of numbers, but the things which gave shape to the purpose of Laudanum Grange, which he, with his sense of the grand plan and his superior people skills, could provide the leadership and inspiration to achieve.

Whenever things started to look confusing, Rick Callow was an expert at identifying something from among the activities of others that he could lay claim to have furthered; things that seemed to him so much more worthy of his attention than the day-to-day mumbo jumbo of details that emerged from within the confines of his computer. Besides, so much of it really seemed to require someone else's attention. Why this stuff came through to him was something that, one of these days, he was really going to have to sort out.

He'd made inroads on this the other day when he'd asked the office ladies to redirect any calls from James Broadbent whilst he sorted out the detail of the things that Broadbent needed to know. It was really all in hand. Besides, talking to James would simply have taken time from the thing that was about to be done anyway. It would simply have raised unnecessary concerns. It would get done, and as it was going to get done, there was no need to get sucked into it right now. No, for now he suspected there were things of greater import he should be directing his attention to, which these minor irritations had been distracting him from. Now, what would they be?

He looked out the window and watched a figure walking towards the library. Fenella Morningstar. Fine looking filly. That was something that he'd normally have done by now. How could he have overlooked it? He always liked to be abreast of what was going on at the place. What better time than now to start familiarising himself with the progress of the visiting fellows? Especially Fenella. After all, Pamela had said her research was on something very close to his heart. Dancing. Ever since he'd been a runner-up in the Young Mover's competition at Butlins he had thought it only a matter of time before his talent would reward him with greater prizes. After he had become CEO of Laudanum Grange he had spent some time learning the dances of the eighteenth century, pacing out the complicated steps across the carpet of his office with a range of imaginary partners. He could offer Fenella the benefits of this experience. Maybe read some of her work, impress her with his insights. Actually, better still, give her some practical instruction. Lead her through the steps of the dances in her work. Allow her to feel the embodiment of her words in the hands of a master practitioner. That's a ticket worth more time than sitting in front of a computer on tasks that could surely be delegated to others. Though delegation itself could take time. He'd get on to that tomorrow. More important now to engage Fenella, make sure she didn't miss such an opportunity. He set off with a pleased skip.

Fenella Morningstar pushed through the revolving door and walked across the lobby of the Grimalkin Library towards the exhibition cases, casting a bright smile and trim wave toward Harvey and Arlene in the café. Her easy stride took her to the case containing the account book of the East India Company from 1808 to 1814. She wanted to look at it because of something Arlene Kendrick had said about Jane Austen's brother, Francis. About the East India Company paying him a lot of money in the early 1800s. After noticing the book she'd wondered if it might be recorded there.

She was aware of the notorious reputation of the nabobs, ruthless profiteers of The East India Company, that made Enron executives pale in comparison, and the possibility of scandal had kindled her intrigue.

She read the card in the display case: 'Accounts, respecting the annual revenues and disbursements, trade and Sales of the East India Company, for four years. 1814.'

The book was open at the page entitled: 'Abstract Statement of the Receipts and Disbursement of the Bengal Government.' She scanned down the column marked 'Ordinary Receipts'. Her eye stopped on one entry and followed it across.

	1808-09	1809-10	1810-11	1811-12
Sale of opium ------	*8,223,431*	*9,359,961*	*9,246,775*	*7,540,000*

So 1811 had been a bad year. She'd read that Mr Darcy's yearly income of £10,000 would have the equivalent spending power of more than £300,000 today, a factor of 30. She didn't bother to do the calculation here, the sums were huge. No wonder smuggling opium into China was worth going to war.

She turned from the display case and sought Giles Skeffinton. He agreed to let her have a closer look at the book and brought it to her at the reading desk.

She skimmed through and made some notes: extra ordinary disbursements £36,007 to the prize agents for the capture of Malwa; Bombay 1811, £16,950 for purchasing land to enlarge the burial ground. Wonder if the two were connected? Stipends to the Nabob of Surat and his officers - £114,936; to the Rajah of Tanjore £302,939. No wonder the Brits ran an empire on this. Looked like it was all oiled through drug deals, back handers, and exploiting the locals.

She was getting towards the end of the account book, beginning to think there wasn't anything on Austen, when the entries turned even more idiosyncratic. Then in the 1808 accounts:

Captn Austen, for his safe conveyance of seven Indiamen from St. Helena - - - £420

So, around twelve grand from a private company straight into the pocket of a Royal Navy captain. For what exactly? As the East India Company was British, wasn't it just his job to protect them? But then to be paid specifically for it? The antennae of her intrigue piqued. Captain Austen embroiled in corruption? High seas racketeering, cash for protection? Having made some uncommitted strides into Jane Austen's papers and manuscripts, she'd not been entirely unsurprised to find little in the way of the dirty jottings that might have pleased her publisher. Now however, with the prospect of a real target to stalk - she only had so much patience for women in bonnets - who may have prowled around the powerful East India Company accepting bribes, that was much more her.

After setting about further research her suspicious enthusiasm had become more subdued. It turned out there was nothing particularly untoward in the payment. It was fairly standard for the time, with private payments and bounty seized in battle an accepted part of a captain's salary, something that had amused her when reading Francis's peeved letter to his fiancée, whinging about the booty he had forgone by missing out on The Battle of Trafalgar. Indeed, Francis Austen had had a very honourable career, rising, like Nelson before him, to become Admiral of the Fleet. No, there didn't seem to be much that hinted at the air of scandal she was hoping for. Oh well, back to scouting around for something other than the pseudo academic sex scenes her publisher hoped for.

She pushed the open book away from her, leaned back in her chair

Cringe

and stretched her arms. She looked absent-mindedly around the library. Harvey Premnas was sat at the reading table furthest from her, reading with his headphones on. The rest of the tables were empty.

Rick Callow walked down the stairs.

Catching her eye he motioned, 'Ah, wanted to see you'. The significance of his purpose stressed in the raised finger that led him as he homed in on her.

Realising she hadn't been quick enough to feign industry and turn her reflective pause into something that might have inhibited his approach, she let a resigned smile settle on her lips.

'Ah Fenella, lovely to see you this bright and ahh sunny morning. How's the old studying going?'

'Oh, it's going fine.'

'Looks like you've got some pretty tough stuff there eh,' he said, pointing at the list of figures on the open page of the accounts book.

'It's an East India Company account book. Not that too many accountants today would feel comfortable with what these guys are listing. Reads like a litany of fraud, embezzlement and corruption.'

'Ahh yees, accounts eh. Not really my forte, got to do them though I suppose. I get an auditor in, does them all for me. Tries to talk to me about them now and again. Between you and me, I don't understand a bloody word,' he said laughing, 'in one ear, out the other, that's the way of it. As long as we all get paid in the end eh, that's the ticket.'

'I guess.'

'Yees. No me, I'm more of your creative type, something I wanted to talk to you about actually. Pamela told me what you're doing, your research. I've got an idea that I might be able to help you with it. Thought I might explain it over a spot of lunch. What do you say, eh, down at the old Ferret and Trouser Leg, eh, hm,' he said, bobbing from one foot to the other.

'Oh I'm not sure Rick, I'm on a bit of a roll here. I don't think I've got the time. What is it anyways?'

'Ah well, I just, ah yees. Just ah, wondered. You see I have quite a bit of experience in the area you're working on and I just wondered, well really it would be helping you. You see, giving you a bit of advice, helping you with the verité as it were. Wondered whether you'd like to join me in getting a bit jiggy, think that's what they call it nowadays, maybe this evening, after work,' he said, springing on the balls of his feet, 'you know get the benefit of an experienced man who's been around a bit. I do like getting down to a bit of frolicking about the floor. What do you say?'

What was he talking about? 'Er, no. I don't think so?'

'Well maybe I could just read some of what you've written so far. The moves in progress as it were. Ah yees, maybe I could sass it up a bit, you know, suggest a few alternative positions,' said Rick Callow, emphasising his physicality by clenching his fists and punching them towards one another.

Fenella Morningstar blanched and her gut recoiled. Had she heard that right? "Sass it up". "Suggest a few alternative positions". Though not a stranger to being hit upon in a library, it was usually a little more subtle than this. However, something in his eager, frozen grin suggested a pleased little boy who, having just presented the most elegant of bouquets, was keenly awaiting the praise it deserved. The mismatch between what he seemed to be saying and his body language caused her enough distraction to pause and pivot towards some enigmatic hedging rather than outrage.

'I don't know what to say Rick. You know I've never had such an offer before, and made in such a delightfully enticing way. However, Harvey and I have struck up, you know, a bit of a thing. I'm not sure he'd approve.' She glanced over at Harvey Premnas, working away oblivious with his headphones in.

'Oh I'm sure he wouldn't mind. He and I could take turns. Or, I tell you what. I'll show the two of you what to do then just step back and watch. Why don't you have a chat with him and let me know? And remember, we could always thrash it out in more detail over dinner. I'd love to roll your bones around. Eh? Offer's there on the table for you. Ah yees, I'll leave it with you,' he said, bending at the waist as he walked backwards away from her before turning, making a tiny skip and side stepping towards the stairs.

Fenella Morningstar's earlier sense of buoyancy shuddered and cowered. This was not the prospect she had envisaged this morning. What had she done to deserve it? She went over to Harvey Premnas and taped him on the shoulder.

'Hey there.'

'Yep,' he said, removing his head phones.

'You've got to help me,' she whispered, looking around, 'Rick Callow just offered me the benefit of his sexual prowess, to help with my writing.'

'What! You're kidding?'

'No. He said it would "sass it up", that he'd show me different positions.'

'Has he cracked a fruity? The guy's as clumsy as a duck in a ploughed paddock.'

'Thing is, I used you to get rid of him. I told him we were having a bit of a thing. So if he says anything you've got to play along,'

Harvey Premnas laughed. 'It'll cost ya.'

'Oh come on Harvey. If he'd hit on you I'd do the same. It was obnoxious.'

'I'd reckon. Naw, no worries. Who'd a thought? The dirty old bugger.'

CHAPTER THIRTEEN

The phone rang in the front office. The sister wearing the half-moon, tortoiseshell glasses looked over them toward her sibling.

'That will be the phone.'

'Yes, the phone. An inquiry no doubt.'

'I would expect so. Wouldn't you think?'

They looked at one another.

'I answered two yesterday.'

'I know, I counted. Two. That should settle it.'

They looked at one another.

'Then that has the matter settled, wouldn't you think?'

'Indeed I would think it is almost certainly my turn.'

'Your turn, almost certainly,' said the sister with the Cherry red glasses, smiling and picking up the phone. 'Bonjour, Laudanum Grange International Study Centre. Yes, hello Mr Broadbent. Why yes of course Rick *is* here today. I'll put you through. Au revoir.'

'James Broadbent, for Rick?' said her sister.

'Indeed, for Rick.'

'And you put him straight through I noticed.'

'Yes, straight through. Just like we were asked not to the other day. But that was then.'

'Yes. Then that it was asked, now, when it was not.'

'We we. Not asked exactly, and so, not done. One shouldn't assume'

'Bien bien. Not asked. Not assumed. Not done. Exactement.'

They smiled at each other and returned to their computer screens.

Rick Callow liked his desk. It had four draws down both sides. As the bottom ones were extra deep, it meant they could hold even more of the stuff he did not do but which he filed carefully away. He was logged into *Plus 500*, an online platform that allowed anyone to trade on the international stock markets. As a director, nay Chief Executive Officer, this was something he thought he ought to do. Not least because when he met other directors, chiefs and men of leadership, they would talk to him about the progress of their investments, so it only seemed right that he should respond in kind. Only thing was, as theirs seemed to be on an ever upward path, his seemed to be ever descending; with some so earthbound, the red lines on the screen resembled the trajectories of a shower of meteorites, doomed for the ground.

Why this happened was something that puzzled him. However, when he turned too much thought to it, his head ached. He'd read the market reports, with the shimmer of numbers and graphs offering such temptations of a rewarding return that he'd place a position with the diamond certainty of a seasoned speculator. But somehow these insisted on taking a deliberately bloody minded turn for the worse. On looking back at these numbers his eyes would become sore, with the blink of a glittering chance turning to the grit of an accusing taunt. Today was no exception.

He'd moved £2,000 from the Laudanum Grange contingency fund and used it to place a position. Only borrowing it after all. Investing for the future. "Maximization of shareholder value", was the phrase they used at the director's meetings. That Laudanum Grange was neither listed, nor had shareholders, seemed to be a minor detail. It was the general mis-en-scene that mattered in these conversations, not the detail. He'd leave that up to those whose nit-picky patience exceeded his sense of the grand vision. No, for he was a man whose view of the big picture was destined to set him in the stars for eternity. Today, however, this picture was clouded slightly by having to ensure there was enough money in the kitty to pay the wage bill at the end of the month. Something that he'd expected pay offs from his earlier strategic investments to cover but which now looked like it was going to need more of his tenacious attention.

The trend line for gold stocks, which had been going up steadily over the last week, bringing him a smile of certitude, now began to beat him about the temples. Why had it done that? He'd watched it carefully before buying the gold shares. He'd pondered on platinum initially but decided upon gold as it was more valuable, there was more of it about. Besides, platinum was just a bit like silver wasn't it? After pegging in his £2,000 for a minimum of forty eight hours, the line on the graph had turned on him and headed quickly south. Maybe it would turn up again soon. He crossed his fingers and tapped his head. He clicked randomly on some of the other buttons on the screen. What were they all for anyway? It was really a very complicated site. Lots of graphs and numbers streaming across the screen, and more buttons than you could shake a stick at. Couldn't they make it just a little more straight forward? He clicked on one particular button and the graph of gold stocks, whose line he'd traced with his finger leaving half an upward grin smeared on the screen, zoomed out to a view showing its trend across the last year. Oh dear, that didn't look so good. The scale which had showed the increase across the week had also changed. What had seemed to be a certain bet, now loomed at him like an unthinkable query, frowning on the lips. The overall trend of the line was downward. Up a little briefly, down a lot longer.

The phone rang.

'Hello, Rick Callow.'

'Rick, it's James Broadbent. How are you?'

The screen of his computer refreshed and the graph line leered. 'Ah Jim. Fine, fine. Good to hear from you. I'd been meaning to call. How's the old auditing going, eh ah yees, still adding up all the old numbers?'

'Yes, that's what I wanted to talk to you about. You see, I don't think some of them do add up.'

'Oh really, well that's not the ticket is it? Not at all. Now you tell me which spread sheet it's on and I'll have a look, maybe the battery on my calculator was running out of juice or something, I'll change the batteries, see if I can't rev it up a bit and do some double checking, eh?'

'I'd tried to talk to you about it earlier in the week but you weren't around. The details are in the e-mail I sent you, have you seen that?'

'E-mail, eh, hang on I'll just check, ah yes, yes got that. I've marked it as very important, to be read ASAP.'

'We'll could you look at it now and get back to me? I think it's just the case that some accounts haven't been included, or aren't running entirely up to date. I'm going to need the gaps filled in by the end of the month at the latest so I can sign off on it and file the report with the national audit office. Can you check the details and get it to me?'

'Check_the_details_and_get_it_to_you,' wrote Rick Callow as he spoke. 'Yep, I've made a note of that, all written down, and ah yees, that'll be done as soon as I can, sooner probably eh, that's the ticket. So don't you worry, I'll get it to you.'

'Thanks Rick, you do understand the importance of this don't you?'

'Of course, of course. Numbers, business, profits that's what it's all about eh. Got to make sure that it's all tickety boo as they say. No you leave it with me, when it comes to detail like this I'm your man. Always drilling down into the detail, that's me. You can rely on it. I'll have it with you before you can say, "who's going to send me that important data as quickly as they can in an e-mail with a spreadsheet attached and everything", well that'll be me, so don't you worry on that one James.'

'Well.. OK then, as soon as you can. Thanks Rick.'

Rick Callow hung up the phone and watched as the red line indicating the live price of gold further wriggled its downward grimace at him.

CHAPTER FOURTEEN

When the world of eighteenth century studies and Jane Austen had heard about the discovery of The Morocco Manuscripts there was immense speculation about their contents. There were those who speculated they contained the missing manuscript of her unfinished novel, *The Watsons*, that Jane had sent to her brother Francis for safe keeping. Though why she would have thought them safer on a British man-o-war during the Napoleonic wars, rather than in Bath or Godmersham, was not something they bothered to explain. Others had argued they might contain accounts of a more personal nature, reflections on his relationship with his parents and siblings, or thoughts on his superiors in the Admiralty and the management of the navy. Some thought this undoubtedly the case since, given his literary ambitions, an unpublished biography and parts of a sea faring novel, it was unlikely that Francis had lost the documents. For them, there was the suggestion that he had probably meant these documents to be destroyed, but in the chaos of re-supply and racing back for the Battle of Trafalgar he had not managed to do so. The general fervour of speculation had received greater impetus when it became known that Laudanum Grange had inserted a secrecy clause as part of the contract with the conservators. That Laudanum had bought the documents in a partially blind auction, without knowing precisely what they were buying, was seen as an act of cultural inspiration by some and by others as the indulgence of a patron whose wealth was exceeded only by his whimsy. For Harvey Premnas the speculation was about to end. The Morocco Manuscripts had arrived at his desk.

The first thing that struck him as he scanned the labels was how much of it there was. He had understood that it was found as one package. However Giles explained that each of the plain, buff boxes contained an array of items that had been classified by their form and date, such as the one he was presently looking at; *Letters and Correspondence 1792 - 93*. There were ten boxes holding forty-one individual documents and three longer manuscripts.

Giles had gone on to tell him something of the state they were found in. They had clearly spent time exposed to the subtropical Mediterranean climate as the paper had dried and become very brittle, with some on the documents breaking along their creased fold lines. When they had been discovered in the National library of Morocco they had all been stuffed into a worn leather satchel and this, along with their general bulk, had offered some protection to the bashing they received whilst becoming lodged between the wall and the back of one of the rolling stacks. A less experienced eye than Deirdre La Faye's might have ploughed on regardless when they had pulled out the crumbling pile. However, she had quickly realised the significance of what she had and helped set in train the events that had led to their reconstruction and conservation. This had included the time consuming process of soaking each document in an aqueous alkaline bath to remove acids and staining from the paper and re-hydrate the cellulose fibres, carefully drying these in batches, then repairing the documents using Japanese mulberry tissue and rice starch paste, in several cases re-building whole documents from many pieces. Those documents that were still in one piece but that remained folded had had to be humidified and flattened before any of this could take place.

After considering the labelled boxes Harvey Premnas had not seen anything obviously indicating that it contained documents relating to family life in Steventon. However, the labels were all fairly general, so he started with the nearest to him labelled: *'Morocco Manuscripts: Miscellaneous notes and documents; Captain Francis Austen, 1804 - 1805'.*

He laid out his desk, placing the reference books and other texts around to form a neat amphitheatre surrounding the now open box, his note book and pencil. He took the first document. It was a large single page and appeared to be the entries for a ship's log.

Monday 10th October 1805
Gentle Breezes and clear weather. We have been Docked at Gibraltar for four days but with our efforts should be able to stay longer. Went on shore with Major Tench and organised moving empty water casks ashore. Message received from C. To meet on Saturday 15th. Re-supply may be completed before this. Must ensure against this.

Tuesday 11th October 1805
Re-supply continues. Received on board fresh Beef and Greens for the Ship's Company.

Wednesday 12th October 1805
The re-supply for Canopus is being handled too quick. HMS Queen

and Spencer also well forward with re-supply. The officers are eager to sail as the Spanish and French fleets were near at hand when we left. Missing the glory of a successful attack on the enemy's ships is something that would be unfortunate for them but I must ensure our other task is well achieved before we sail. Major Tench has seen to it that the men under his command are confused in their purpose. Progress on the other ships has slowed. Received news of the progress of C. We are now to meet on Friday.

Thursday 13th October 1805
Set some People to repair the Sails and the Caulkers to Caulk the Ship; the rest of the People employed in the Hold and about the Rigging. Punished John Thurman, Seaman, with 12 Lashes for refusing to assist the Sailmaker in repairing the Sails, even though the repair, though required, was not necessary.

Friday 14th October 1805
Close cloudy weather. Employed getting aboard Rum, Water, and other necessaries. Went ashore with Major Tench at night. Passed the documents at the meeting with C. in The Star Tavern, Bomb House Lane. C. says T was well pleased with the last dispatch. C. passed communication from B. and T. It seems I am still trusted. Major Tench also passed on the copy of FR's orders intercepted ten days ago. They had come from contacts outside Madrid. This was a risk. Cadiz is 3 or 4 days ride. V. should be informed by Monday 17th or Tuesday 18th.

The entries didn't particularly surprise him. Since the discovery of the documents in Morocco the one thing the speculative scholars agreed on was that they were more than likely lost or misplaced around the time he was re-supplying *The Canopus* prior to The Battle of Trafalgar. The details were interesting and the meeting might be something worth checking against other sources at some point. However, the events were peripheral to his interest, though possibly not to Arlene's, so he made a brief note on the contents and moved on to the next document. This appeared to be a list of gunnery items. The next was a letter whose script looked so impenetrable he put it aside for later. The next item was in the same hand as the log entries, safe to assume it was Francis's then. As he started to read the thrill of seeing something that locked so immediately with his hopes caused him to try to read faster than he was able to. He took a considerate pause before starting over at his usual speed.

I write of the life and times of Francis Austen. At the age of twelve he travelled from his home in Steventon to The Royal Naval Academy in Portsmouth. Very soon after his admission into this seminary, he was distinguished by all the Masters as a youth of superior abilities, which joined a possessing appearance and a regularity in his conduct but rarely seen in so young a boy, gained him the esteem and regard of them all, and especially Mr.Bayly who he was sure would treat him to the day of his death with the most flattering marks of attention. On his occasions of leave he would pass around the town of Portsmouth and he observed amongst the women a sort of flippant air which seemed rather at variance with the retiring modesty so pleasing in the generality of English women his mother most surely being one of these. He could not but rejoice at the memory of his mother and father in the times at the vicarage in Steventon. The earliest occasion of this was when he was four years old and watched his father playing with his younger sister Jane.

He turned the page over. It was blank. He took the next document from the box. It was another letter in the almost indecipherable script. He browsed through the dozen or so other items in the box. None of them picked up the tantalising theme of the previous document. He exhaled deeply. This seemed like some exquisite torture. However, experience told him not to become disheartened. The manner in which items were collated for cataloguing, though theoretically codified through precise protocols and procedures, was often idiosyncratic, and particularly so with such a large batch of documents new to scholarly attention. He started to make notes on the documents in front of him, peering more closely at the indecipherable script of the two letters.

'See you've got them at last.' Harvey Premnas looked up to see Fenella Morningstar.

'Not without a bit of a wrestle,' said Harvey. 'I've only just started on them. This is promising.' He pointed to the page he had just read. 'It looks like an early draft for part of his autobiography.'

Fenella regarded it for a moment. 'What's this?' she said, pointing to page with the dated entries.

'I think it's a page from his ship's log.'

Fenella skimmed down the dates. 'I know what you mean, but wouldn't it be ripped?'

'Why?'

'I'd always assumed a ship's log was a book. So if this was a page of the log shouldn't it look like it was ripped out?'

Harvey fingered the edge of the paper. 'I suppose so. I'm not sure.'

'I'd always assumed a ship's log was pretty sacrosanct. Not something you rip pages from.' Fenella read through the entries in detail. 'Does that seem right to you?'

'What?'

'Him and his mate, Tench, trying to take as long as possible?'

'I didn't really think about it. I supposed it was something naval. It's not really relevant to what I'm doing. I'm looking for stuff on the relationship at home. I was thinking of letting Arlene take a look at it.'

'Can you get access to his ships log? That would be something to look at.'

'Yeah. But I want to see what else is here first.'

'Would you mind if I take a look?'

'No worries. Go on,' said Harvey, gesturing to a seat at the table.

Fenella sat across from him, pulled out her lap top and started to search. Harvey returned to sifting through the contents of another box.

After ten minutes or so Fenella gave a low whistle. Harvey looked to her. 'I couldn't find his log book, but then I remembered something. I came across this the other day. This doesn't sound like a man who wants to waste time.'

'What?'

She turned her laptop towards him.

Harvey was looking at a digitised image of a letter, held by The British Library, from Francis Austen to his fiancée Mary Gibson.

Fenella stood up and moved behind him. 'He wrote it over four weeks, just after he had received orders to sail to Gibraltar. Here's the bit,' she said, pointing at the screen.

As a national benefit, I cannot but rejoice that our arms have been once again successful, but at the same time I cannot help feeling how very unfortunate we have been to be away at such a moment, and by a fatal combination of unfortunate though unavoidable events to lose all share in the glory of a day, which surpasses all which ever went before, is what I cannot think of with any degree of patience, but as I cannot write on that subject without complaining, I will drop it for the present till time and reflection have reconciled me a little more to what I know is now inevitable.

Harvey Premnas looked up at Fenella Morningstar.

'He's talking about being disappointed at missing the Battle of Trafalgar,' said Fenella.

Harvey looked back to the log entries. 'When was it written?'

'Seventh of October eighteen-o-five, that's when he started it,' said Fenella.

'When was the Battle of Trafalgar?'

'Twenty-first of October.'

Harvey looked for a long time at the letter and the dates of the entries in front of him. 'So this,' he said, pointing to lap top screen, 'is written after the battle and it seems like he's slowing re-supply before it. You couldn't find the actual log book?'

'It's held in the archives at Admiralty House. It's not digitised, so you'd have to go there to see it. But neither it, nor this,' said Fenella, pointing at the screen, 'get lost for a couple of hundred years.' She read through the dated entries again. 'Doesn't it sound like he's doing something dodgy?'

'Mmmm, I don't know. I know what you mean, but it might just be some kinda normal naval procedure. That's why I was thinking of Arlene. I'm not really that familiar with the events leading to Trafalgar.'

'No, me neither. But I will be. Quick and dirty,' said Fenella, as she sat down pulling her laptop towards her.

CHAPTER FIFTEEN

'Gus-tav Crum, Gus-tav Crum,' said Pamela Larrup, her tongue trying out the name, releasing a small expulsion of spittle from the top of her pallet on the second syllable. 'Gus-tav Crrrrrum.' All Danish and delicious, just like a pastry. She picked up the confection that she had brought from the café to her office and licked at some of the sugary icing. Gus-tav Crum hm, mm, mm. True, he was younger than her, but you know, sometimes a younger man likes to be taken in hand. Taken in hand. She licked at some of the cream from the centre of the pastry. There was a knock on her door.

'You may enter.'

As the door opened, and Gustav appeared, a slight heat rose to her cheeks. She quickly put down the pastry.

'Ah Gustav, how are you getting on?'

'I have finished the preliminary work that you asked Doctor Larrup. I thought I would come early for our meeting for I wish to be ripe to use my time here.'

'Oh yes, that is wise. Sit down,' said Pamela, pulling a file from her desk drawer. 'These are the outlines of the research projects that I would like you to take over.' She handed them over the desk. 'If you just look at the first page you will see that I have listed them. A lot of it is hunting out documents and references and writing a first draft of the literature review.'

'I see,' said Gustav Crum, 'is there anywhere particular you would like to start me Dr. Larrup?'

Pamela Larrup looked at him a moment, re-ordering the words. She pursed her lips. It would be the logical thing to start at the beginning, but if he did it would take her longer to get the Morocco Manuscripts away from Harvey. How much longer was he here anyway? Another month? Time enough for him to miss the most important things. True, she would be meeting with him regularly which would give her space enough to pull at the bones of his progress, but that was no substitute for handling the manuscripts herself. If she'd had less teaching and liaison with Northrop

University she would probably have got to them by now. She ran her tongue around the back of her teeth dislodging a large flake of almond which she masticated, savouring the bitter taste. That she had managed to persuade them to fund a temporary research assistant was some recompense. She looked at Gustav considering the list and notched an idea two places higher in her standing.

'You know Gustav, it occurs to me that I did not list those in the correct order,' she stood up and walked around the desk to peer over his shoulder. 'This one here,' she leaned in closer and caught a whiff of aftershave and kippers. She inhaled slowly letting the fragrance linger, 'this one here,' placing her finger beside item number five: "Literature search and review for life and times of Francis Austen - timeline of significant historical, political and naval events against his own duties and activities.", 'should really be your first priority. Just focus on that, see how quickly you can get it down. I am very eager to move forward with that.

'I will start now,' said Gustav, straightening himself more formally in the chair. 'Research, like life, can only be understood forwards.'

'That sounds very profound Gustav.'

'It is based from my favourite philosopher, Søren Kierkegaard. "Life can only be understood forwards; but must be lived backwards." '

'Well how very wise that is, I think I will make a note of that, what was it again?'

He repeated the misquotation as Pamela Larrup wrote it down.

'Another one is, "Anxiety is the freedom to be dizzy," said Gustav Crum, pleased.

'That is so true, is it not. If you do choose to be dizzy it would make you a bit anxious.' She looked at her watch. 'Are you hungry? We could discuss the other projects over lunch.'

'I am afraid I have eaten. However, I will enjoy doing the business with you on a meal. Why don't we do it this evening? I will work on the Francis Austen this afternoon and tell my results. It will be my treat.'

Pamela's cheeks flushed. 'Oh you do not need to do that Gustav, but I think that would be a nice idea. We can get to know each other a little better. Bring that file with you and bring a pen. You will need to make notes.'

Gustav reached into the satchel at his side, pulled out a pencil and held it up.

'Excellent, I like a man who is prepared,' she said. Oh please, do be prepared.

Gustav Crum peered over the balcony of the Grimalkin Museum, down through the atrium to the reference library and reading room two floors below. Harvey Premnas and Fenella Morningstar were sat at one of the tables with a trolley of archive boxes beside them. Fenella must be Harvey's research assistant. She'd said she was researching Austen. If it had been him he would have chosen someone more qualified. At least with a PhD from a decent university - Oxford and Cambridge were the only ones worth bothering about in this country. Ahh, but she is American. Even more difficult when it came to ones over there. Anything outside of the old world had barely had enough time to civilise itself, let alone the populous. The hasty scrabble to employ academics of standing at these places seemed an unsightly way of trying to curry academic prestige against a culture so little steeped in the values they were attempting to foster. Indeed, places like America seemed to have deliberately slunk passed civilisation, opting either for decadence, degeneracy, or both. A view he had been pleased to share with Pamela at his interview. Though it would be interesting to talk to Fenella and Harvey. To see what they had found. That way he could get a jump on the literature review, focus it on the materials that were most pertinent to those in the Morocco Manuscripts. Dr. Larrup would be more pleased.

When he arrived in the reading room Fenella Morningstar was alone.

'Hello Fenella. You are researching the Morocco Manuscripts?'

'Huh,' said Fenella, her gaze taking a moment to pull Gustav into view.

'I have the work to do for Dr. Larrup on Francis Austen. I need to know what you find.'

'You'll have to talk to Harvey about that.'

Gustav looked about. 'He is not here. Will you tell me the things you have to find?'

He stood expectantly.

'You want to know what I've found?' asked Fenella.

'Yes'

'Well that's not really my call. It's Harvey's research. I'm just kinda helping out.'

'You are his assistant?'

'No, not exactly.'

'I see. You are his expert on Jane Austen then?'

'Again, not exactly.'

'You are helping but not assistant or expert?'

'That's about it.'

'How can you help?'

'Sorry?'

'If you are not expert?'

'I'm following some leads for him.'

'I see. So you do know what is found?'

'Yes I do.'

'So you can tell me, or I can read,' said Gustav Crum, gesturing to the notes.

'No. No I don't think I can, and nor can you,' said Fenella Morningstar, closing Harvey's note pad.

'Dr. Larrup is the Director of Research. She needs to know that I am her assistant to do her the work. You will help her. She will know.'

'Hmmm, yes. But this is Harvey's research. So as I said, it's his call.'

'He is not here.'

'Right again.'

'I will look through the boxes then, yes?'

'Nope. You know, I don't think that would be appropriate either. At least not without asking Harvey first.'

Gustav's forehead tightened, puzzling her answers for a moment. 'Ahh I see the problem. You are not working for Harvey and you cannot say. You do your own research, yes?'

'Yes,' acceding in exasperation to what she didn't entirely comprehend.

'Ah, so I wait for Harvey and ask him?'

'Yes.'

'Hmmm,' Gustav Crum looked around. There was still no sign of Harvey. 'Harvey is fortunate you are not the research assistant, if you are not the expert. And you only have the masters,' he said, partially to himself, folding his arms as he turned away.

'Oh really?'

Gustav turned back. 'It is not enough for the importance.'

'The importance of what?'

'The importance of the manuscripts. You must be owning the PhD. Yes.'

'Like you?'

'Yes.'

'Where was it you got yours again? I've forgotten.'

'Oxford.'

'And I suppose you've published a few books as well?'

'Not yet. But I have published an article in the journals.'

'Written in English?'

'Yes.'

'Hmm, that'd be interesting to read I bet.'

'Yes. You are correct.'

'More than your bloody English I'd imagine,' Fenella muttered under her breath, turning back to her lap top screen.

Gustav stood motionless behind her watching her computer screen as Fenella continued scanning material on The Battle of Trafalgar. As she moved to obscure his view he moved closer, closing down what little personal space remained. She continued to click between different pages, making some notes, and moving to try to obscure Gustav's view. Eventually, she folded her arms on the table, turning her head away from him behind her shoulder, her gaze looking off, trying to banish his presence to the middle distance.

'It is for Harvey you do this?' Gustav said, eventually.

'It is.'

'Yes. I think it is not Jane Austen.'

'Nope. I've not really written anything on her yet.'

'No. You are not the expert.'

Fenella's gaze pulled back from the distance and returned to her screen. 'You know Gustav. I'm not the expert. You're absolutely right. I'm here to write an entirely different kinda book.' She started to type something into the search engine above the images of full-masted men-o-war.

'Yes?'

'Oh, yes.'

'It is on Jane Austen?'

'It is. You see Gustav,' Fenella said, as she typed, 'I've got this theory that there was more to Jane than meets the eye.'

'Ah, I see.'

'Yep, a lot more. Yu see, I reckon that underneath she was a lot more like this,' she said, clicking on one of the returned search engine terms.

Gustav's chin started back and he blinked rapidly.

'Yep Gustav. Ah reckon Jane was a chick with a dick. Frigging in her rigging'

Gustav regained his composure and nodded slowly at the pictures of naked Filipino lady-boys. 'I see. You are a slut?'

Fenella froze, stretched her fingers and pulled them into fists.

'G'day there. How's it going?'

They turned to see Harvey emerging from the door to the stacks followed by Giles Skeffington.

Fenella took a deep breath. 'Gustav wants to steal your research,' she said, smiling.

'No no no, I am doing the research for Dr. Larrup. To see what you have found would be..ah..helpful,' said Gustav, looking back and forth between Harvey and Fenella's lap top screen, now returned to H.M.S. Victory in full sail.

'I'm not really at any stage to say what I've found,' said Harvey, 'I've only just scratched the surface.'

'That's what I told him,' said Fenella.

'If you let me know what Pamela's interested in I'll keep an eye out,' said Harvey.

'Ah. You will still be helping?' Gustav asked Fenella.

She shrugged her shoulders and pursed her lips in an inquisitive appeal to Harvey.

'Yeah, if she wants to,' said Harvey, acceding to Fenella.

'She will not be doing the, ah, "figging in the rigging"? That is not Dr.Larrup's interest.'

Harvey gave Fenella a puzzled look which she returned with a slight smile and tiny shake of the head. 'Er, no,' he said.

'It is well.' nodded Gustav, 'I can help you too?' he asked.

Fenella's eyes widened askance at Harvey.

'I have the PhD. From Oxford. I would not waste the time,' said Gustav, looking at Fenella.

Why the chinchy, mizzle-witted....

'You know, that's really kind Gustav but ah reckon Fenella and I'll be OK.'

'Very well,' said Gustav Crum, moving off towards the shelves across the room.

CHAPTER SIXTEEN

The oldest part of The Ferret and Trouser Leg had stood in the village of Cragg since the 1600s. It had seen additions and remodelling over the years and had variously been used as a farm house, stables, a barracks for the Parliamentary forces during the English Civil War and part of it had been a brewery in the 1890s. It had fallen into disrepair during the nineteen twenties but had been saved by the National Trust in the 1950s. The low ceiling hung from a black timber frame that was reinforced in places where it had moved over time and the wooden floors inside bowed and sloped.

Harvey Premnas had to stoop and bend his knees slightly to get through the door as he followed Fenella Morningstar into the pub. His eyes adjusted slowly to the dimming light as they moved down the straggling corridor. At the end, before they turned into the bar, there was a large painting on the wall. It commanded the space in a portentous manner, demanding inspection, yet eluding Harvey's immediate attempt to resolve its subject. It was smoke stained and defaced, yet within it there was something compelling. Hovering at its centre was a long, limber, furry form, writhing amongst a black mass of some blasted hyperborean heath. Within this, two red eyes stared down your gaze. Something about it made Harvey feel nervous and distracted. The indefinite, half attained figure pulling at him like chaos bewitched.

He dragged himself away from the painting and went into the bar, noticing a poster: "Wednesday 25th, Trouser Legging. How Long can you keep 'em down?"

'What's that about?' he asked the barman.

'The Trouser Legging lad? You've never heard a the trouser legging? Eh up Greg,' he shouted to an old man sat in the corner nursing a pint, 'this lad wants to know about the trouser legging.'

The old man looked up slowly from under his cloth cap to regard Harvey Premnas with a wizened gaze. The right-hand side of his face held a deep groove of age that ran like a scar up his cheek onto his forehead and disappeared into a streak of white hair across his scalp. He lifted his pint and took a pull on the bitter. Half of his little finger was missing.

'So. Thy wants to know about the trouser legging eh? Thinks ye can challenge?

There'd be plenty o room for the little buggers in those,' he spoke slowly, with slight Yorkshire disdain, nodding towards Harvey's long legs.

What was the guy on about? Having frequented the bar often over the last two weeks he thought he'd come to know most of the ins and outs of the locals. Nothing he'd heard had gone beyond what he assumed was the usual farmer's gossip and local's banter. Though he'd not seen this bloke before, and he seemed a little more eccentric than the usual characters, there was nothing about him to worry an outback boy. Nothing to compete with the bikies, cops, drugs, guns, and drunken bar room brawls. Nothing to warn off a boy from Kalgoorlie. He'd play the old fella.

'Reckon I might if I know what it's about. What'd ya say?'

'Why lad. George, here that?' said Greg to the barman, 'reckon's he might challenge,' he narrowed his eyes as he continued, 'reckon ye's got the nerve to take on King Greg eh. To take on two o the little bah-stards eh. Mind there's no jock straps and no underpants allowed, ye have to be naked underneath. An' no drink, thou hast to be sober.

What says ye to that then? Reckon ye can keep 'em down?'

Fenella Morningstar looked between Harvey and Greg. Harvey's eyes had narrowed. They were grim and unflinching, the muscles around them taught and determined, however, they made a sudden flick to Fenella. She detected a whisper of hysteria. What was he getting himself into?

'OK old timer, why don't you tell me more? What exactly are we keeping down?'

The old man laughed hoarsely. 'Why dons't thy know lad, dons't thy know? Ferrets, ferrets lad. Sharks o the land, piranhas wi feet, fur coated devils. They make the weasels weep, the rabbits run screaming and the rats tremble. Teeth like carpet tacks and claws like needles.'

He stood up, picked up his walking stick and shuffled towards the back door of the pub, the iron shod foot of the stick thudding slowly across the floor.

'Come on, ah'll show ye.'

Fenella Morningstar looked up at Harvey. What are you doing? His eyes widened and he shrugged. Twitching his head, they followed Greg towards the back door.

'Untrustworthy beggars that live only to kill,' he said, as he disappeared into a shed followed by a rattling and banging. 'Come on ye little blighters.'

He reappeared holding two dirty weasel like animals, with eyes as hard and red as rubies, which were squirming in his grasp like snakes, trying to twist and sink their teeth into his hand.

'They must have a full mouth o teeth, no clipping or filing, and they must be hungry enough so as they'll eat yer eyes to get at ya brain. Here I'll show ye,' he said, thrusting the ferrets towards Harvey. 'Why tak hold o them lad, tak hold a them. They will bite, so keep tight ahold.'

He transferred them into Harvey's grip who squeezed the steel cable of their necks at arm's length.

As Greg was tying up the bottom of his trouser legs with string a young man with a green Mohican haircut appeared in the yard on a bicycle.

'Eh up Greg, you puttin' 'em down again?'

'Aye lad, show yon foreigner what he's up against.'

'Ye gonna challenge Greg them?' asked the young man.

Harvey Premnas did not answer and kept his gaze fixed on the writhing forms in his hands.

Greg looked towards Harvey. 'Now then lad, give em here,' he said, undoing his belt.

He took one of the animals and stuffed it down his trousers, quickly followed by the other before cinching the belt tight. Holding his fists clenched by his sides, he stared up into the grey Yorkshire sky. There was a whirling of legs, claws and squirming bodies inside his trousers as two bulges circled round and round one leg, across his crotch and down the other.

'Don't they bite your...bite your - you know?' said Fenella.

'Do they!' thundered Greg, as the tussling bundles reached his crotch again. 'Why,

I had 'em hangin' off me...', he looked towards Fenella Morningstar and grinning asked, 'Are ye cheeky, luv?'

'Oh yeah, she's cheeky,' said Harvey, nodding.

'I am?'

'Why,' Greg roared, 'I had 'em hangin' from me tool for hours an' hours an' hours. Two at a time—one on each side. I been swelled up big as that,' he said, pointing to an empty, rusting, five-pound can of instant coffee.

Fenella Morningstar and Harvey Premnas winced.

'Do you think it's your age that gives you the nerve?' asked Fenella Morningstar.

'And what do ye mean by that young lady?'

'Well, I just thought, since you probably aren't going to have any more children....'

'Are you sayin' I ain't pokin' 'em no more? Is that your meaning? 'Cause I am pokin' 'em for sure,' Greg growled with menace scowling up into the sky.

'What do you say then, are you still reckoning on a challenge?' asked the barman when they returned inside. Harvey Premnas was about to say 'no' when Fenella grabbed his arm.

'Yes, he is, he is. Aren't you Gustav,' she said winking.

'Err, ah yeah. OK honey if you say so,' the initial ghost of alarm furrowing into question across his forehead.

'Should I sign you up?' said Fenella.

'Arrr, if you think it's a good idea,' said Harvey.

Fenella Morningstar took a pen from the bar and printed "Gustav Crum" and the address of The Terrace on the form.

'And if he doesn't turn up this evening for some reason, feel free to bring the ferrets down there, or send someone to collect him,' said Fenella.

'Think he might chicken out love?' asked the barman.

'No, not really but he can get distracted. You know, when he's studying. He gets so engrossed he forgets the time, don't you?'

'Yeah, it can happen. What do you want to drink, a Martini?'

CHAPTER SEVENTEEN

As the last of the light faded from the evening sky, Gustav Crum walked down the road to The Ferret and Trouser Leg. He'd thought tonight might be the best time to make clear just how much Dr. Larrup's fastidious, unforgiving nature aroused feelings he had hither to been oblivious of. However, as this was a state even Kierkegaard hadn't prepared him for, he had arrived early in order to engage in, what he believed the English called, Dutch Courage.

He opened the door and walked into the hubbub of the busy bar. As he queued to order a drink he was aware of a small crowd starting to form around the raised seating area in front of the bay window. The tables and chairs had been pushed to the side forming a low staged area. A man was standing at a microphone and next to him was an older man wearing a cap who looked like he had taken out his false teeth.

'Now then ladies and gentlemen, I'd like to welcome ye to annual trouser legging competition. Once again we've got King Greg here ready to take on all challengers.'

The barman nodded at Gustav. 'What'll it be lad?'

'I will have a pint of bitter please.'

'So, we haven't got many challengers on the list,' the man at the microphone continued, looking at the poster that he had removed from the pillar, 'so there's plenty o' opportunity for anyone who hasn't signed up. Anyhow, let's mek a start. Rules are simple. Challengers first, Bert there has the stopwatch, then we let Greg see if he can keep 'em down longer than any o challengers. Longest wins. Right then, let's see who we got? First up, Brian Sedgewick. You 'ere Brian?'

A balding man with a large beer belly raised his hand from the back of the small crowd. 'Aye, here,' he said, easing his way through to the front.

'Brian, you'll remember, was runner up two year ago wi one minute twenty five seconds, a marvellous effort for a beginner. Now then lad, reckon ye can top that today?'

Cringe

'Ah'll give it a go.'

Gustav Crum stood at the side of the crowd and watched with fascination as Bert, with a stop watch round his neck, bent down and started to tie the bottom of Brian Sedgewick's trousers tight with string, whilst Brian loosened his belt and pulled the top of his baggy trousers open. Bert stood up and looked into the cavern of Brian's trouser front. Nodded and turned to the microphone.

'Nought on.'

The other man turned his back to the audience, slid a panel open on the top of a wooden crate and pulled out two weasel like animals with fearsome eyes.

'Here we are ladies and gents, Gerty and Fred,' he said, holding them up to the crowd. 'Is thy ready Brian?'

Brian bent his legs slightly, braced himself, and holding the front of his trousers open with the ends of his undone belt, pursed his lips and nodded.

To Gustav's consternation the man then proceeded to stuff both the animals done the front of Brian Sedgewick's trousers, with Brian quickly buckling his belt. He braced his arms in a body builder's pectoral pose and waited. The audience fell silent. The front of Brian's trousers began to rustle and rumple as the two ferrets scuttled from one leg to the other, trying to find a way out. Brian's face contorted. Gustav Crum watched with growing concern. Surely they would bite.

'Ooh ya bugger,' shouted Brian Sedgewick, 'oh ya bastard, that hurt.'

Gustav Crum flinched. He had come across some unusual customs during his time in England, Morris Dancing and the burning barrel races on Guy Fakwes night in Sussex, but none where the aim was to endure pain for entertainment.

'All right, all right, that's it. Get 'em out,' said Brian Sedgewick, undoing his trousers.

Bert stopped the watch and, shielding Brian's modesty with a towel, he and the other man detached the ferrets from Brian's scratched and bloodied legs. After the blood had been wiped off and plasters applied the man at the microphone said:

'Well Bert, what have we got?'

'Fifty-two seconds.'

'Not bad, let's have a big round for Brian.'

Brian smiled and raised his hand to the crowd.

'Aye, not bad. Now let's see, who've we got next?'

He looked at the poster.

'Ey up, reckon we've got a visitor. Is there a Gustav Crum in the house?'

Gustav's eyes widened in trepidation. The man at the microphone craned his neck, looking across the crowd through to the other section of the pub.

'Maybe he's through in t'other bar. Gustav Crum?'

The audience looked around at one another as Pamela Larrup walked into the bar.

'One last call, Gustav Crum?'

'Why Gustav what have you done? Why do they want you?' Pamela said, as she reached Gustav's side.

'Ey up David, here he is. Young lad here,' shouted Brian Sedgewick, stood next to Gustav and Pamela.

'Come on then lad, don't be shy.'

'Oh Gustav, have you entered a competition? What is it? Cragg's Got Talent? Are you going to sing?' said Pamela Larrup in admiration.

'No no, I think there is a mistake, I do not do this.'

'Come on then lad, up you go.'

'Oh yes Gustav, do. I'd love to hear you sing,' said Pamela, as she pushed him through towards the front, an action repeated by other audience members as Gustav peered around in rising panic, making small noises of protestation. When he arrived at the front of the crowd Greg looked at him from under his flat cap.

'Where be ye from then lad?'

'I am from Denmark, but I do not do the Trouser Legging. There is a mistake.'

'Aren't you Gustav Crum?' asked the man at the microphone.

'Yes I am but I did not put my name on the list.'

'Why, there ain't many other Gustav Crum's around here lad, so this must be you.'

'Yes it is me, but..'

'There ye go, lad's just a bit shy,' said Greg, 'though thy trousers are a bit tight. Ye need some like these,' he said, pulling his baggy legs out to the side. 'Dos't thou want to borrah these?' he said, starting to undo them.

'Hang on there Greg, is't thou naked under theyor?'

'Oh aye lad, hadn't thought o that,' said Greg, stopping.

Pamela Larrup began to suspect that this was not Cragg's version of *The Voice* and looked about see another poster behind her. Realising the mortal danger that was about to befall Gustav she barged her way through the audience to the front. 'There has been a misunderstanding,' she said to the man at the microphone. 'He *is* Gustav Crum,' Gustav stood at her side nodding, 'but he would not have entered himself for something like this.' Gustav shook his head. Pamela took hold of the poster that was hanging from the man's hand and looked at the names. 'Your name is here Gustav.'

He looked at it. 'Yes, but that is not my writing. I think someone is setting me down.'

'Up,' said Pamela.

'What? Said Gustav, looking up.
Setting you up, not down.'

'Ah,' he nodded, 'setting me up. That is not my writing.'

'So thou dursn't fancy a go then?' said Greg, disappointed. 'What wi you an' t'other tall lad, ah thought we'd gone all international this year.'

'Very tall?' said Pamela Larrup, holding her hand high above her head.

'Ay, foreign lad.'

Pamela Larrup's eyes narrowed. She looked at the list. Harvey's name was not on it.

'Well now, I think I know what has happened. It is a mistake, someone has made a big mistake,' she said, guiding Gustav away through the crowd towards the door.

'Let's get out of here and eat across the road,' she said.

'Oh thank you Pamela, that is a good idea. You have saved me.'

'Yes, I have haven't I,' she said, with a grin.

CHAPTER EIGHTEEN

Rick Callow had told the ladies in the office he was attending a meeting on good governance at the West Yorkshire Institute of Directors. However, the forty minute drive to Bradford had ended up with his yellow Smart Car weaving along a rubbish strewn back lane and turning into the back yard of an amusement arcade, Crouchmoor and son, on the shabby red and white sign above the entrance.

For Billy and Henry Crouchmoor fun was a serious business and came in a variety of diverting pastimes. Like his father before him, Billy's meaty fingers extended across Yorkshire and beyond, to massage and pummel the operations of a fraternity of enterprises which provided them both with a constant source of pleasure. In its day, the amusement arcade, now seemingly harmless, had attracted gangs of youth which Henry had hitched to ambitions of an entirely less legitimate nature. Growing up with the Crays in London's East End, he had acquired a skill set which he'd gleefully set about utilising further north. From racketeering and extortion, through fencing stolen goods and bankrolling the plans of other innovative entrepreneurs, Henry Crouchmoor had risen amongst the local community to occupy a most enviable position. Through careful delegation he had organised his affairs so that the amusement arcade provided the facade of respectability required for the Chairman of the local Chamber of commerce, whilst his other operations, run at a distance, provided the unspoken muscle to persuade anyone caring to look, that any dirty dealings were someone else's rubbish, to be thrown out by the bins. Though levity was on offer through the front door, it was the rubbish strewn backyard that Rick Callow had arrived at.

He had met Billy and Henry Crouchmoor at a social held by the Chamber of Commerce a couple of years ago. Over several glasses of wine Henry and Billy had recognised the unique business opportunity that Rick Callow presented and had nursed the association with him. This had paid off around twelve months ago when Rick Callow let slip evidence confirming their earlier suspicions that his financial judgement might not be quite as well honed as he liked to pretend.

Billy and Henry had been talking about ideas to further diversify their creative investment activities when they spotted Rick Callow in the room.

'Hey there Rick how's it going matey?'

'Ah good, good. Listen, I've just been talking to Stephen Skullington over there and he's given me a hot tip.'

'Oh yeah, what's that then Rick?' whispered Henry Crouchmoor, putting his bear like arm around Rick's shoulder.

'Ostrich farms.'

'Ostrich farms eh, tell me more.'

'There's a chap in the West Country down in Devon, he's got this plan to import a whole load of ostrich eggs, hatch them, grow the birds and then sell the meat. He's looking for investors. Stephen says it tastes just like chicken. And you'd get a lot of meat off a bird like that. Why imagine, a Christmas ostrich rather than a turkey. I think it's a real goer. He's going to market it as the height of culinary sophistication. Apparently,' Rick Callow paused and looked around, then dropping his voice further, continued, 'apparently Jamie Oliver might be getting on board.'

'Oliver eh. The golden boy.'

'Exactly, everything he touches just rockets. It's a dead cert. But, you know, keep it to yourself,' he said, tapping the side of his nose.

'So you're planning to invest?'

'Why, I'd be a fool not to. I'd advise you to as well. Never look a gift ostrich in the mouth eh, eh,' he said, chortling, gingerly elbowing Billy Crouchmoor in the ribs. Henry and Billy looked at one another and joined Rick in his pleased laughter.

'He's a fucking nutter.' said Billy, as Rick Callow walked away.

'Too right my son, too right. But he's just the sort of nutter that might come in useful. You just watch, you watch my son.'

Henry and Billy Crouchmoor had watched the fiasco of Orlando's Ostriches unravel with some glee. The initial impounding of ostrich eggs by customs. The shoals of hatchlings scurrying around the warehouse floor, with TV cameras catching hapless customs officials flapping their caps at them. Eventually the stench of ostrich shit and protests from RSPB activists drove customs to reconsider their decision, releasing them into Orlando's care. When the company eventually tried to sell the meat there was no interest, with the market testing showing that the great British public preferred their ostriches in a zoo, rather than gracing the Christmas dining table. The company spiralled into debt and bankruptcy shortly followed.

It was a more subdued Rick Callow that Henry met at the Chamber of Commerce Christmas dinner six months later.

'No ostrich on the menu I see,' he said, as he sat down next to Rick.

'Oh, ahh, no. That didn't quite work out did it. Very sorry about that. Did you lose much?'

'Nothing. I thought it was an interesting tip at the time. Held possibilities. But no I decided to go for Royal Mail shares. Quite a nice little earner so far. You invested much did you?'

Rick Callow paused in mashing some carrots and turkey onto his fork. 'Ah, well. Yes, a bit, but not exactly me. You know how it is.....look Henry. We've known each other for some time. I like to think of you as a friend..'

'Why yes, of course Rick, you are a friend. Is there something I can do for you?'

Rick Paused. 'Weel, ah yees. It's just I really could do with getting hold of some cash. Quickish, if you know what I mean? Bit of a cash flow problem. Do you know of anything that is, you know, good for a quick return? ....You know, any sort of under the table tips, strictly between us, you know...?'

'Ah yes, I see. I think I know what you mean. There is something that I've been wondering about for a while. A kind of special deal that I thought only someone like yourself would have the intelligence and foresight to appreciate.'

'Ah yees, that sounds like the kind of ticket, something special eh, just the kind of ticket.

'You see I've got these acquaintances. Fellow businessmen, like ourselves. Sort of in the import/export trade.'

'Ah yes, importing and exporting, yeees. I see.'

'Yes, you see, it's really something for the specialist. Something for a man with an eye for the main chance. Something that I think you would appreciate being in your position.'

'Ah, yes, I like to think so.' said Rick Callow, growing eager.

Henry Crouchmoor stopped and inclined his head to the side.

'But then...I don't know. You know it's such a good opportunity. With your talent you've probably spotted it already. I wouldn't want you to feel like I'm patronising you.'

'Ah, well, yees I can spot them. Go on, tell me anyhow. Maybe I could help out.'

'OK. What do you know about exporting antiquities to China?'

'Antiquities eh. China, a lot of money to be made there. Selling the nips some of the old world eh. Yees I could go for that. I do know a thing or two about old things, we have a lot of that kind of thing at Laudanum you know.'

Oh yeah, of course, I'd forgotten about that. A lot of that kind of stuff eh?'

'Yees, place is full of it. Books, paintings, furniture. You name it we've got it.'

'Place is full of it eh, probably pushed for space I'd imagine?'

'Oh yes, we're always buying more new old stuff, if you see what I mean. Making use of rich sponsor's gifts and donations. Sometimes I don't know where we put it all.'

'Overflowing by the sound of it.'

'Oh yes. Why you know only the other day Giles was telling me about a whole bunch of old books that were coming in. Said he didn't know what he was going to do with them. He wasn't there when they were delivered so I told them to just stick them in one of the outhouses. Still there. Must tell him about them.'

'You know, when Mrs. Crouchmoor, she likes to shop, when Mrs. Crouchmoor goes on a spree, I like to have a bit of a spring clean. Bit of a sort out, get rid of the stuff she doesn't use any more, make some space. And you know, she hardly notices. Does make the place more tidy.'

'Yes, sounds very sensible, sensible indeed.'

'So you see, you could kill two birds with one stone, clear just a little bit of the stuff nobody uses. Give you a bit of ready cash for the place. You know re-invest it and you get more space to house new old stuff that somebody might want, if you get my drift.'

'I think I see what you're getting at,' said Rick Callow.

That evening Henry Crouchmoor took advantage of the business opportunity that Rick Callow had inadvertently informed him about, directing some of his associates to quietly look through the outhouses at Laudanum Grange and remove anything that looked like a large package of books.

'Have you given any further thought to that business proposition Rick?' said Henry, when they met in Henry's office the following week.

'You know I have, but I haven't spoken to anybody about it yet. I quite like the idea, but some people get quite precious about some of our stuff. I'm not sure they'd understand, you know, see the business sense of it.'

'Yeah, I know what you mean, not everyone sees the advantage of taking an inventory, getting shot of old stock, but it's one of the things that makes for an efficient business Rick.'

'I know, I know.'

'Is it something that you think you should take a lead on? I mean you are the CEO, it's up to you to set the direction.'

'Yes, I know you're right but..'

'I mean, in a way you already have.'

'I have?'

'Yeah, I took you up on sorting out your overstocking problem. My colleagues in China were very generous. Here's your share. I've taken out my facilitation fee,' said Henry Crouchmoor, handing over a fat envelope.

Rick Callow took it and looked inside. It was stuffed with £50 notes. 'What's this for?'

'The crate of books that you said you didn't know what to do with. I took them off your hands. Like you suggested.'

Rick Callow looked panicked. 'You did what?'

'Nobody's noticed have they?'

'Well no. I hadn't told anyone they were there.'

'There you go then.'

'But I wasn't asking you to take them. And you've sold them?'

'Yeah, that was our agreement, wasn't it?'

'No no, I wasn't asking you to do anything like that,' said Rick, looking at the envelope.

'Oh dear, but it was very profitable Rick. There's three grand there. You said you could do with the money.'

'Yes but..'

'And you see now, well, we're business partners. Our transaction is all on film,' said Henry, pointing to the CCTV camera of his office.

Rick Callow opened the door of his yellow Smart Car. There was a stench of rotting rubbish coming from a pile of black bin bags in the corner of the yard. He took a black brief case off the passenger seat, closed and locked the car door. The outside metal stairs rang as he walked up to the first floor. He pushed the button on the intercom.

'Yeah?'

'It's Rick Callow here for Billy Crouchmoor. I have an appointment.'

'OK.'

There was a buzz and click. Rick Callow pushed open the door. He could hear the sound of bells, and coins falling as he walked past the open door into the arcade and followed the corridor to the flight of stairs at the end. He peered through the window in the door at the top of the stairs and knocked. A man's chest and thick neck appeared in the window, clad in an open necked white shirt. A head bent down and Rick Callow's gaze was met by a pair of mean narrow eyes underneath a low brow and a vertical cliff of a forehead that looked as though it would be useful in the demolition business. Billy Crouchmoor opened the door and let Rick Callow into the office.

'Wotcher matey, how's it going Rick?'

'Ah, er, alright I suppose.'

'Come in, sit down. I gather you've got some business for me?'

'Ah, er, yes business. Your father sent me a list of things. I haven't been able to get all of them.'

'Riiiick,' said Billy Crouchmoor slowly, 'that sounds a bit disappointing. Look at me,' he stuck out his bottom lip and pointed at it, 'I'm disappointed.'

'I know, I'm really sorry but it might look suspicious if I took too many of them at once.'

'Well, let's see what you have got, shall we. It might cheer me up, but if it doesn't...' said Billy Crouchmoor, wagging his finger.

Rick Callow lifted the brief case onto the desk, opened it and turned it towards Billy, who reached in and took out a book, looking at the spine.

'Sense and Sensibly eh. Now that is good book. A book that is sensible. You should have listened to it Rick. Been sensible yourself. What do you think?' said Billy, holding the book out in front of him and looking between it and Rick Callow. 'Should we ask the book what it thinks? Eh?' He lifted it up to his mouth. ''Ere book, don't you think that Rick should have been sensible like you, eh, been sensible and brought everything on the list?' He moved the book towards his ear. 'What's that you say? He's a fucking wimp, 'ere you want to watch your language,' he looked at the spine, 'you want to watch your language Jane, a bit less of that cussing and swearing, I'm a delicate flower.'

Rick Callow's hands fidgeted in his lap. 'I know, I understand. I will be able to get the other things. But you must understand that, you know, in order not to attract attention, if I take too much then, you know, things might get noticed more, then where would we be?'

Billy Crouchmoor regarded him slowly before turning his face to the copy of Sense and Sensibility and raising it to his ear again. 'What's that Jane? You want to give the little fucker a slap, make his arse wear his teeth. That's not very lady like. What do you think Rick? Is Jane being sensible here?'

Rick Callow smirked tensely. 'I'll get the rest for you in a couple of weeks, promise. There's the map in there as well,' nodding at the brief case.

Billy Crouchmoor looked into the bottom of the case.

'Oh, hello, didn't see that.'

He placed *Sense and Sensibility* on the desk and took the rolled map out of the case, untied the string, and pushing the case back towards Rick Callow, unrolled the map.

'Oh, now that is lovely,' he said, looking at the 1507 Wytfliet map of California, 'that is lovely, he should of told us about this first shouldn't he Jane? Saved getting you all upset. What's that?' he said, leaning towards the book on the desk. 'He's not so much of a plonker, just a stupid fucker. I agree.'

Rick Callow's grimace twitched and relaxed a little.

'Alright, we'll let him off this time. But he must bring us the rest of the stuff by next week. Is that alright Rick?'

'Oh yes, oh yes, I think I can do that.....er, I er, will be getting my usual commission, er, upfront?'

'Oh I think so, can't have you going hungry now can we.'

He went across to the safe and pulled out a fat roll of fifty pound notes. 'Mind, don't you go holding out on me. I wouldn't like to have to turn up at your gaff and tell everyone what you've been up to now would I?'

'No, no. No you won't need to do that,' said Rick Callow, taking the bundle of cash, sticking it in his case and retreating backwards towards the door as he closed the case. 'Absolutely won't be necessary at all. I promise.'

CHAPTER NINTEEN

'I think it's a cover up,' said Fenella Morningstar. 'He was a traitor. This moaning about missing the battle, he's trying to cover his tracks.'

After mulling upon the documents her research had taken her to a place where she had begun to put potential names to some of the initials in the dated entries of the log page. Harvey Premnas was looking at her notes.

1. Francis Austen's ship and five others ordered to leave fleet and sail to Gibraltar to re-supply - 2nd October 1805.
2. Captains went reluctantly. Thought they might miss battle.
3. If not there and Nelson won, they would miss out their share of spoils, prestige, rewards, promotions etc. - Francis' letter to Jane.
4. Battle of Trafalgar - 21st October 1805.
5. Six ships in Gibraltar did miss battle - ditto letter.
6. Pierre-Charles-Jean-Baptiste-Silvestre de Villeneuve ordered combined fleet of French and Spanish sail from Cadiz - 18th October 1805 - despite light winds. Had received intelligence of the six British ships anchored at Gibraltar.
7. The British - 33 ships, Franco-Spanish - 40.

'Is there another way of looking at it?' asked Harvey.

'Well, let's look at the evidence. Austen and Tench, whoever he is, are slowing down re-supply to meet with a person C, whom he gives documents to. C goes to Cadiz, where the enemy fleet is. He's able to move through Spain. So he is either, or appears to be, Spanish, who the Brits are at war with. Francis is expecting C. to pass the messages to a V. at Cadiz. The commander of the enemy fleet is Villeneuve, V. He's passing on intelligence. Which when Villeneuve gets it, causes him sail for battle. He's spying for the French.'

'But why? What's he got to gain? Also, if he is a spy, why is he writing it down in his ship's log? Why write it anywhere, but especially why the log book?'

'But it's not the log book. It's log like entries but this is separate,' said Fenella, pointing to the document.

'Yeah, OK.'

'And these documents,' she gestured to the boxes on the trolley, 'aren't lost at all. He got rid of them to cover his tracks, which seems to have worked pretty well until now.'

Harvey Premnas looked at her. 'I'm not entirely sure. Something like this, I mean you'd have to have it cold,' he said, 'stone cold. I can see why you'd draw those conclusions. But it may just be circumstantial, coincidence. V may stand for something completely different and the comments in the log are fairly cryptic, we may be reading more into it.'

'Exactly, if you were perpetrating treachery you'd want to make it cryptic.'

'Then why write it at all? No record would be better than a cryptic record,' Harvey paused. 'Though if it were true it would be sensational. The man that goes on to become Admiral of the Fleet, the highest position in the Royal Navy, tried to ensure it was defeated,' he said, his voice drifting off into a realm of speculative haze, 'trying to help Napoleon defeat his own side. No,' shaking the temptation of what seemed too easy a claim, 'in order to reach those allegations you'd have to have it absolutely stone cold sober. I wouldn't want to be in the firing line without substantial corroboration.'

'Yeah, OK, agreed. But you're not going to discard the possibility?'

'No, by the same logic, you'd need evidence the other way to do that with any certainty.'

'So OK, I agree. Let's work out what else we'd need to know? One,' she started to write another list, 'Who C. T. and B. are? Two. Confirmation that V. is Villeneuve. Three.'

'Three. What information was passed on? Four. What his motivation was?'

'And Five. Who Major Tench was?'

'Ah, well I know that, and there's a letter from him,' said Harvey, smoothing out one of the pages of indecipherable scrawl.

'Can you read that?'

'This'll help, took me an age but I think it's right,' he pushed his note pad across.

> 23 Pike Street,
> Plymouth,
> September 1792.

My Dearest Francis,

The wind was fair and the passage favourable since our meeting in Batavia and we arrived to sight Spithead in June. Indeed, previous to leaving Sydney Cove in December we expected the journey to take fully two months longer. The event of our meeting was fortuitous, though, if an opinion on the subject might be risqued, our agreement on the political motives of our friend gave quick confidence to our meeting.

As some doubts on the French experiment are commonly expressed in England, I cannot, however, dismiss the subject without expressing a hope, that the candid and liberal of each opinion will unite in wanting the result of a fair trial to an experiment, no less new in its design, than difficult in its execution.

I am presently engaged writing a full account of the settlement of Port Jackson in which I mention my meeting with the French. The following is a fair copy:

About the middle of the month our good friends the French departed from Botany Bay, in prosecution of their voyage. During their stay in that port, the officers of the two nations had frequent opportunities of testifying their mutual regard by visits, and every interchange of friendship and esteem. These ships sailed from France, by order of the King, on the 1st of August, 1785, under the command of Monsieur De Perrouse, an officer whose eminent qualifications, we had reason to think, entitle him to fill the highest stations. In England, particularly, he ought long to be remembered with admiration and gratitude, for the humanity which marked his conduct, when ordered to destroy our settlement at Hudson's Bay, in the last war. His second in command was the Chevalier Clonard, an officer also of distinguished merit.

In offering this little tract to the public, it is my wish to persuade some others that the French are less a set of desperate and hardened villains leagued for the purposes of depredation and iniquity, but are engaged in ploughing tracts of land around which will bring to perfection whatever new ideals shall be sown in them.

-Adieu!

Watkin Tench

'So who is he?'

'Marine Major, Watkin Tench. Set sail from Portsmouth 1787 on board HMS Charlotte, arriving in New South Wales to help establish the new convict colony in January 1788,' said Harvey, reading aloud from his lap top. 'One of the first Europeans to arrive in Oz on The First Fleet, and one of the first to write about it. He published popular accounts back in England. Though I'm not sure what, if anything, this has got to do with the log entries.'

'Where's Batavia?'

'Jakarta now. Capital of Indonesia.'

'So he meets Austen there, what, on his way to Australia?'

'On his way back, I checked the date.'

'And Tench met the French in Australia? Is that right?'

'Yep, that's historical record. Some of our republicans argue that we could have been French.'

'There's your French connection,' said Fenella, she looked at the letter. 'They met in 1792, that's thirteen years before Trafalgar. And this "experiment", that's the French Revolution.'

'Maybe, I just think we ought to be careful. It would mean re-writing the history books and..'

'Uh oh, look out,' Fenella interrupted.

Gustav Crum appeared at the bottom of the dark circular staircase, wearing a sloppy brown knitted jumper and blue jeans. He raised his head to look disdainfully down his nose at Harvey as he walked across to a computer terminal at the far side of the library.

Fenella's gaze followed him. 'I think somebody may have been approached about a little trouser legging last night.'

'He was looking at me. Do you think he thinks it was me?' Harvey whispered.

'Who knows? I'd love to have seen it,' said Fenella Morningstar, smiling and widening her eyes.

'He's Pamela's research assistant, she's already after me for writing dirty poems. What if he tells her?'

'I am afraid it is worse than that Mr Premnas,' said Pamela Larrup, appearing from behind one of the tall run of shelves, 'he did not have to tell me. I witnessed first-hand the frightful situation your tomfoolery placed poor Gustav in. What you may have thought was a harmless bit of fun, something that no doubt passes for acceptable horseplay in Australia,' she said distastefully, 'here it is unacceptable, highly unacceptable.'

Gustav had turned in his chair, his arms folded. 'It is OK Dr. Larrup, let them have their fun, it is as Kierkegaard says "At the bottom of indifference between strangers lies enemies." '

Pamela's words froze Harvey with a deathless alarm before a layer of bemusement was added by Gustav's.

'Hold on, now hold on there. I think there has been some major misunderstanding here,' said Fenella. 'I put your name down Gustav.'

'You put me down?'

'I thought you'd want me to. I meant to tell you but I didn't see you. I've been so busy working with Harvey, I guess it just slipped my mind.'

'Why did you put me down?' said Gustav.

'I thought you'd be interested.'

Gustav's head twisted on his neck into a question mark.

'You know. You said you wanted to explore more English traditions, the other day. I thought it looked really typically English. Isn't it typically

English?' asked Fenella.

'No, Miss Morningstar, it is quite the crudest thing,' said Pamela Larrup. 'Quite the crudest.'

Fenella looked horrified and placed her hand across her mouth. 'Crude? The poster said they had trouser leggings, I thought it was something to do with horse riding.'

A series of puzzled faces ranged around the room.

'Chaps. Leather chaps. Like you need for horse riding, leather over trousers?' said Fenella.

'It is not what goes over the trousers Miss Morningstar but what goes down them,' said Pamela.

Fenella feigned perplexed distress.

'They tried to put ferrets down poor Gustav's trousers,' said Pamela.

'Oh my lord,' exclaimed Fenella. 'I thought it was the Brits equivalent of something like a cattle drive, or wrangling, like at the rodeo. I'm so sorry Gustav. Aw geez, I'm sorry. I really did think I was doing you a favour Gustav. I saw your name wasn't there, so I put it down. I meant to tell ya, I thought it'd be a great experience.'

Gustav Crum regarded her, his arms unfolding as she explained. 'I see. I suppose it was quite the experience. Was it not the experience Dr. Larrup?'

'Pamela, please. I suppose you could certainly say it was an experience,' she said, recalling Gustav's gratitude.

'So, were you OK?' asked Fenella.

'It was a close run thing Miss Morningstar but I am happy to say that I was able to extricate Gustav in the nick of time,' said Pamela.

A small smile passed between Gustav and Pamela.

'Yes Dr. Larrup. I was extricated,' said Gustav.

Pamela blushed and started to shuffle up the papers she had laid on the table. 'Anyway it is over now, if you are happy with that Gustav I think we can leave the matter.'

'Yes, Dr. Larrup,' Gustav nodded and turned to the computer.

Having collected her papers Pamela started off before turning back. 'Harvey, did you get my e-mail?'

'Aw yeah, you wanted a report on my progress? Some point in the next couple of weeks?'

'A report yes, but much sooner than that. I thought I had made that clear. I assume you are progressing?'

'Yeah, some interesting developments.'

'Good, then perhaps we could talk about them now, in my office. I will see you up there in ten minutes,' said Pamela.

After she had gone Fenella smiled, slowly shaking her head at Harvey who rolled his eyes.

'See ya later,' he said, getting up. 'and thanks,' he mouthed, with a wink.

Fenella watched his back disappear up the stairs. She checked something on her lap top. Stood up and considered for a moment, before gathering her belongings and stepping quietly over to Gustav.

Speaking from behind his head and smiling, she said, 'Gustav, thought you might like to know. It's "At the bottom of enmity between strangers lies indifference". Not what you said.' Shaking her head warmly, as a gelid murk of trepidation began to seep within Gustav's mind.

CHAPTER TWENTY

There was no reply when Harvey Premnas knocked on the door to Pamela Larrup's office. After knocking a second time he opened it slowly. It was empty. He looked around and, deciding to play it safe, closed the door and ambled to the landing window.

It was a cold, overcast day, with dark clouds drifting in on the horizon above Stoodley Pike. He could just make out the monument on the edge of the moor in the distance.

Built in 1814 to commemorate the defeat of Napoleon, it seemed a curious coincidence initially. Australia, Gibraltar, Morocco, Cragg. That he and the documents had passed through these places to come together here, within view of this obelisk, erected on the skyline of such a bleak part of Britain; it felt more than fortuitous. But then, for those on this island at the time, living under the prolonged threat of Napoleon's imperial ambitions, to erect such an isolated monument must be a sign of the collective relief that passed across the nation. If Fenella's speculation was right, and the documents were a paper trail of betrayal, they represented what would have been the equivalent of Field Marshall Montgomery selling out Churchill at Alamein. Must get out there sometime and see that monument up close.

'Oh Harvey you are here,' said Pamela Larrup, emerging from Rick Callow's office.

'Rick needed to talk to me, some problem at the bank. Come in.'

He sat down and sank into a low arm chair, his knees raised up above his thighs. He struggled to get more comfortable as she walked around to the far side of the desk.

'Now, how have you been progressing with your little project?'

'Well I'm not really too sure yet. There wasn't too much in the existing collections. I've found some suggestions of ambivalence towards Austen's father in the letters.'

'What about the Morocco Manuscripts?'

'It's still early days. I have found a short biographical piece of Francis's which was intriguing.'

'Oh yes?'

'Yeah, I'm hoping there's more but I've not come across anything yet.'

'What more have you found? You have had them for a few days now.'

'Ah yeah,' Harvey made a show of flicking through his note pad, 'just a mo.' He pretended to read something he had written. 'Yeah. I mean, I have come across stuff, but, well I'm not sure what to make about it yet.'

'Yes?'

'I don't really want to jump to conclusions. I need to do some more digging to corroborate what they suggest.'

'What is it they suggest?'

'Mmm, well that's part of the problem, what they seem to suggest is,' he hesitated, 'well, it seems to be at odds with the historical record as is. I wouldn't like to get ahead of myself and...'

'Oh come on Harvey, let us have it out.'

'Well, there's this, like log, a ships log and some letters. They suggest he may have been involved in something in Gibraltar just before the Battle of Trafalgar. I'm not sure what exactly, but it looks unusual.'

'How so?'

Harvey Premnas hesitated again.

'Well, it looks like it might have been spying,'

Pamela Larrup smiled indulgently. 'It would not surprise me if he had. It would be part of his job to report enemy movement.'

'No not spying for the British. That wouldn't really be spying. I mean, well it seems he may have been passing information to the French, spying for them.'

Pamela's indulgent smile flickered momentarily before spreading wider. 'Oh, I hardly think that is likely. He was admiral of the fleet remember. No one gets promoted to such a position unless they are very certain of one's loyalty.'

'Yeah, I know...'

'Remember Harvey,' Pamela said, the Scottish brogue broadening to an indomitable tone, 'there are many different ways to interpret historical correspondence. One needs to consider the intended audience, their motives, the backdrop to this, and the background they share. Which of course, you do not. In your case, this is even further removed because of your Antipodean nature. There is plenty of room to make mistakes there. This is your first visit to Europe isn't it?'

He nodded.

'I should think you need to ground yourself for at least a couple of years here before you would really be able to pick up on the nuances. Just because you speak a sort of English does not a shared meaning make. If I were you I would brush up on that first, then go back and take a careful look at it.'

'Yes, I do know that. That's why I didn't really want to mention it at this stage. However,...'

'And anyway it doesn't really sound like it falls within the scope of your thesis, bit of a wild goose chase,' Pamela Larrup laughed. 'Do you not think so? After all, your time here is limited. I should not waste it on something that you cannot hope to have time to disprove. It is only likely to be wrong.'

'I agree, it isn't within the scope of my thesis as it stands. But, just for the sake of argument, if it were only partially true, that Francis Austen had been involved in previously unknown events, that in itself would provide more than enough for a thesis; I could still change it, analyse and interpret the manuscripts within that context.'

'Harvey, Harvey. You are not saying that you are thinking of abandoning your current thesis?'

'No No. Not yet at least, but I'd have to be led by the evidence.'

'Don't you have a financial award associated with your current thesis? And I think you would need to be careful about how much trust you can put in the evidence in this instance. Given the lack of any reference to these documents anywhere else, their provenance is still to be established. That's one of the reasons I was hesitant to let you start on them. Their provenance was something that I was hoping to establish first. Before that is done anything else that is said of them runs the risk of being built upon very shifty sands. You would not want to look like a fool would you? Not in your early days.'

'Of course not. But as I said, I've only just started on them and that's what seems to be suggested...'

'Try to be more discriminating Harvey my dear. You said you had found some biographical material. I would keep your focus on that. Skip over anything that isn't pertinent to it, so you make the best use of your time here. Don't waste it on idle speculation. I know I am not your supervisor, only here to advise after all. But if you are intending to go off track, I would consult your supervisor in Sydney first, before you waste any more time.'

Until now he had managed to calm the ire that was pulsing around his temples, telling himself not to rise to the irritation growing about him. He wasn't at all sure that she gave any consideration to the effect that her comments had on people, and as such, he suspected that to respond to them would be to place their credence on to more conscious and combative ground, something he suspected she played for, and which would only serve to confer substance on her lack of consideration, encouraging her to entrench.

'Well, thanks for that advice Pamela. I'll just get on and do that right now,' he said, hauling himself out of the armchair and towering into the room.

Pamela Larrup looked towards the back of the door after it had closed, her gaze focused far away. She took a note book out of her desk drawer and made some notes. If this were true? How much longer was Harvey and his crew due to be here? She looked at the calendar on the wall. Longer than she thought. She put the note book back in her drawer and picked up the phone.

'Hello Giles, is Gustav down there? Could you put him on? Hello Gustav, could you come up to my office. I would like to discuss something with you.' Yes, that would be the way to play the thing. That would be the way to do it.

'How'd it go?' asked Arlene Kendrick.

'Don't. Don't go there. Don't ask me who the most condescending fuck wit in this country is. Don't ask me who's as dumb as a box of rocks, because I don't know, I don't know anyone at all like that,' said Harvey.

'She is a bit of aginner. Don't let her get to you. I don't think her judgement is that good. Look who she picks as a research assistant for a start.'

'Yeah I know, I know, but it's the whole cringe thing. You'd think people would have moved on.'

A puzzled frown crossed Arlene's face. 'What are you cringing at?'

'Sorry. The Cultural Cringe. Supposed feelings of inadequacy we Australians used to display when faced with the culturally sophisticated "mother country". When we felt like poor hick cousins invited up to the big house to watch how things should be done. Seems Pamela thinks I shouldn't get above myself. Just chuck another shrimp on the barbi and leave the sophisticated stuff to someone more qualified,' Harvey simmered.

'Is there something wrong Harvey?' asked Giles Skeffington from his desk.

'Er, aw, no mate, nothing. Just a misunderstanding.'

'Oh, sorry to hear that. Come and have a look at this, it'll take your mind off it. A book I bought last month has just arrived from America. It's going into the Shakespeare collection, right up your street I would have thought.'

He waived Harvey and Arlene over to the service desk. They crowded round as he opened a heavy cardboard box revealing wads of packaging which he removed to uncover a book, about six inches by nine, wrapped in layers of tissue paper. He unwrapped it carefully, laid it on a book pillow and opened the embossed brown leather cover, releasing a feint whiff of lignin and vanilla.

Of ghostes and Spirites Walking by Nyght, and of strange noyses, crackes and sundry forewarnyngs, whiche commonly happen before the death of menne, great slaughters, and alterations of kyngdomes. One Booke, Written by Lewes Lauaterus of Tigurine.

And translated into Englysh by R. H.

1572.

'May I introduce you to Ludwig Lavater's *Of Ghostes and Spirites*,' said Giles Skeffington.

'Wow. How rare is this Giles?' asked Arlene.

'Very, very rare. There are about a dozen or so scattered around the world,' he said, turning the pages slowly.

'What's it got to do with Shakespeare?' she asked.

'Hamlet?' inquired Harvey.

'Well done, yes. It is universally accepted that Shakespeare consulted this book when writing some of his works, and as Harvey has correctly pointed out, it clearly served as a source for Hamlet.'

'So, is it like, a book of spells?' asked Arlene.

'Not exactly,' Giles smiled warmly. 'It's a demonological study of ghosts and spirits. What Lavater presents us with is historical and contemporary accounts of ghosts and lemures.'

'What's a lemure?' asked Harvey.

'It's a certain type of ghost, and something that Lavater wanted to put the record straight on. You see some writers at the time thought of your lemure as the shade or spirit of the restless dead, inherently evil and unsettled. However, Lavater argues here that they are actually angelic or demonic entities that are haunting the earth as some sort of divine or satanic plan, watching the daily comings and goings, influencing events by making interventions which us unwitting mortals are oblivious of.'

'So they could be good guys or bad guys,' said Harvey.

'Yes, very much so, and though we can joke about it, this type of thing was taken very seriously in the sixteenth and seventeenth centuries. There would be heated debates played out in books like this, between those who accepted claims of the existence of demonic witchcraft and those who challenged them, with lives quite literally hanging on their outcome.'

'Witch hunts?' said Arlene.

'Exactly. Though this is less about witches and more about spirits and haunting.'

'So this is where Shakespeare got his ideas on Hamlet's ghost,' said Harvey Premnas to himself, then louder, 'I never expected to see something like this when I set out.'

'It was a bit of a surprise to me too. We had a rather large, anonymous donation specifically stipulating we use it to buy a copy of this should one become available. So I put my feelers out and found this in the collections of an American physicist who had just died.'

'Does that happen often? People giving you great wads of cash?' asked Arlene.

'No unfortunately. Not as often as I'd like. I'm jolly glad we've got it though. I'm going to write about it on our blog.'

'I'll look forward to reading that,' said Harvey.

CHAPTER TWENTY-ONE

Something was unsettling Fenella as she walked back from lunch at The Ferret and Trouser Leg. Normally another notch on the winning post would be a source of uplift, yet somehow her humbling of Gustav left a vacant distraction whittling away at her. Was this guilt? That would have been unusual. Maybe Gustav didn't really deserve it. Had she returned more than he'd dealt? A disproportionate response? He was very young after all. Callow even. She shuddered. Probably naive and uncertain under that pompous exterior. Should she have given him more latitude, spoken softly and simply hinted at the big stick?

When she had completed her masters, the distinction had set her eyes on a prize which had quickly tilted. In a world where academic assets increasingly lost their value to the rapacious growth of the education market, what she had considered a hoard of shiny new currency, turned out to just about cover the entry fee for the next proving ground. However she'd quickly realised this and set about making herself a more unique commodity. Rather than cashing up to do a PhD, she had pitched straight to the publishers, with her books attracting enough prestige in certain circles that offers of employment from universities followed. It was, she concluded, what you made happen that mattered and that was something that no amount of letters after your name could guarantee. For Gustav, however, these letters seemed to have skewed his opinion of himself to such a degree, that no amount of starch could further stiffen the disdainful resolve of the stick up his butt.

He'd have spent years grafting away in the archives of god knows where, to produce, what to him, must feel like the apotheosis of scholarly endeavour. Only now he seemed to expect his worth to be appraised as at least equivalent to the professorial airs he gave himself. His puffed up demeanour seemed beyond any reasonable expectation of a newly minted PhD. A little humility before the elders never went amiss. However, it seemed as though he'd been pushed out into the academic playground, eagerly waving a handful of newly printed cash, without realising that the local kids dealt in reputation.

She'd seen plenty of intellectual obsession among the postgrad community. However, the extent to which this crowded out those normal human relations which ease the progress of any project, often left her bemused. What mattered at least as much, was the manner in which you establish yourself in the eyes of your peers. After all, to let the opinions of yourself become all-consuming ran the risk of obscuring how the opinions of others may consume you, especially if they're sitting on the grants committee. Trust and integrity. These were the values that bred faith in your convictions. Not the bald presumption that as you have a PhD the only appropriate position for those that don't, is to submit to your obvious superiority. It was these values that had to be built in relationships with others, and they took time to wed to the expression of your ambitions. That he behaved in such a high handed manner was possibly something he'd been led to believe appropriate by senior academics he'd worked with. She'd seen it before. However, whilst their reputations may have insulated them from the fall out, for him to behave so, spoke of a serious lack of playground insight. He's got his PhD all crumpled up in his grubby little hand but has still to show he knows how to behave when the grownups aren't around.

The sky appeared to be darkening over towards the West as she entered the library. The lobby and exhibition areas were empty. She headed towards the circular stairs down to the reading room and ran her hand along the rail at the edge of the atrium, her palm letting the cool steel move through it with the cogency of a well-controlled exposition. She looked down onto the heavy maple reading tables below. They were empty except for one figure. And that did not look right.

Gustav Crum was sat at the seat normally occupied by Harvey Premnas. She watched him sift through Harvey's papers, looking around furtively and making notes in a small notebook, replacing the papers in the position he had found them. That did not look like something that Dr. Crum PhD should be doing. He stood up and looked around before making towards the circular stairs up to ground level where she stood.

Fenella stepped quickly across the marble floor on the balls of her feet and stood out of view behind one of the exhibition shelves. Gustav emerged and continued up the next flight of stairs to the museum. She followed him at a distance, through the museum, across the glass walkway and watched him quietly knock on Pamela Larrup's door, before letting himself in. No, that was not right, not right at all.

She had herself occasionally experienced the temptation to let slip the vigilant strictures between creative borrowing and slender plagiarism, allowing her references to creak faintly, before being woken up by the gentle terror of an outright accusation, revisiting her prose to punctuate it with the ugly stumble of more attributions. However, what she had just seen went well beyond anything that might simply gnaw on the doubts of a watchful conscience. Of course, she couldn't say she'd witnessed plagiarism unless and until there was published evidence. However, it seemed to her that the perfidious Crum was engaged in a form of treachery that was so heinous it was yet to be formally censured by any academic code of conduct. Any such theft of Harvey's research before it was published meant that he could hardly prove anything subsequently. How very creative of Gustav, or should that include Pamela too?

Her previous uncertainties fell away. Not disproportionate at all. Simply getting my, or rather our, retaliation in first.

Returning to the library she started to scan various courses of action before leashing them for later discussion with Harvey. To quiet her outrage she imagined Gustav on horseback, as settled as a badly seated Action Man, wobbling around and grimacing, with a couple of ferrets hanging from his butt. She'd have love to have seen that. And there was definitely something going on between him and Pamela. They deserved each other. She seated Pamela behind Gustav, hanging on for grim death, and sent them galloping off with their machinations out to the distance of the Wyoming plains, the figures wavering smaller and smaller against the huge sunset, which they would ride into forever, or at least until Harvey and Arlene returned from the long lunch they'd planned in Mytholmroyd.

She let her mind turn back to the tasks she had planned for the afternoon. With the Morocco Manuscripts promising a far more satisfying game she had dismissed any intentions of writing dirty Austen. She turned back to one of the documents she'd been studying before lunch, nothing more than an undated scrap she and Harvey had come across earlier.

> *My Dearest Francis,*
> *I am writing you quickly with bad news of the investments I made for you. They have not eventuated in the outcome we hoped for. Indeed, I may have overstated our position so that further monies may be necessary. I spoke to father about this. As you know, though I value his advice, since his problems with East India shares we cannot expect the financial help that he would like to give.*
>
> *Henry*

Though she couldn't be certain she suspected this Henry was Francis' brother, the banker, his failure in banking perhaps further evidenced by this note. The lack of a date was frustrating as mention of the East India Company rekindled the payment made to Francis listed in the accounts book she had looked at previously. However, this had set her on the path to finding out more about the company. Though she respected Harvey's circumspect approach she wanted to be able to parry his carefully fenced caveats, move her suspicions from chance to conspiracy, and had used his caution to galvanise her pursuit of the challenge it presented.

She was building a picture of a company, if that's what you could call it, that had operated in a manner that today would have been seen as that of a rogue state: running its own private army, waging war, administering swift and sometimes brutal justice, minting coin and collecting revenue. The conflict of interest in these activities had resulted in widespread comment and scandal at the time. The company basically ran India and the man in charge, Warren Hastings, was impeached and put on trial for corruption by the British parliament in 1788. The same year Watkin Tench set out with the First fleet. She had found a list in the manuscripts that looked as though it had been torn from the type of East India Company accounts book that she had looked at previously. It read like the acquisitions for a small army.

She'd started to formulate some ideas of association from this which were sent into a spin upon finding direct correspondence from Warren Hastings to Francis Austen in the Morocco Manuscripts. In the first of two letters, dated May 1792, it appeared that Hastings had been on close terms with Francis and Jane's father, George. It referred, amongst other things, to George Austen losing a lot of money when East India Company shares had crashed in 1769, with Warren Hastings feeling bad about this as it had caused substantial hardship in the young Austen family. A second letter, dated 1795, talked of his relief at being found not guilty at his impeachment trial; his resentment at being put on trial in the first place, especially since there was so much favourable comment from India; and how public opinion now saw him as somewhat enlightened, curbing the worst excesses of the company. Hastings appeared to see it as the result of a personal vendetta run against him by the prime minister, William Pitt, in order to sure up his political base. He'd also asked whether Francis was in a position to help with the debts he had run up in defending himself over such a long period, £70,000. Millions today she supposed.

As she was reading she heard footsteps coming down the stairs. She looked up to see the wilting grin of Rick Callow approaching.

She smiled. 'Hello Rick.'

'Hello, hello. I was looking for Giles, have you seen him?'

'No, the place has been empty since I came back from lunch.'

'I suppose he could be in the stacks. I'll just pop down. You still hard at it eh, getting stuck into those books I see.'

'Yeah, that's right.'

'You know I'm still up for it if you change your mind.'

'Sorry?'

'You know, bit of the old, hoo haa, hoo haa,' said Rick Callow, thrusting his hips and pumping his arms back and forth.

Fenella's eyes widened. The man's ability to plumb the depths of lechery was uncontrollable. Didn't he realise?

'I must get on if you don't mind,' she said, glancing down at the books in front of her.

'Of course, of course, wouldn't want to disturb you.'

Really? Then why did you? She watched him cross floor toward the door down to the stacks, making slight swaying motions with his hips. An involuntary spasm jerked her shoulders, sending a goosed shudder down her arms. Odious. She mounted Rick on a mangy donkey and sent him bouncing out to join Gustav and Pamela, tiny specks on the skyline, letting her irritation spin out to an unfocused mantle against intrusion, marking the distance with the resolution to do something about them all in the near future.

She let her mind ruminate back across the centuries. She didn't suppose that Francis Austen would have had much in the way of funds to help out Hastings, he was a naval lieutenant at the time. The fact that Hastings felt he could ask suggested something personal and beholden about their relationship. Why would these letters be with the other papers? If these manuscripts did document some conspiracy, if Francis Austen was involved in treachery against the British, then how was Warren Hastings implicated? Betrayal would explain why Francis was eager to get rid of the documents, to cover his tracks after the British had won at Trafalgar. No doubt if the French had won he would have used them somewhere down the line to demonstrate where his true loyalties lay. Maybe that was it? Hedging his bets, stashing the documents against the overall outcome of the war. If Hastings was involved, that too would require some reconsideration of his actions and place in history.

She paused, took her eyes from the notes and books and looked about. Where were the others? They'd been gone a long time. It seemed to be getting dark. She looked up through the light well. A storm seemed to be threatening.

Giles Skeffington carefully placed Lavater's *Of Ghostes and Spirites* on the shelf and rolled the stack back into place. As it slowed to its resting place, Rick Callow's grin mooned into view from the opposite end. Giles started.

'Oh, Rick, you gave me a fright. I didn't hear you come in.'

'No, that's me, quiet and nimble,' he said, placing his hand on his stomach, raising the other arm and making a swivel with his hips.

'I've just catalogued *Of Ghostes and Spirites*.'

Rick Callow nodded slowly. His normally immobile face beginning to morph in a manner that seemed to take it by surprise. The brow between his eyes furrowed and he pursed his lips, giving the momentary impression of some newly recovered wisdom awakening within him.

'Isn't that one of Shakespeare's?'

Giles was momentarily stupefied. 'Why, well you're in the right ball park.'

'Thought so.' The muscles of Rick's face were now so unfamiliar with the expression it was wearing they began to slip, the purse of his lips over extending and his eyes, which had narrowed towards an impression of fierce intelligence, began to twitch and bulge. ' "Best laid plans of ghosts and spirits", though I thought it was men. "Best laid plans of ghosts and men," ' he said.

'It's mice,' said Giles.

'Hmm?'

'Mice and men.'

'Oh that's right, mice and men. Though funny, you never really think of mice planning. Not like us, eh, always got a plan eh, eh. So what's this book about then?'

Giles explained.

'Ah, I see, yees, yees,' he nodded. 'How much did we pay for it again?'

'£10,500.'

Rick Callow nodded again slowly. His eyes sloping away from Giles', making peremptory halts as they circled their orbits.

'So, do you think it'll be popular? Do you think you'll get many, ahh, punters coming to see it?'

'I would think there will be a number of Shakespeare scholars who would be interested and I'm going to post a blog about it. I suppose we might get some alternative types in to look at it.'

'What, you mean hippies?' asked Rick Callow.

'Well, people into black magic, Aleister Crowley, witchcraft, that sort of thing.'

'Smelly lot.'

'What?'

'Hippies. Smelly lot. Joss sticks. Muddy too. We don't want that lot in here.'

'Well, we can't really legislate to keep them out. I can hardly ask people, "By the way, are you a smelly hippy?", when they phone to book an appointment.'

'No, see what you mean. Pity though. So it's going on the shelf there is it?'

'Yes.'

'Good place for it I'd imagine. But, weeel, it's a bit squashed in isn't it? Shouldn't it have a bit more space, to let it breath. Important book like that.

Not that I have the expertise or experience to know, only you've got that eh, but you know. Er, ah yees, puts me in mind that, something that, something that I thought only you, with the expertise that comes with your experience, prowess even, that comes with the mastery of your subject, being librarianship, something that I thought only you could know the answer to.'

'Yes?' said Giles.

Well you see. It seems to me that libraries are all about knowing. I should think you'd know that.' Giles nodded, despite himself. 'And that provides us with the opportunity from time to time, I would imagine, to ask ourselves the question: "Do we really know?" and, "Are there things getting in the way of knowing?" You see, it seems to me that one of the things that might get in the way of knowing, is whether or not there isn't too much knowing going on in the library. Too many books that stop us from knowing the wood from the trees, as it were. When really all we need are those trees which would help us see the wood in the first place, as a place to stroll through without the canopy obscuring the light of knowledge which we are seeking to let in. Surely if there is too much knowing going on, it would darken the understanding within the place. Don't you think? Ahh, yees, so there was just something I wanted to ask.'

Giles waited for the salad of words to settle into something meaningful.

'You see I wondered,' Rick continued, 'how are we doing for space?' He looked around at the stacks.

'Space?'

'Yes, aren't we a bit, well, overflowing?'

'Not really, why?'

'Ah well, just a thought. I was thinking of the development plan. The Strategic Development Plan,' said Rick, portentously running his hands along an imaginary banner in front of him. 'Thought I might write a section on contingency planning, you know, if we do run out of space. Work out how we could create more, maybe plan to get rid of some of the less popular stuff, eh.'

Giles Skeffington drew his head back. Writing the strategic development plan? Rick had been dropping that into conversation for the last three years and nobody had seen anything yet. But this "contingency plan", that was a new one. 'Well, firstly I cannot see us running out of space anytime soon, and if we did, then I'm sure we could enter into an arrangement with Northrop University for them to hold some of our archives. There are lots of other contingencies before we have to "get rid" of anything.'

'Are you sure?' said Rick, looking about the stacks, 'it all looks a bit stuffed up on the shelves in the reference library, and look, this one here is full.'

He pointed to the stack in front of them.

'The reference library is deliberately full. That way, those texts that are most in demand are immediately accessible, and should we need to shelve anything further here,' said Giles, pointing to the stack, 'then. Stand back.' He rolled the stack across. 'Then, I'll move some of them along to this empty space here.' He pointed, over playing the gesture as the stack came still.

'Ah, yeees, good plan. Excellent, excellent. Knew you'd be on the case. Of course, of course, you're the expert, and that'll be what I write in my contingency plan, "Giles is the expert,"' said Rick Callow, gesturing another banner headline. ' "Consulted with Giles Skeffington, our resident expert." '

'What made you think we might be running out of space?' asked Giles.

'Oh nothing really, just trying to anticipate. Thinking ahead. Planning for the foreseeable, and maybe the unforeseeable, and what we might foresee but which is unexpected and what's expected but then unforeseen, as it were. But, as you say, not an issue. More than enough space. Never know what stuff someone's going to need eh,' he said, backing towards the door with his hands behind his back. 'Thanks for your input on that, very helpful, very helpful indeed.'

He turned and pushed open the environmentally sealed door. It closed with a heavy thud. When he had come up with this scheme Rick thought it might provide him with a way to escape the brawny clench of the Crouchmoors. Though their grip had set about wringing his nerves, he couldn't help feeling that, under slightly different circumstances, the deal they had alerted him to would have been the type of opportunity that he would have inevitably come to himself. If Giles had been just a smidge more dynamic surely he too would have spotted it for the ingenious boon that it was. He could then have sold off some of the less popular items in a much more agreeable manner than he was currently embroiled in with the Crouchmoors. This would have given him a much improved bargaining position.

He'd really been surprised by Giles. He'd thought he would have been quicker to see the plan's obvious merits. But once again he'd been reminded that the penetrating insights he took for granted were seldom grasped by those whose feet were set in more pedestrian ground. Giles' rejection of the type of idea that would have tempted Faust, meant that, for the time being, he was going to have continue his present arrangement with the Crouchmoors.

The thought perturbed him momentarily before he shook it into the dissipating realm of annoying inconveniences that sometimes stalked him, attempting unsuccessfully to nag at the scale of his ambitions. He wasn't one to be put off. He would undoubtedly come up with an alternative that was so alluring it would even cause the mundane imagination of a librarian to swoon. A business proposition so beguiling in its formulation that the Crouchmoors would stagger in admiration, only to be left consoling themselves in the wake of his enterprise.

He'd find a way to offer them some graceful solace of course. Show them how their blunt approach to business was hardly a style that was going to persevere with the inscrutable subtleties appreciated by the Chinese. A market that he, with his suave appreciation of the unspoken nuance, was far better suited to.

He imagined Billy and Henry conceding, their physical bulk waning as the smooth resolution of his plan enfolded them; wilting into the velvet words that overlaid his iron will. He hadn't formulated this scheme yet. But he could picture the grand vista it was to be found in. Callow country. A land so fecund with prospects he had only to sweep his hand through its hinterland to come up with a fistful of possibilities. Yes, it was only a matter of time before the business of Laudanum Grange was back within his command, its income stream dutifully flowing from his tenacious mitt.

On returning to his office he noticed the voicemail light on his phone flashing.

'Rick, you old spunker. It's Billy here,' Rick's spine wept into a mucilaginous slump, 'we need to talk. It's about those other items, the ones on the list. Our clients are very keen, very keen Rick, to purchase them. So, you know, we need you to deliver. Give me a call and tell me some good news mate, and none of your wanking around eh, just get your hand off your cock and make this happen.'

He hung up the phone and pushed his chair back from the desk. How had it come to this? He tried to reach back to his earlier resolve but the jangling boom of his nerves drowned it out in a deathless toll.

He clicked on an e-mail attachment. The list the Crouchmoors had sent zoomed into view. He considered it a moment, printed a copy, and shaking, folded it into his jacket pocket.

CHAPTER TWENTY-TWO

'Here come the wanderers,' said the sister with the half-moon tortoiseshell glasses, taking a deep drag on a brown cheroot and exhaling. Dark clouds were scudding across the moors and large, singular drops of rain started to plud onto the drive.

'Mai we, the wanderers, they return,' her red glasses sister replied, stood on the opposite side of the porch, looking down the drive and tapping her black and gold cigarette holder.

'They have been away the whole afternoon.'

'The whole afternoon.'

'That would be the right thing to do, wouldn't it? If one knew.'

'The right thing, if it were to be done at all, would be to go. But then to return?'

'I know. The egos are circling. To return, to struggle. Certainly it is brave.'

'Or ignorant?'

'It cannot be ignored for long. To ignore it would be to know and not notice, do nothing.'

'They have become too involved to do nothing. It is something for them. They have begun to become something,' said the red glasses sister, removing her cigarette from its holder, grinding it out with her foot and kicking the butt down the steps. 'They come.'

'Bojour mon amie. Bonjour,' they both chimed, smiling.

'You have had a very good walk?' said one of them.

'We've had lunch down at Mytholmroyd,' said Harvey Premnas, 'The Dusty Miller.'

The two sisters let their gaze follow the fellows as they passed, then turned back to look long at one another as the front door closed with a heavy thud.

Harvey and Arlene went up the creaking wooden staircase to the common room on the first floor. Fenella Morningstar was sat at the large table gazing out of the lead mullioned windows across the moor.

'I saw you coming back,' she said. 'You missed the rain.'

'Just', said Harvey, looking at the heavy drops on the windows melting the view.

As Arlene Kendrick made a drink Fenella Morningstar took Harvey's elbow and guided him towards the windows. 'Can I have a quiet word?'

'Sure, what's up?'

'Have you said something to Gustav about looking through your papers?'

Harvey looked puzzled, 'No.'

'Well look, I saw him going through them in the library and making notes. I suppose it could be harmless, but I don't think so. It looked suspicious. There was no one else there and he looked shifty.'

Harvey's countenance bore down on his concern. 'He didn't see you?'

'No, I was watching from upstairs. And, well, I was suspicious, so I hid and followed him to Pamela's office.'

Harvey looked intently at Fenella before turning a preoccupied gaze out of the window.

'He didn't take anything did he?' he said, turning back.

'No. I don't think so, I don't know how long he'd been there. I thought you should know.'

'Yeah. No thanks, you're right to tell me. What was he up to? You say he went to Pamela's office?'

She nodded. 'He had the notes and went straight in. It looked like he was taking them to her. I may have misinterpreted it, but I don't think so.'

'No, somehow I don't think so. She's already made it clear that she wanted to work on the manuscripts. But why get Gustav to do the dirty when she could just ask me? And she thought I was running up a blind alley, a misinterpretation at best. Would she be that scheming?'

'What?'

'Well, tell me she thinks I'm wrong, then send Gustav to sneak through my notes.'

'She wouldn't be the first academic to pinch the work of a researcher.'

'Really?'

'Oh, I know of several situations like it. Mostly it gets swept under the carpet. A junior researcher, PhD or early career. Less clout than someone established, a professor in one of the cases I heard about, who quietly went about pinching ideas then published them as his own.'

'I wouldn't stand about and let that go by.'

'No, but the researcher involved felt she couldn't say anything as she'd be seen as a trouble maker, and lose the support of her supervisor. He could've gone on to make things awkward, cast doubts on her credibility. She thought it easier to just shut up and plough a slightly different furrow.'

'Really? Well, Pamela Larrup isn't my supervisor. If she has put Gustav up to this I'll be doing something about it.'

Leaving Harvey to consider the implications of Gustav's actions Fenella went back to the reference library. Giles Skeffington was sitting at the service desk. Having set loose her account of Gustav's deeds it was time to rein in the attentions of Rick and watch the consequences settle.

As she stepped across to Giles her gait spoke of a resolve that seemed to make time run a little more slowly; a horologist laying bare the tiny mechanism of a time piece, stilling the balance wheel.

It wasn't that she'd found Rick's approaches upsetting. Irritating, dumbfounding, laughable, yes. But upsetting? No. They'd simply left her wondering how often the naive ten year old Rick had been subject to ridicule in the sexual playground, viewing his inept attempts at a sexual pick up, as the entertainment of older boys egging him on to make a fool of himself. Something that he seemed to excel at but which had run its course. The absence of any peril meant she'd come to observe his overtures with some amused remove. But this didn't level her concern over his apparent myopia regarding how others perceived him. That he seemed so oblivious, meant he might at this moment, be gratuitously preening himself with the prospect of his success, imagining her teetering around giddy in expectation of her next encounter with him. She shuddered. To see to it that he was left with no doubts, and ensure the embarrassment was exquisite, she'd publicise his attentions. After all, why should she be the only one to benefit from his experience? She flicked the balance wheel.

'Giles, hey there, I need to talk to you about something,' she said, approaching him.

'Why Fenella, hello, certainly, what can I do for you?'

'Well, it's a bit sensitive and I wasn't really sure who to talk to at first, but it's something that needs to be dealt with, and I think you should at least know about it. Even if you can't sort it, you may know who can.'

'Oh really, what seems to be the problem.'

'It's Rick.'

'Oh yes. What exactly..'

'It's his behaviour. I don't know if there have been problems in the past, but..'

'Yes.'

'Well, he keeps making these inappropriate sexual invitations to me.'

Giles' disconcerted features fixed abruptly. 'No, surely not.'

'Yeah, I mean it's not like he's just simply hitting on me, I can blow that off. It's the way he does it. Basically he just comes straight out and asks to, you know, do it.'

Giles Skeffington blinked and raised his head slightly, trying to be sure he had heard what he thought he understood. 'Are you sure? I mean, sometimes it can be a bit difficult to understand what he's getting at.'

'Yep, he does like to yagger on.'

'No but I mean, sometimes he talks and I find it difficult to follow, you're sure you're not getting the wrong end of the stick?'

'No Giles. He's pointing at the stick and saying, "Hop on".'

Giles Skeffington reddened a little.

'Oh, I see. Well that doesn't sound like him. At least no one has ever complained about him propositioning... you're quite sure?'

'Giles, quite sure. Look, basically I feel sorry for the guy. He's not got much going for him looks wise and he's clearly an idiot, I just want you to warn him. If he continues I'm going to take him out. I'll make such a row that the stink will stick like skunk juice.'

'Well, I, err. I'm not sure what to do exactly. I've never had to deal with anything like this. I don't know what the channels are.'

'Do you think you could just talk to him? Tell him that he's out of line and I'm going to make a stink if he doesn't stop? If he continues, then, you know, you can worry about channels after that.'

'Er, yes. Very well. I will do that.

Fenella nodded. 'OK'.

Harvey Premnas had come down to the reading room and was sifting carefully through his papers. Fenella Morningstar joined him.

'Anything missing?'

'No, it seems exactly as I'd left it, I wouldn't have noticed a thing if you hadn't said anything.'

'What are you going to do?'

'I don't know. I'm not going to do anything immediately. I'll let it sit for a bit while I get on.'

'OK, you'll let me know if I can help? I'd like to.'

'Sure, no worries. You have a think too, eh?'

'I will,' said Fenella, sitting down and arranging her materials. 'You know that note we were looking at, from Henry?'

'Yeah.'

'I'm pretty sure he was Francis' brother, the banker.'

'Mmm yeah, makes sense.'

'I started to do some background on The East India Company, and then I found these.'

She passed him the letters from Warren Hastings and told him about the powerful conflict of venal interests that served as the modus operandi of The East India Company.

'....this was one of the first mega corporations, though it operated more like a rogue state, the institutional rules that we're used to simply didn't exist then, so the vacuum was filled by the merchant classes and their aristocratic sponsors.'

'Sounds like something today's corporations wouldn't mind too much.'

'I'm not so sure they're that far away from it, but they did make a show of reining in the company's excesses. Hastings was put on trial by parliament for corruption. He was found not guilty but had a mountain of debt. He knew Austen's father, and he's asking Francis if he can help with the debt.'

'If it is a paper trail for a conspiracy what part does Hastings play?'

'What links the former governor of India, who is in debt and feeling pissed at the establishment, with the future admiral of the fleet, who we suspect of giving, or maybe selling, secrets to the French? Follow the money.'

CHAPTER TWENTY-THREE

Giles Skeffington thought no cause irredeemable. As such, he lured himself with the belief that there was hope in most things. This even extended, on occasion, to allowing himself the thought that Rick could not be as blunted to reason as the memory of any previous encounter suggested. That somehow it was he who was at fault. Failing in some way to give due consideration and attention to what had been said, or lacking in some facility that Rick assumed he had, and which, if he'd just concentrate enough, would unlock some meaning that he had previously missed. With this in mind he'd start out with the bright step of optimism evoked by a crisp sunny morning only to return slopping through the muddy sludge of a winter's thaw.

Sullied and irritated, he'd berate himself for having allowed a susurrus of hope to drift among his wits. He supposed this was born of an inability to believe that anyone could so determinedly mangle language in a way that seemed to pay so little respect for its purpose; to communicate meaning. Having spent a career devoted to words and their various collations, clarity of meaning, and its collected reason in a well framed and classified collection, was something he could only understand in terms of striving to achieve it. If he were to classify books, monographs, codices, manuscripts and the like with the same unrelenting sense of obfuscation that Rick employed, the collection at Laudanum would resemble nothing more than a decomposing rubbish dump; a fetid heap of unbound texts degraded to the highest pitch of entropic gibberish.

He'd never come to a firm conclusion about how conscious Rick was of this. At times he was convinced it was deliberate, a way of avoiding something he was asking Rick to do. At others, it seemed a half conscious attempt to try and use words and phrases to impress, but which were clearly beyond his command. And then there were times when it appeared an unfortunate habit that made him feel embarrassed for Rick. However, there were occasions when he was entirely clear. It was these that aroused what all too often became a bootless hope, dashed by some lugubrious encounter.

He was still struggling to come to terms with what Fenella had told him and the thought of broaching it made his will stumble. He liked to confine his interactions with Rick to those that were essential; things to do with the library; books, acquisitions, donations, preservation, and so on. To engage Rick in a conversation about his sexual behaviour meant being sent out to bat on a particularly sticky wicket. The dark, messy unctions of the bedroom were something he preferred to keep locked in the blanket box under the bed. Opening this with Rick left him dreading all sorts of verbal googlies and swinging balls, which delivered amidst the wrangle of Rick's management language, made him feel he was about to face the seamiest of deliveries.

He straightened up some books on the returns trolley. Moved them from one side to the other then back again. He looked towards Fenella who was writing. These books should really be shelved. He looked at the clock, ten past four. There would be time to do it today. But Rick would have left by the time he'd finished. He could always talk to Rick tomorrow. He looked back to Fenella who raised her head and smiled. He smiled back. The thought of Rick propositioning her seemed as likely as that of a spinster aunt in a Bronte novel. He couldn't square what he knew of the man, Fenella's accusations, and the thought of having to raise them with Rick. He had no reason to doubt her, she had been the epitome of scholarly rectitude and breezy professionalism, raising no qualms about her judgment previously. If he put it off until tomorrow he was in for an uneasy night. He rolled his shoulders a couple of times, alternately squeezing the muscles above his shoulder blades. If he was going to do it today he should really go now. Though the library closed at five Rick would be off before this. He started to click aimlessly through the unsolicited emails from publishers and auction houses that he would normally just delete. He opened a catalogue attached to a mail out from Bonham's and browsed through the forthcoming lots without paying attention, glancing up from time to time at Fenella. Sexual harassment was something to be taken very seriously. Did they have a policy on it? He started to look through his files. A trot of urgent heels forged down the stairs.

Pamela Larrup rounded into view, her face set on him. 'Giles.'

Harvey and Fenella looked up and Giles rose from his seat.

'Pamela. Yes, what can I do for you?'

'I have some important visitors coming tomorrow.' Her Scottish border brogue suggested a toad was on offer. 'I need you to put out a display for them.'

'Well it's a bit late notice. What time are they coming?'

'They are important local business men. They want to sponsor the

Shakespeare Collection.'

Giles looked at his watch. 'What do you want out? I'll probably have to stay after closing. It's a bit much leaving it this late.' said Giles, hushing his reprieve.

'I know. They have only just been on the phone. It is the first enquiry we have had.'

When Pamela had suggested advertising for sponsors for the various collections Giles had assumed, or hoped, that children, animals and church spires would be well ahead of what he was happy, in this instance, to present as boring, stuffy old books. He didn't want the grubby interference of local businesses intruding on how the collections were promoted.

'This is exactly the type of philanthropy we need to encourage Giles.'

Letting just enough annoyance ahead of his relief, he said, 'Yes, I suppose. What is it you want out?'

'They are very interested in the Shakespeare, so we need all the headliners, The Portfolio and put out the Lavater too.'

Giles sighed. 'What time will they be here?'

'Around eleven.'

If it were going to be done properly, with some written interpretation and context, particularly for the Lavater, which he'd not done before, then he should start now, finishing it off in the morning. If he didn't need an excuse to avoid talking to Rick he wouldn't have contemplated starting today, also hoping that a slightly lack lustre effort might put off any sponsor.

'You can be around too.' said Pamela.

'Oh really? Do you think that'll be necessary.'

'It will make a better impression if you can tell them something about what they are looking at. I would have thought you'd want to be there anyway.'

'Why's that?'

'To discuss the branding.'

'The branding?'

'Yes. They'll want their name on it, and I imagine they will have some ideas about slogans.'

'Slogans? Who are they anyway?'

'William and Henry Crouchmoor. They have a number of concerns across Yorkshire, including a chain of amusement arcades.'

He could just see it. "The Crouchmoor Shakespeare Collection. Sponsored by Crouchmoor and son arcades. Slots of Fun for all the Family, Come on down!" Accompanied by a picture of rows of neon lit machines in a dowdy red boudoir with flock wallpaper. He could smell the stale beer and candy floss, and feel his feet sticking to the carpet.

'I nearly forgot. Rick asked if you could drop in before you go,' said

Pamela.

Giles let his computer screen take a long pull on his gaze.

'Oh, and can you remind him that I'll be dropping by with the Crouchmoors tomorrow morning, after they have seen the books.'

'I'll let him know,' said Giles.

For now he still had the option of saying nothing. He knocked on Rick's door.

'Come in.'

Rick was sat behind his desk with the phone to his ear. He gestured for Giles to sit.

'Yees, ahh, yes. I think that would very much be the ticket. I certainly will. A bird in the bush is worth two in the hand, eh. Yes, I'll move the money in a jiffy, should be available for you by tomorrow morning. OK. Yes, good bye.' He placed the receiver down. 'Just sorting out some investments an old mucker of mine put me on to. What can I do for you then Giles? You know if you ever want any investment advice, just let me know. I've got some pretty tasty little earners. You should think about it. I do like to play the old stock market. Makes a man of you. All that bustle and shoving and the funny jackets. They are smart though aren't they? All stripy, like the old school tie. Many's a mate that I've helped out on the old investment front. Bull markets that's what you want. Charge through. Makes a man of you running in front of all those bulls,' he said, pumping his arms. 'Like at Pamplona, you know. Ahhh, yees. I've made a bit of a mint at times I don't mind telling you. Slap it on when the price is low and let it ride the market. It's all about demand and supply. Demanding the price you want and then supplying the money to pay for it, though I like to keep a bit of money in reserve. Hold it back. Make them think that's it, then slap on a bit more when the price is going up. Helps drive it, lures in the suckers. Then pop pop. Make the decision, buy it all. That's the ticket, though mum's the word,' he said, tapping the side of his nose and winking, 'don't let on.'

'Er, no I won't.'

'So what can I do for you?'

'Pamela said you wanted to see me?'

'Did she? Can't think what for. Don't recall saying anything,' he puzzled, 'never mind. How's things going?'

'They're fine. There's a couple of things. Pamela asked me to remind you that she has some visitors coming to see you tomorrow.'

'Oh yes? Who's that then?'

'A couple of local business men thinking about making a donation, to sponsor one of the collections?'

'Oh yes. Business eh, just the ticket, more of that kind of thing, eh. Ah yees. I suppose I'd better meet them, give them the old Callow charm, ehh, just to smooth the thing along.'

'Yes. I'm putting out a small exhibition. I'll show it to them before they come to you.'

'Ah, yes, that's it eh Giles. Show them a few books eh. Get some old dusty ones out, lay on a few stories, eh. Yeees, tell them this was Dickens' personal copy of something or other, and Shakespeare wrote in the margins of that, eh. Bamboozle them with a bit of the old history eh, that'll always get a bit of money out of them.'

'You do know that there's nothing annotated by Shakespeare and we don't have any Dickens?'

'Oh, don't we? Well given 'em a story eh, nudge nudge, eh, eh.'

'I can't just make things up Rick.'

'Oh no, I know, wasn't suggesting it. Just, you know, if we have got anything like that, maybe get them out. You know, put on a show?'

'Yes, well I know what's expected and I'll see what I can do.'

Giles started to get up.

'What's the other thing?'

'Sorry?'

'The other thing. You said there were a couple of things.'

Giles Skeffington hesitated, half standing, then sat again. 'Well, yes there was, is. It's about Fenella Morningstar.'

'Ah yes, fine filly that one, how's she getting on?'

'Well that's it. It's that type of thing that's the problem. You see she's been finding your, er, attentions a bit, well, she feels they're inappropriate.'

'Inappropriate? What do you mean?'

'Well, like what you said just now. "Fine filly that one". You can't say that type of thing.'

'Oh, lord Giles, I know that. I have been on courses you know. Mind was a time when you could. But you know, I know what's on and what's not nowadays. I'm up on all the correctly political. No, that's just between you and me. You know, couple of professional men behind closed doors, mum's the word. Would never say that to her face.'

Giles Skeffington's eyes widened as he looked down at his knees.

'Well, you see that's it. She thinks that you have been saying things like that to her, and, well frankly, she said you'd were making very crude suggestions to her.'

Rick Callow looked genuinely perplexed. 'Crude? I don't understand, that's not my style at all. You know me, I'm all about the suave,' he said, spreading his hands and waving his fingers.

Giles Skeffington's face remained expressionless.

'Not that I've been making any kind of suggestions anyway. All I've really spoken to her about is her research. Ah yees, offered to give her some practical guidance if she wanted, you know, to help with the veritas.'

'Oh,' said Giles, raising his eyebrows. 'How did you do that?'

'Offered to give her some dancing lessons, show her a few moves. I even said I'd give her and Harvey some joint coaching. I think they are having a bit of a thing, if you know what I mean,' he said, pursing his lips and nodding.

'What makes you think she's interested in dancing?'

'Why, that's what she's researching. Pamela told me. Jane Austen and dancing. You know me, I'm a bit of a mover,' he said, holding his palms up and shimmying his shoulders, 'I know a bit of all the styles, including the eighteenth century formals, the Cotillion, the Quadrille,' he made gestures and circling movements with his arms.

Giles cringed at the image of Rick's impromptu performances in the great hall for unwitting and embarrassed visitors.

'Yes, I know Rick, I remember, but Fenella's work doesn't have anything to do with dance.'

'Really? I err, I could have sworn that's what Pamela told me she was doing. What was it she said...?'

'She's researching sex. Well writing pornography really. She was intending to see if she could find evidence of Jane Austen having written any racy scenes or notes. If she couldn't, she was going to make it up. I don't think they were to be exceptionally graphic, though I can't be sure, but it was definitely sex, not dancing.'

Rick Callow was blinking quickly, his mind teetering on the brink of a chasm while his mouth made small movements towards words that puttered into soundless air.

As Giles waited for a response the seconds slowed. 'Rick, you're not saying anything.'

Rick Callow's head started to shake in a palsied tremor.

'Rick? ....can you remember what you said? When you were offering assistance?'

'I......I.....oh Giles, I think I may have put my foot in it, I....I, oh dear, oh.' His face, usually fixed with its Styrofoam grin, had dropped into an unfamiliar repose that left his cheeks pooched around his mouth giving him the look of a saggy cushion left out in the rain. 'Well, ah yes, clearly there has been a miscommunication, Pamela shouldn't have told me she was writing about dancing,' he said, his face starting to gain some of it's more usual fixed cast, though missing the grin. 'Pamela will have to explain to Fenella that she made a mistake.'

'Don't you think you should say something as well? If it's entirely innocent on your part? I don't think she was particularly perturbed by what she took to be your, er, overtures. She'll probably find it funny.'

'Funny? I can't have people laughing at me Giles. What exactly did she say?'

'Ahem. Well. She said that you were asking, well asking to, you know, asking to do it. Have sex.'

'What. There and then...though...if she thought, if she thought... Oh dear, this is really very embarrassing Giles. Pamela really ought to have been clearer. I don't think it's for me to clear up. I can't have my position, and my my, well my gravitas, undermined by having to apologise for someone else's mistake. Ah, yees yes. Yeeees. So Giles, I think, in order to keep this, you know, tickety boo, I think it would be better coming from you, don't you think? I mean, you know, I don't want Pamela feeling embarrassed by me having to summon her and, well, let it be known that she's made a mistake. No we can just keep it on the down low, as they say. If you had a quiet word with Fenella, you know, ah yees, just say that you realised she had got the wrong idea, and you didn't want to make a thing out of something, that was really, well, just ah errm, just a misunderstanding. That way you can keep me out of it, and Pamela never need know that I know that she made such a mistake. I'll keep mum,' he said tapping the side of his nose, 'and well, you never know, Fenella may actually appreciate being offered dancing instruction when she realises that's what it was. I mean, after all *she's* likely to be quite embarrassed by *her* mistake, don't you think? It was her dirty mind, and her intentions that led to this in the first place. After all, it is the institutional capacity involved in knowing that we know how to deal with situations like this that allows us to understand, with inevitability, that such situations should always be devolved within the institutional hierarchy. That's what makes us all leaders in situations like these, our ability to all lead in a way that suggests that to lead is to control, and of course knowing when to lead as an act and when to lead to delegate, and in this sense I'm leadering you to take the lead on this one Giles. In a sense we are not only all leaders, but "leader" should now be the verb that guides not what we are, but what we do in all of our institutional thinkings, ah yees. Ah, yees, I think that is definitely the way to go. So, if you could just have a quiet word with Fenella, then we can get the whole thing sorted out eh, eh, Giles?'

Giles Skeffington's mind was snatching at the words as they drifted into the space between them. As he grabbed a hold of one, he noticed with dismay that there were two or three others which had just conjugated out of reach in a way that sounded like it was sense but which remained senseless. Had he really just said that *leader* should now be a verb. I leader, you leader, he she it... As he wallowed in the verbal soup, he tried to focus on the centre of his resolve. He was not going to apologise for Rick.

He was about to speak when the phone rang. Rick Callow held up his hand and picked up the receiver. 'Hello, ... Ah yes, yes. I see, oh, just a moment,' he placed his hand over the mouthpiece, 'Giles this is important and I need to deal with it now.....so if you wouldn't mind.'

Giles Skeffington stood up slowly. 'OK, but we still need to speak about this.'

'Oh, I know, I know, it will need your expert skills. Thank you very much Giles, let me know how it goes. Eh.'

Giles Skeffington left the room and Rick Callow hung up the receiver. Well done old boy eh, well done, expertly handled.

CHAPTER TWENTY-FOUR

The door of the black 1980s Jaguar XJ6 closed with a solid clunk. Henry Crouchmoor settled into the worn seat and buckled up the seat belt as Billy lowered his head through the door frame and folded himself into the passenger seat. Henry punched the cigarette lighter into its socket with his fat finger before turning the ignition key whilst Billy fumbled through some cassettes, selecting one and pushing it into the player. Jennifer Rush, *The Power of Love.*

'Nice choice Billy, very classy. I love a bit of Jennifer, she really moves me,' said Henry Crouchmoor, applying the glowing cigarette lighter to his half smoked cigar. 'Now, let's go and see if we can put the frighteners on our old mate Rick and get him to be a bit more generous with some his stuff, eh,' he said, as he looked over his shoulder and quickly reversed the jag out of the yard of Crouchmoor's amusement arcade.

Billy smiled and nodded his large blunt head. 'Yeah, I don't think we'll have to say much, reckon the little berk will shit himself the moment he sees us.'

'Let's hope so. He didn't get back to you the other day?'

'Naw, I left a message, saying come on my son, let's get with the plan. Where's the rest of them items? But nothing.'

'So he does need a little reminder then. I want to get a gander at this new book that was on the web site, Lavatory or something, about ghosts. Our friend in China says it's very rare, he knows a few people who might be interested.'

The black jaguar slowed and turned onto the drive leading up to Laudanum Grange, the tyres crunching on the gravel.

'We're going to meet with some tart called Pamela, I've told her I want to make a donation, so they should be giving us a nice arse licking. She's going to introduce us to Rick. Act like we've not met him before. See what he does. And be nice,' said Henry Crouchmoor.

'Oh, I'll be very polite, don't you worry about that.'

The jag pulled to a stop in the car park half way up the drive and Henry Crouchmoor yanked on the hand brake.

'What else was there on the list?' he asked.

'Hang on,' said Billy, reaching into the pocket of his sheepskin coat. 'Let's see. There's a couple more of them books by Jane, some Thomas Paine and a couple of maps.

'So, we're a few items light eh. You did tell him that we'd be making personal calls if he didn't deliver?'

'Oh yeah, told him that his teeth might be meeting his arse hole too.'

Henry Crouchmoor pulled a concerned face. 'Aw Billy, Billy. That was a little hasty wasn't it? You ought to at least have given him one chance of asking before you use that sort of language. Sometimes you can be subtle you know with these educated types, you don't need to spell it out.'

'Sorry pops, I was just enthusiastic.'

'I know me old China. Can't fault you for that, and I like it. Besides, I'm just a bit jealous I wasn't there to clock his boat race.'

He laughed and Billy Crouchmoor cracked a smile revealing large nicotine stained teeth. They got out of the jag and started to walk up the drive.

'You been here before?' said Billy.

'Nope.'

'Looks old.'

'Yeah, I reckon so.'

'Don't know why they didn't just knock it down and build a new one when they was tarting it up. Makes sense.'

They reached the porch. Henry Crouchmoor pushed the bell. It rang deep in the house. The intercom clicked to life.

'Bonjour.'

Henry Crouchmoor turned to Billy. 'Bon-fucking-jour,' he mouthed.

'Oh 'ello, this is Henry and Billy Crouchmoor. We're here to meet Pamela Larrup.'

'Aw we, we, come in. First door on your left.'

The lock buzzed and Henry Crouchmoor pushed open the door.

'Bonjour, I've called Pamela, she'll be down in a moment,' said the sister wearing tortoiseshell glasses when they entered reception.

'Did you have a pleasant journey?' asked the other sister.

'It was alright. Straight through on the A58, no bother.'

'I see, the weather didn't trouble you too much then?' Henry Crouchmoor puzzled and looked out of the window at the weak autumn sun radiating behind the thin patchy cloud.

'Nope, sunshine all the way my lovely.'

The two sisters giggled.

'What's funny?'

'Oh we are not used to being "lovely",' replied the sister in the red glasses.

'Not lovely,' echoed the other.

'What? A couple of stunners like you? I'd have thought you'd be turning all the boys' heads,' said Henry Crouchmoor.

'Oh, he thinks we would turn heads.' said the sister in the tortoiseshell glasses smiling.

'Well, we have done it before. Remember? Though he wouldn't know it.'

'Ah, bien sûr, of course, no he wouldn't know about that.'

Henry Crouchmoor looked nonplussed towards Billy as Pamela Larrup bustled into the office.

'Good Morning gentlemen, Pamela Larrup, very nice of you to come and see us.' she said, holding out her hand. 'If you will follow me, I'll take you across to see the library and museum,' said Pamela, leading them out of the office.

The sister in the red glasses looked toward her sibling watching Billy Crouchmoor's frame shamble out of the office over the top of her half-moon, tortoiseshell glasses

'They won't be expecting it,' said the red glasses sister.

'No, not at all. But it is expected. It will be coming?'

'No doubt, it's always been coming. Etre. And it will be again, in that other way.'

'It will have been happening before they can even know it has passed.'

'And then it will all seem like it has been, again.'

'Settled down?'

'And ever present.'

'Ever present, again?' the half-moon sister said.

Her sister looked at her and said nothing. They both smiled.

Henry and Billy followed Pamela outside and around the corner to the Grimalkin Library and Museum.

'Gordon Bennet, what a two-an-eight,' exclaimed Billy Crouchmoor as it came into view.

'It is impressive, is it not?' said Pamela Larrup. 'Richard Rogers.'

'What?' said Billy.

'The architect, Richard Rogers.'

'I'll say he does,' muttered Billy.

Pamela Larrup strode ahead as Henry and Billy stared up at the stumbling edifice hanging onto Laudanum Grange.

'I don't like the look of that,' said Billy, pointing to the Grimalkin Library.

'Ah know what you mean my son. But it's a typical bit of your postmodern irony. Something these university types think is a kinda witty comment on the relationship between the form and function of the past, its formal restrictions, and the unrestrained freedoms of the present. Me, ah reckon it's just bullshit. Some lazy arsehole just letting his pen slop about the page, knowing that yer modern building techniques can render anything.'

'Fuckin' university types. They ain't got no idea about style, pops. No idea.'

'Too right my son, too fuckin right. Come on, lady lah-di-dah's waiting,' said Henry, nodding towards Pamela stood by the side of the revolving door into the library.

'We have been putting a lot of effort into developing some of our collections recently. I'm very keen for you to meet Giles, our librarian. He has arranged a display of things you that might interest you,' said Pamela Larrup, as they walked across the marble ground floor and down the circular stairs to the reading room.

Billy Crouchmoor looked towards the exhibition space and took note of the security cameras. When they reached the bottom of the staircase a neatly dressed man in a tweed waistcoat was laying out some books onto wedges of foam on one of the large tables and placing what looked like thick laces across the pages. He looked up and pushed his glasses onto the bridge of his nose.

'This is Giles Skeffington, our librarian. Henry and William Crouchmoor.'

They shook hands.

Giles Skeffington wrinkled his nose slightly at the smell of stale tobacco. 'Pamela told me that you were interested in our Shakespeare collection, so I've put out some of the more important items for you to look at,' he said, gesturing towards a number of books, open on the table. 'What is it about the Shakespeare collection that interests you?' said Giles Skeffington to Billy Crouchmoor who looked unnerved for a moment before Henry replied.

'Aw, well, it's me that has the interest. I think that Shakespeare and me would have had a thing or two in common if we'd been around at the same time.'

'Really? What type of things?' asked Giles Skeffington.

'Aw, well. Like me, he was a man of the people, and he was persuasive. Knew how to make his characters do things they didn't really want to, even though they knew they should. Cos, well. It's what was good for them.'

'I see,' said Giles.

'So what have we got?' said Henry Crouchmoor, removing a pair of Pince-nez from his glasses case and placing them on his nose as he moved closer to the table.

'This is our most recent acquisition which I am particularly proud of,' said Giles Skeffington, pointing to Ludwig Lavater's *Of Ghostes and Spirites* open at the first page.

The firste parte of this Booke, concerning Spirites walking by night
Wherein is declared, that Spirites and sightes do appeare, and that sundry strange and monstrous things do happen.

'I like the sound of this. Here Billy, come and have a gander.'

'Is it one of his plays?' asked Billy.

Giles Skeffington smiled. 'No sorry, it's not Shakespeare. I should explain. This is the book that Shakespeare consulted when he was writing anything about ghosts or the supernatural.'

'Oh right, so Macbeth, Hamlet?' said Henry.

'Yes, almost certainly,' said Giles Skeffington.

'Fascinating, don't you think Billy?'

'Yeah, yes pops.'

'So when Hamlet, when he's going all Gert and Daisy with his dad's ghost, that comes from here?'

'Sorry? I don't quite...' said Giles.

'Oh yeah, forgive me my son. When Hamlet's letting on that he's a few bob short of a nicker,' said Henry Crouchmoor, circling his forefinger by his temple, 'you know to check out if it's really his dad or Old Nick playing the Bengal Lancer?'

'Oh yes, I see. Yes, Lavater, the author, precisely codifies the different types of spirits, a ghost, an evil spirit or the devil, Old Nick as you say, or indeed angelic spirits.'

'Codifies them does he? Very interesting,' said Henry, nodding slowly. 'You say you got this recently?'

'Yes, it's come across from America. It was in the collection of an eminent physicist who passed away.'

'Expensive?' asked Billy Crouchmoor.

'Well, there are very few of these, so they don't come cheap. But I thought it was worth it. It complements the rest of the collection. This for example,' said Giles Skeffington, pointing to another large book open on foam wedges.

'Mr William Shakespeare's Comedies, Histories and Tragedies: published according to the true original copies, 1623,' Henry Crouchmoor read aloud, as he scanned across the black and white print of the bard occupying the rest of the page.

'Yes, it's Shakespeare's First Folio. It was the first attempted compilation of his plays. It's one of the most important books in the history of the English language printing and publishing.'

'Worth a few bob then?' asked Billy Crouchmoor.

'I would say that it's priceless. Though, of course, they do have a price. They go for millions when the odd one comes up for sale, but for me, it is priceless.'

'Pheeew,' whistled Billy Crouchmoor, 'millions for this?' he said, placing a large finger on it. 'Who would have thought?'

'Yes, so you see, if you do decide to sponsor the collection then you would be doing some important work,' said Pamela Larrup. 'The money will allow us to ensure that the collection remains conserved to the highest possible standards. You would be associated with a very prestigious collection and contributing to preserving the heritage of the nation.'

'Cor blimey, you hear that Billy. "The heritage of the nation." Crouchmoor and sons, associated with the heritage of the nation, ah like that, I do like the sound of that.'

'Of course something as important as this, well it would need to be done, well, in a manner that is fitting. You know, tastefully,' said Giles Skeffington.

'Oh don't you worry my son, don't you worry. Me and Billy here,' said Henry Crouchmoor placing a bear like arm around his son, 'we can be very tasteful, can't we Billy.'

'Very, tasteful pops, very tasteful indeed.'

CHAPTER TWENTY-FIVE

Warren Hastings, wearing a calico shirt and knee breeches, paced up and down the bare wooden boards of his estate room in Calcutta and wondered how good Phillip's aim was.

He had not been challenged to a duel before but things had reached such a pitch, this was the only way honour could be satisfied. To have taken the word of Maharaja Nandakumar against him was one thing, but to have behaved so scandalously in his private affairs; to have taken away the sweet wife, Catherine, from his dear friend George Grand. Why, that was something that could not be tolerated. So he had had recourse to no other action. However, when he had presented the minute to the council board of the East India Company he had not expected it to lead to this. Now that it had, honour must be served.

In presenting the minute he had intended to shame Phillip Francis into resignation and a dishonourable return to England. However, Phillip was more pugnacious and stubborn headed than even he had given him credit for. He wondered if he could have worded the minute differently; whether this would have led to a different outcome. If he hadn't written that he judged the public conduct of Mr Francis by his experience of his private, which he had found to be "void of truth and honour". If he had toned it down, would Phillip have still challenged him to the duel?

No. It was the correct thing to have said, and needed to be done. Anyway, the thought was moot. There was to be a duel. He hefted the flintlock pistol in his hand and practiced his aim, taking a bead on a man walking with a donkey on the far side of the dusty courtyard. A duel it was and we would see whose side honour would satisfy.

Harvey Premnas' gaze wound back across the moors from late eighteenth century India to the here and now, and the library cafe. He turned his head from the view and took a mouthful of luke warm coffee. Warren Hastings had gone on to win the duel, seriously wounding Phillip Francis, who would later take his revenge upon Hastings by leading the accusers, and providing much of the evidence for his impeachment, eight years later. That he was eventually acquitted of this would, he supposed, have been some recompense, and though the trial had left him impoverished, he was not to remain without power and influence.

One of the beneficiaries of this, Harvey had recently learned, was one Francis William Austen. Hastings had put his shoulder to the wheel of nineteenth century patronage and lobbied strongly in favour of Francis Austen's rise through the ranks to become Admiral of the Fleet. To see this as evidence of unscrupulous dealings, however, would have been to misplace judgement. Patronage, dispensing favour and position to one's friends and family, was an expected and accepted system in the eighteenth century and played the role that merit and academic achievement played today. Harvey knew this and was keeping it in the forefront of his ruminations. However, could the line of association belie something more?

Warren Hastings, friend of George, Francis Austen's father, if not culpable, at least feeling some unease at the precarious finances of the Austen family after George's losses in East India Company stocks, reaches into the system to promote his friend's son across the years. This was no evidence of wrong doing, and indeed, Austen would hardly have been allowed to rise irresistibly if it was only Hasting's patronage that was the source of leverage. There would have to have been some talent too. But was that the sole motivation? What if Francis had found a way to help with Hastings' debts? And if he had, where had the money come from? Would he, could he, have been selling naval secrets for money? Cash for plans. That didn't seem likely, too high a risk for someone else's debts, unless certain promises had been made and certain sympathies were present. Austen was ambitious. And then, what if these ambitions were also coupled with a certain ambiguity towards the French? Not in support of them exactly, but sympathetic to some of their ideals, as his friend Watkin Tench appeared to be. What if Austen had become radicalised?

'Brrrrr, it's getting cold out there.'

Harvey turned to see Fenella Morningstar emerging from the revolving door. He smiled. 'G'day, how are you?'

'I'm good.'

She bought a coffee and sat down. He told her about the role Warren Hastings had played in Francis Austen's naval career.

'You're not suggesting Hastings was in on the plot to pass information to the French? That he was a traitor too?'

'No, I'm just speculating on it as part of an overall picture. If Austen did pay off some of Hastings debts in expectation of his support, then it paints him in a slightly different manner than otherwise, says something about his character. Not undue to thinking in the long term, planning, plotting something, that whilst not unethical by the principles of the time, it does suggest a certain venality. And if he did, there's the question of where he got the money from.'

Fenella Morningstar nodded slowly. 'Have you had any further thoughts on what you're going to do about Gustav and Pamela?'

'Well yu know, I have. I'm writing two sets of notes. One that reflects my real interpretation of the documents and manuscripts. The other? Well the other is a little more creative and should, I hope, cause some, er, tensions to arise should certain persons see it.'

'Oh yeah.'

'Yeah.'

'Well, don't just sit there. What? What are you making up?'

Harvey grinned, looked about and leaned over. 'Well. Apparently there is a letter from Jane thanking her brother for writing her another first draft of a book to work on.'

'No?'

'Yep. Francis Austen wrote Jane's novels. I think that'll cause some commotion don't you? Make someone eager to move.'

'But, she'll want to see the evidence, won't she?' said Fenella.

'You think so?' Harvey paused. 'But to do that openly she'd have to acknowledge how she'd come to know of its existence. Admit that she, or Gustav, have been rifling through my notes and pinching my research.'

'Oh exquisite. Even if she can't believe it, she won't be able to contain herself.'

'What do you think she'll do?' asked Harvey.

'Depends on how big her ego is. Whether it's voracious enough to consume her judgement. At worst, she'll just be eaten up by an infuriating sense of impotence. Which'll be a lot of fun to watch,' said Fenella.

'From what I've seen I reckon her ego's big enough. She seems to consider anything that isn't about her to be beneath her, or at least a suspicious waste of time,' said Harvey.

'Does this letter from Jane say which novel he's just sent her?'

'No, I thought I'd leave plenty of room for the imagination to run riot.'

'Oh, I can't wait. How are you going to know whether she's seen it?' asked Fenella.

'I hadn't thought of that. You're right, it's hardly going to be fun unless we know that she knows.'

'I know. When you arrange your papers leave a hair lying across one of them. If it's gone, someone has moved them.'

'Fair Dinkum.'

'James Bond. In *Doctor No* he puts a wet hair across the closet door, same thing.'

'Very crafty, only mine's a bit short,' said Harvey, tugging at very little.

'Here.' Fenella said, running her hand through her hair and passing him a dark strand. 'Unless you're looking for it, you'd never notice.'

Harvey took the strand, wrapped it around a pencil and put it carefully in his pencil case.

CHAPTER TWENTY-SIX

He stretched out his arms, yawned and looked up from the computer screen. It was Friday. Friday, Friday. Not a day to be taken seriously. More a day to be undone. A day to....well, a day perhaps just to be, today. He stood up and looked out at the view over the moors. The sky ran with thin patchy cloud to the horizon, where it seemed to give way to darker stuff. He watched a black car turn from the road onto the drive leading up to the house. No, Friday was a day that was always waiting to be the weekend, so one shouldn't take it seriously. At least not this Friday, or indeed, perhaps any. The car pulled into the car park half way up the drive. Two figures got out. Maybe he would finish early. Finishing early, that's the ticket. That way he could focus on getting something really purposeful done, just a small task, and that would be it for the day. They must be the business men Giles told him about. That would be the thing. Meet with them, then lunch and that would be the day. That would be Friday done.

He watched the men approach closer up the drive. There was something familiar about them. Their gait. One of them shambled along with a long lumbering roll to his shoulders as he paced.

Something numb began to creep across Rick Callow's mind. That couldn't be. Icy pins and needles started to collect and insert themselves around the back of his neck. Business men. He should have thought to ask. He struggled to stare closer at the two men, to make their faces resolve to something other than what they seemed to be. The icy grasp on the scruff of his neck began to move into his marrow. It was them. That was Billy Crouchmoor leaving heavy treads in the gravel below, and Henry following. They had come. He became more rigid as the slow cold began to rise from his feet as well, freezing his ability to feel in control. He shook himself and started into movement, turning from the window. What to do? To do, what? Where? Now? What to do? What was it Giles had said, what was it? He took a hold of the edge of the desk and steadied himself. Think. Think Rick. Yes, that was it. They were meeting Giles first weren't they? Calm, now calm. Wait.

The phone rang in the office. The sister with the half-moon tortoiseshell glasses looked at it, then up at her sibling.
She nodded at her. 'Il aura vus.'
'Oh, we. Yes, he will have. But should we?' She looked over her glasses at the phone.
'Should. Could. Would we? Will we?' The phone continued to ring.
'We could. But then when we do, we could, you know, undo the raison d'etre and let something else come to begin?'
'To begin The Begin?'
'And begin again.'
'Bien sûr, bien sûr,' said the sister with the red glasses as she picked up the phone. 'Bonjour Rick, comment allez-vous? Yes, they were just here. Do I know where they've gone? Why yes, Pamela said they were on their way up to you.' After they have visited the library, she mouthed silently across to her sister. 'Yes, I think so. OK OK, au revoir.' She smiled and her eyes beamed as she hung up the phone.

Rick Callow looked around his office. Nowhere to hide. He walked on the balls of his feet across to the door and placed his ear against it. Silence. He cracked open the door and peeped through. An empty corridor. He opened it further and listened. Still silent. There might be time. Stepping into the corridor he closed the door carefully behind him and moving quickly on the balls of his feet, he resisted the temptation to do a passo double, he reached Pamela Larrup's door. He listened, knocked quietly and opened the door. He started to go in, then looking around the corridor again, stepped back out and pulled the door closed. She might go in here when she found his office was empty. Quick thinking Rick. Where to? Quickly. He heard a creak on the stairs. Quick, quick. He stepped across to another door and opened it. The broom cupboard. Good thinking Rick. He stepped inside and closed the door quietly as he nuzzled in amongst the brushes, mops and smell of disinfectant, almost tripping over a metal bucket with a clang. He froze and listened. Nothing. He waited and listened, stretching his neck forward to catch the slightest indication that anyone was coming. He waited. Still nothing. He looked at his watch. Blast, he couldn't see it. He put his ear to the door. The silence was impassive. Try as he might he could not detect the slightest creak from the old wooden staircase and his eyes strained against the darkness in a doomed attempt to pull some image into view. What would he do when he did hear them? They would knock on his door. Then knock again. Pamela would open it and find him gone. She'd apologise. They would...they would what? They would go back down to reception then...reception. The women in reception knew he was in his

Cringe

office. They knew. Maybe Pamela wouldn't ask. Maybe she would just see them out the door. No she would ask, she would. She knew Giles had told him about the businessmen. He grabbed onto a soggy mop and squeezed it to steady himself. He felt cold water run down his sleeve. What to do? He could just wait it out. The women in the office, they would say he called, but now he can't be found. They would just go, "Oh sorry, don't know where he can be. We'll call to rearrange a meeting. Yes, very disappointing but.." No, no, but no. What if they said something? Billy and Henry Crouchmoor, what if they said something? They hadn't come to talk about donations, they had come to see him. To see him because they wanted the rest of the items on the list. He felt the folded paper inside his jacket pocket. But they had said they'd come for donations. Business men making donations. Told that to Pamela. So this might just be a warning. Wouldn't blow their cover to her. He might get another chance, or at least be able to get out of any immediate danger, then he could plan what to do next. That would be it. He would wait until they had knocked on his door, started to go down stairs, wait until they were half way down, then appear at the top of the stairs. "Hello hello, Rick Callow here. Hello gentlemen, so sorry I missed you just now. Just in the little boy's room."

Ah yees, that's the ticket. Tell Pamela he'll speak to them alone, and then say, "Sorry, I know, I know. Definitely get you those other things, yees definitely. Just a question of timing. No, of course no problem. Just a misunderstanding earlier. Of course, of course." Shake hands, show them out. That's the ticket, that'll be the way to go. He listened again. Waited. Maybe there had been a change of plan? Maybe Pamela had decided not to bring them up to him? He listened only to hear the throbbing of his own blood in his ears. Maybe? That was it. Maybe he would go and find them? Take control of things. Rick Callow, always good at taking control. A steady hand on the tiller. That was Rick Callow. Calm and suave, steady as she goes. Ah yees, that's the ticket. He started to crack open the cupboard door, manoeuvring himself forward through the brooms and mops that had fallen in against him, sliding his feet through the metal buckets on the floor. He peered through the crack and listened. Nobody there, good.

He had eased the door open half way when he heard distant voices and the thud and creak of footsteps coming up the staircase. Cockney voices. He tried to move himself out of the clutch of the mops and brooms. As he did so, they started to clatter out of his grasp and fall through the half open door. He clutched at them desperately, trying to control the sloppy mops and dusty brooms. Stop them from banging on the door and floor. He managed to grab an armful as he slipped back and tripped back over one of the metal buckets, stepping backwards and clattering his other foot into six inches of cold water. He continued to fall backwards into some cleaner's coats hanging on the back wall. He heard sounds outside the door.

He froze, half propped against the back wall, one foot in a bucket with armfuls of brushes and mops on top of him. He could smell the soap and disinfectant and felt water seeping through his jacket onto his chest. The door opened to reveal a puzzled and concerned looking Pamela Larrup with Billy and Henry Crouchmoor's faces, grinning like hyenas, attendant over her shoulders.

'Why Rick! What on earth are you doing there?'

'Oh, Pamela, just looking for a duster,' he said, trying to untangle himself from the mops and brooms, whilst slipping further down the wall.

Henry Crouchmoor moved past Pamela. 'Here, let's give him a hand,' he said.

'Yes, thanks,' said Rick, accepting Henry's hand. 'Just thought my office was looking a bit dusty, so I thought, just give it the quick once over, and well, I sort of stumbled and the door shut behind me. Then everything just started to fall. I'm so sorry, I'm not usually this clumsy.'

'Don't you worry my old son, could have happened to anyone, here you go,' said Henry, pulling Rick to his feet through the tumble of cleaning equipment.

'Phoof, thanks,' said Rick, brushing himself down and smearing half dissolved soap powder down his suit. 'Oh dear.'

'I think you need to clean yourself up Rick, you are a bit of a state,' said Pamela.

'Yes, suppose so. Not a great first impression. I'm really very sorry about this gentlemen.'

'We will wait in your office whilst you sort yourself out,' said Pamela.

'Yes good idea, shan't be long,' said Rick, walking off in the direction of the gents.

Henry Crouchmoor looked out of the window in Rick Callow's office. Not a bad day. Nice day for a spot of shooting. Maybe bag a few grouse. Not that he was a great shot, but he did like to have a go. He liked the kick of the recoil.

'Do they have any shooting around here? Grouse shooting?'

'Yes I think they do, over on Ilkley Moor. Though I do not know much about it. Do you go shooting?'

'I have done. Just looks like a nice day for it, sociable too. Though I don't own a shot gun. I normally borrow one. Suppose I could buy one,' said Henry.

He turned back to the window. The door to the office was open. Rick Callow's footsteps approached along the corridor.

'Ah, Rick, that looks a bit better. Henry was just talking about getting a shotgun.'

'A shotgun! I don't think it's come to that. I mean guns, no one mentioned guns before,' said Rick, holding up his hands.

Henry Crouchmoor smiled. 'For shooting birds, grouse shooting.'

'Oh yes, I see. Yes, yes. Er yes.'

'Rick this is Henry Crouchmoor and his son William,' said Pamela.

'Oh please, call me Billy, all my friends call me Billy, I like to be friendly, if you know what I mean,' he said, engulfing Rick's hand in his meaty paw.

Rick Callow grimaced. 'And Henry, nice to meet you too,' he extended his hand and braced himself, only to be met with a firm, yet not painful, handshake. 'So, shall we sit down,' he gestured towards two chairs.

'I'll just pop next door and get another one from my office,' said Pamela Larrup.

Billy Crouchmoor pulled a piece of paper from his jacket pocket, unfolded it and holding it up to Rick Callow tapped on it as he winked and tipped his head. Rick Callow held up his hands and mouthed "I know, I know."

Pamela Larrup returned with a chair which she set beside Billy as he folded up the paper and replaced it in his pocket. 'Henry and William have been looking at some of the items in the Shakespeare collection,' she said.

'Yes, you've got some very interesting acquisitions there, very interesting,' said Henry Crouchmoor.

'And very valuable too. Do you lend them out?' asked Billy.

'Oh no no, mister Crouchmoor. We are not a lending library. They can only be used in the safety and security of our reading rooms,' replied Pamela Larrup, 'we need to ensure they have the best care possible.'

'Bit like an old folks home then,' said Henry Crouchmoor.

Rick Callow grinned fixedly.

'I'm not sure I follow,' said Pamela Larrup.

'Well they're a bit rackety round the edges. You don't want them out on the streets, you know, where any old so-and-so could knock 'em about. They're not up to that anymore. So you wrap 'em up in blankets, and they're wheeled out for the relatives. You know, the likes of us, for visits every now an' again,' said Henry Crouchmoor.

'Well, I suppose there is a certain analogy,' said Pamela Larrup.

'An' that's why you need us,' said Billy Crouchmoor, ' 'cos running an old folks home costs money. Only the old books, they ain't got it like the old folks, and that's where we come in.'

'Exactly,' said Henry Crouchmoor. 'Now I was impressed with some of the things in your Shakespeare. The folio an' the Lavatory, it was Lavatory wasn't it?'

'Er no. Lavater,' replied Pamela Larrup.

'That's it Lavater. Silly me. I think we could work something out here. You see, I think it would raise our profile a bit. You know, get a different class of customer into our business if we was associated with it. Pamela, was saying on the phone the other day, that we might be able to name it, and you know have our pictures next to it on your web site.'

'I don't think I said anything about pictures,' said Pamela Larrup.

'That would be alright though, wouldn't it? You know, a little bit of a splash, like a, like a, what's it called?'

'A press release pops?'

'That's it, a press release. You know, a bit of a story and a nice picture with me and Billy either side of Rick, arms round his shoulder and the books in front of us. You know, with some kind of headline, "Crouchmoor and sons sponsor Lavatory at Laudanum Grange".'

'Lavater,' said Pamela Larrup.

'Sorry. Stupid me, I did it again. Lavater. What do think Rick? You could arrange that couldn't you?'

Rick Callow grinned and nodded.

CHAPTER TWENTY-SEVEN

As he watched the black jaguar turn out of the drive, spewing gravel across the road, Rick Callow felt a draught of relief pass across his shoulders. As Pamela had left his office for another appointment, he'd told her he would iron out the details of Henry and Billy's sponsorship suggestions. Though it had been a tense affair, he had handled it in an exceptional manner. Quite exceptional. All he had to do, they assured him, was provide the rest of the items on the list and that would be it. They would call it a day. It would be worth it to get them off his back. However, this did present him with a slight problem in the long run.

The long run. He liked the phrase. It was all managementy. Like profit margins, emotional intelligence and leadership. He could see himself at the tiller of Laudanum Grange. Hand shading his eyes, focused on the horizon, as he looked off into the future, vision in view. The long run. Yes, that would be something he would need to think about once these last few things had been passed on to Billy and Henry for the appropriate fee. He had, of course, ensured that. You can't out fox Rick Callow. And it would be enough to fill the gap. But after that? After that, there was the long run.

He pictured himself striding out across the moors brandishing a rolled up copy of the financial times, beating off the mosquitoes of bills, debts and balances as they dared to bother his quest to fulfil his destiny. A giant of business. Colossus across the management landscape. Rick Callow, director and manager extraordinaire. But what was that? That something. Something there, something nagging. Something that, though he knew he should be paying attention to it, somehow left him slightly confused when he started to think about it. It was something so far off, that it seemed paltry to expend effort in trying to grasp it. Somehow, as his thoughts ranged around his position in the firmament of business managers and directors, the trend lines on the graphs of his share portfolio ranging ever upward, somehow, he found there was some plea that was gently begging for his attention, tugging at the back of his trouser leg. However, when he considered paying it some heed his eyes would lift, take in the light and skies around him and he would know. He would know. Know, that his path towards his future was not something that a barely conceivable detail should be allowed to distract him from. He owed it to those who looked up to him. Viewed him as a role model. The other members of the North Yorkshire Institute of Directors, and the members of the Guild of CEOs. He owed it to them to leader. He couldn't let himself get distracted by any silly, slight nag. Any tiny, silent incessant doubt. And how could he doubt? To doubt was to lack decision. And decision and decisiveness, those had been the words that had allowed him to take charge of those defining situations, those key moments, and turn them to his own ends. Rick Callow, ah yees, he knew how to make a decision. So he decided to forget about anything that was nagging him. It would be too little of worth to be worthy of consideration, so it would not be considered. After all, there was his vision and mission to fulfil. That's the ticket. Ah, yees, get on with that mission. He turned from the view and sat down at his desk. Now what was it he should be doing?

Henry Crouchmoor wound down the window and exhaled a cloud of smoke. He looked at Billy, smiled sardonically and roared with laughter. 'What a fuckin' full blown, arse about elbowed, diamond berk,' he said, as they both exploded with laughter. 'Could you Adam and Eve it. "Ah yeers, that's the ticket". What was he talking about? Did you understand him? I've never heard so much blather in all my born days.'

'I think he just shit himself, only he forgot which was his arse hole and which was his mouth hole. But I think,' said Billy, catching himself, 'I think he got the message pops. I don't think he'll be holding out on us in the future.'

'Let's hope so my son, let's hope so. Once we've got this lot out of the way I think our friend in China would be very interested in the Shakespeare stuff.'

The light well that ran the height of the reference library was turning from grey to black as the autumn dusk settled. The view up and out of it through the trees was darkening to an increasingly solid wall of obsidian glass: a monolithic reflection of the shelves of books and the exhibition space above. Harvey Premnas became aware that he was staring at himself.

Except for Giles Skeffington, he was alone in the reading room. The reflection of a movement on the floor above caught his eye. Gustav Crum's image floated along behind the handrail. Why would he agree to do Pamela Larrup's dirty work? It suggested a certain lack of self-determination; a deference to seniority which was out of proportion to that normally expected. She could certainly be over bearing but surely that wouldn't extend to her insistence on him doing something that he must know is unethical? Unless being a Dane at Oxford conjugated in a manner that led to some inevitable expectation of complicity? Maybe he was just in thrall to her. His first professional post. He's eager to make a good impression. She, somehow, presents a case that makes pinching his ideas seem a reasonable act under the circumstances. He wants to please her. As she's more experienced, senior, he assumes she knows what she's doing. Somehow it makes sense to him.

It wouldn't have been the first time. Intelligent people often became very good at rationalising the unacceptable. Faking data, plagiarising, creating false documents. He recalled the Hitler diaries.

The German magazine, Stern, had paid millions for them, publishing excerpts before they were proved to be fake, written on modern paper dyed with tea. They had even fooled some eminent historian that Stern had asked to verify them.

Harvey wondered, ran his hand across his scalp, ruffled his short hair and shook his head. No, that would be taking it too far. Besides, creating a convincing eighteenth century letter would be too time consuming. Whatever Gustav's motivations, if he did it again at least he would know.

He shuffled up his papers, separating those he would leave and those he would take with him, opened his pencil case and took out the hair that Fenella had given him. He held it up to the light. Dark brown. He placed it carefully across a corner of the pile of papers he left, packed his bag and started towards the stairs up to the ground floor.

'G'night Giles.'

'Yes, goodnight Harvey. Have you had a prosperous day?'

'Yeah, not bad mate, thanks.'

'I suppose you'll be feeling the weather a bit?'

'Yeah, bit colder than Sydney. How much colder will it get?'

'It won't be too bad by the time you go. But once winter bites, well it's got down to minus ten in the past, with all the snow and wind that goes with it.'

'I won't be sorry to miss that,' said Harvey Premnas, as he started up the stairs.

'Yes, good night Harvey.'

Giles Skeffington switched off his computer, tidied up the service desk, turned off the lights in the reading room and walked up the circular wooden stairs. He turned off the ground floor lights and left through the revolving door, locking it as he did so.

"During the first period of a man's life the greatest danger is not to take the risk." He had checked this when it came to him. That was a stupid mistake the other day. He liked to get his Kierkegaard right. Pamela had asked him to keep an eye open for opportunities to check on Harvey's progress. This was almost certainly one that was worth the dare. He stepped forward and lost his footing momentarily as he gained the rail and looked down from the museum to the darkened reading room two floors below.

He stepped quietly down the stairs, letting his weight down slowly on to each foot. "There is nothing with which every man is so afraid as getting to know how enormously much he is capable of doing and becoming." But now was not a time to be afraid of what he was capable of. Now was a time to be capable of the task which ought to be done. A leap of faith – yes, but only after reflection.

Pamela had told him how Harvey's research was not really specified in a rigorous enough manner; how it presumed to be something more than he was capable of delivering; and how this would be an embarrassment. Both for Harvey, he would appear as a pint pot scholar trying to down a quart, and for Laudanum Grange. When Harvey announced, it would seem that Laudanum Grange had paid a lot of money for a game that was hardly worth the candle. They, and she, would be a laughing stock. So they really could not afford to let Harvey release his misinterpretation of such important material without preparing the ground to soften his fall. They had to pre-empt him; get their more far-reaching, careful, nuanced account out first. Not to do this would be to fail the academic community, and indeed the wider world. They could not risk leaving one of the more momentous historical revelations in the hands of an amateur. He had not even completed his doctorate yet, and this was precisely the type of revelation that Laudanum Grange had been set up to achieve. To be associated with such a project would also be a very good feather for the start of his own career. Doctor Gustav Crum, assistant to Doctor Pamela Larrup, though she had mentioned a professorship in the offing, responsible for uncovering and interpreting the puzzle at the heart of the Morocco Manuscripts. He would have been in there at the beginning.

There was also a sense in which they were helping Harvey. He would get a mention. He was, after all, providing them with the ground work for a proper reveal, even though it was unwitting at the moment. Pamela had assured him that when the time came she would let Harvey know. That if he wanted to, he could have a mention when she and Gustav released Laudanum Grange's account of the manuscripts. However, they were also keeping Harvey from exposing his own inadequacies as a scholar. Embarrassing himself. "One can advise comfortably from a safe port." Once Harvey saw the account shaped by her and Gustav he would quickly realise his mistakes. It would give him a second chance. It was an act of altruism.

Gustav Crum approached the desk where Harvey's papers were laid out. He took out a small torch attached to his key ring, a note book and pen, and began to leaf through the papers, making notes as he did so. As he got to one page he paused, looked around, and returning to the page, reread it. He copied it down, then checked again to make sure he hadn't misunderstood it. He translated it carefully for himself. No, it seemed that he had been correct the first time. Did this mean what he thought? He would have to let Pamela know immediately. He took out his mobile phone and was about to call when he paused. He should take a picture of the notes. Just in case there was some English nuance he was missing. Just in case Pamela was incredulous and called his interpretation and translation into question, though he doubted it. He put his phone back in his pocket, better to get out of here first, and left the library via the walkway from the Grimalkin museum.

The card catalogue in the Grimalkin Library was housed in a large wooden chest of draws across the other side of the reading room from the light well and reading desks. Rick Callow opened the draw labelled 'Pa' and started to flick through the cards with one hand, whilst the other held his mobile phone as a torch. He stopped. *'Paine, Thomas. The Rights of Man. 1791.'* He pulled out the card and put it in his jacket pocket. He flicked through a couple more until he came to *'Paine, Thomas. The Age of Reason. 1797 published by Thomas Williams's.'* He took this too. Crafty Rick. No cards, no books. The idea had come to him that afternoon. Resolved as he was to provide the last of the items on Henry and Billy's list, he had decided he needed a few more arrows in his quiver when it came to covering his tracks. This was a stroke of genius.

The final items on the list didn't require this level of sophisticated skulduggery. They were maps. Petrus Plancius's, 1594 double-hemisphere world map and John Speed's 1627 map of North and South America. He knew where the books containing these were, having removed another map previously with a craft knife. And no one would notice this. He closed the draw in the card catalogue. Stage one successfully completed. Now for stage two.

He went to the service desk, opened a draw, removed a small bunch of keys and went down the stairs to the floor below. Beside the door into the stacks was a small wall safe. He opened it with one of the keys on the bunch, took out another key, closed the safe, then unlocked the door into the stacks and let himself in. He turned on the light and, consulting the cards, wound his way through the stacks to find the Paine books. After he had collected them he laid out the map books and carefully sliced the two maps from them, rolled them up and tied them with book ribbon. With the books under one arm and the maps in his hands he retraced his steps through the darkened library and museum back to his office.

Harvey took his time walking back down the road to The Terrace and into the mind of the never knowing, never certain and not understood. The future.

In ten years' time, he would have been in a professional post for say, five or six years. He looked back on the day of his appointment. How the appointment committee had commended him for his thesis and the ground breaking analysis of the Francis Austen Manuscripts. He would have been deferential and wondered out loud whether he was just lucky. He would have remembered Giles bringing them to him. The trolley appearing as the lift doors opened. Would that become one of those times that defined a life? Where its memory became so preternaturally real, the world seemed to pull back from its edges to fold this point to the centre of his mind's resolve? And who could know that anyway? It only became so, as the rest of the world turned, and returned, and that point took on the past as something more than the rest of the moments around.

He paused by the gate that led up to the porch of The Terrace and turned to look at the lights twinkling across Cragg Vale. And how would his thesis have carried itself in the world? Would it too have become a memory toward what seemed a sealed future? Not many PhD theses went beyond being defended, presented and filed. Beyond being the evidence of achieving a certain standard of critical and analytical discourse, such as to make a body of evidence coherent and substantial enough to satisfy one's peers. There were some. You heard of it happening. Of theses published as books, a handful being declared works of genius, with profound insights or ground breaking. Insight would be nice, profound better. But if he was right, if the hunches he and Fenella had developed over the last few weeks became something more solid, would it be seen as anything other than a lucky break? If not him, then someone else? Come on Harvey, now is not the time to doubt. Now is the time to let the leading edge take the strain and follow where the evidence beckons. Don't push it, or force it to fit hoped for expectations. Let it be, and become what it has been, what it wants with certainty to reveal. Once that has been set, then there may be room for speculation. Or at least a set of questions, guiding insights toward an interpretation of the past for a future that is never known, uncertain and only about to become. He turned into the path and closed the gate behind him.

Gustav Crum listened to the phone ring in what he knew to be a neatly organised, primly appointed living room.

'Hello, Pamela Larrup speaking.'

'Pamela, it is Gustav.'

'Why good evening Gustav, how nice to hear you. What can I do for you?'

'I have some of the news for you. I kept the eye open on his research.'
'Oh yes, something interesting I presume?'
'I think so. His notes reference a letter. It was from Jane to Francis. The notes they said, Jane thanks Francis for sending her, "a draft manuscript for another story",' he enunciated carefully.

There was silence on the end of the line. 'Say that again Gustav.'

' "A draft manuscript for another story." Jane thanking Francis.'

'You are sure it wasn't the other way around. Him thanking Jane?'

'No, I was very careful, I could not believe it. I took a photo of the page.'

'Could you e-mail that to me? Not that I doubt you, but I would very much like to see it with my own eyes.'

'Yes, I will do that. Do you think it is correct?'

'I don't know Gustav, I do not know. Send me the e-mail. I will speak to you tomorrow.'

The e-mail arrived shortly afterwards. It revealed nothing more than what had been related. She read and reread the photographed notes, trying to divine something more below the surface of Harvey's pencil scribbles. They looked as though they had been written quickly. Excitedly. There were no comments of surprise or exclamation marks. Just the statement as Gustav had related it and a date, 1802. Jane Austen would have been twenty-seven. Her first published novel, *Sense and Sensibility*, did not come out until 1811. According to the accepted accounts this started life as *Elinor and Marianne* some years earlier and it was well known that she had started several of her other novels years before they were published. Could it be? To say "thank you" for "another" manuscript? Others previously?

She stood, took down a book from the book case and opened it at a timeline. Yes, 1811, starting and re-writing several of her other novels, including *Northanger Abbey* and *Pride and Prejudice* in the period between then and the date of this presumed letter. If this could be established... why, it would turn the world of Austen studies on its head. Never mind if her brother was a traitor, this was far more important. After all, we won Trafalgar, beat the French. But to think that Jane Austen was not the sole author of her books....why....why. Pamela Larrup snapped the book shut. It hardly began to bear thinking about. But surely, surely it would have been realised by now? You would think so, with so much scholarship poured over her across the years, such a revelation could hardly hinge upon just this? But then, was that not the same as the claim of Francis being a traitor. Was Jane a traitor too? A traitor to all of us who have built our reputations on her? How much of her analysis of Austenian prose had been the analysis of Francis' rather than Jane's? Shouldn't she have picked up on a different tone, a different voice from somewhere behind the narrative? Wouldn't it depend on how much it was over written, worked over? Though of course, it had never occurred. Never occurred to her, to anyone, to be looking for this. Would this be better to be known about or better kept secret? How would it cast the conclusions, not only from her own research, but that of thousands of others? It must be a fake. It could only be a fake. To be otherwise... surely she would have spotted it. But then, wouldn't the same be true of Francis' treachery. The possibility had never crossed the desk of any journal or academic that she was aware of, there had been no evidence to provoke it, and yet, here she was considering the way that Laudanum Grange should handle the announcement of the findings about Francis. Should she confirm one and deny the other? Maybe the presence of this letter, along with documents suggesting treason, confirm that both are true. Both secrets that were intended to be kept. Would that be best for both? To ensure the authors' intentions? The world knew, or expected, that revelations were to come from these documents. But maybe too much truth was a bad thing, too much truth after all of this time of things being the way one expected. Maybe it would be intolerable to now have to admit to living a life in a different way? Having to re-think all the safe assumptions that had allowed you to build yourself and your reputation up to now. Although. Everything would now require re-evaluation, a major re-evaluation. Major research projects for years to come that could completely revamp the study of Austen. Symposiums. Conferences. It would not deny the importance of her writing and the beauty of that witty, sardonic prose. That would still stay. Only now we have to rethink who the author really was and how the identity of her brother, Francis, now came to the fore in these works. Why this was a whole new life for someone, a whole new way to play the discipline, a whole new set of academic positions, papers, journals. She could see the future coming and somewhere she was at the head of it. No, this would be OK. This would be somewhere she could go. Pamela Larrup, out in front, leading the charge, whose work was not denied. How could it be? She had worked, as everyone else had, with the state of the subject as it was agreed to exist. She had not slipped up. It was simply never something that had been thinkable before. Now however, with it arriving as a reality, well. She would need to get a look at that original letter, and what if there was more. She would have to get a look at those documents.

CHAPTER TWENTY-EIGHT

She knew about him from her undergraduate studies and had come to understand that he would have been able to play at any table, at any level, at any time, and yet remain a known enigma. You could see his hand everywhere in the purpose of events in the eighteenth and nineteenth centuries, but of the man himself there was but the shape of a deliberately abstruse presence. As if the continental mistral, blowing across a great French maze, had been drawn down by the hand of a magus, held in the thrall of his own cryptic illusion. A felt presence. A made up countenance that was now beginning to slip into the pages of herself and enfold her thoughts into the parade of history that she was reading.

Fenella had been worrying away at the identities of T and B in the log entries. T had been pleased with the last dispatch from Francis, presumably carried by C who had reported this to him, and who in turn, C had passed a communication from along with another one from B. That was it. Not much to go on. But, with Harvey having deciphered another letter from Watkin Tench, her suspicions at their identities were forming.

23 Pike Street,
Plymouth,
3rd November 1792.

My Dearest Miss Burney,
It is with great pleasure that I recall our meeting at my recent marriage to my beloved Anna in October. Your presence on so joyful an occasion, needless to say, blessed the conviviality which was dictated in your every sentiment. The divine service that was performed by Rev. Mr. Johnson was the most distinguished with regard to the attentions of the duty of marriage which Mrs. Tench and I hold dearly to our future destiny.
I found the subject of our conversation on the French situation most enlightening. Though I must confess myself a stranger to your

political sentiments at the time, I thought your conversation, given with such friendly and informed manners, has done favour to my own thought. I have intentions to publish a six penny paper on the matter of supporting the less distasteful aspects of the French affairs and would ask whether a meeting with the French Constitutionals at Juniper Hall is something that is within your possession to arrange for me, so it would seem, that on that occasion, they might receive me with great cordiality. That such a connection might be established would, I believe, tend to the interest of both parties.

- Adieu!

Watkin Tench

Fanny Burney and the French Constitutionals at Juniper Hall? She was a friend to the great and the good, a courtier - second keeper of the robes to Queen Charlotte, a diarist, as significant as Pepys, and a novelist. Always there in the background, self-effacing and taking note. Amongst the French Constitutionals one in particular had her attention. M. de Talleyrand. They were almost exact contemporaries and both were witness and party to the defining events of the era.

Talleyrand was a chameleon-diplomat, who revelled in the inability to pin him down. By turns admired and feared, his poker faced gravitas, sardonic self-possession, intelligence and constant contact with the world of power, had ensured that he was indispensable to all but the most radical of the French regimes. Yet to others, he was a scandalous, tireless schemer, stirring the pot for his own amusement, a revolutionary, a scoundrel, a rake who kept a mistress, Catherine Grand, who became as famous for her prodigious stupidity as for her dazzling beauty. That Talleyrand had once said that he was content with "the mind of a rose", only seemed to condemn him further in the eyes of those who distrusted him. And the final coup de grace to be used against him - he had a limp.

Fenella Morningstar had felt herself slide in her opinions of him in the way that Fanny Burney had also seemed to do. He had arrived in London in January 1792, seeking a commitment to British neutrality in the face of Austrian and Prussian hostility. However, British snobbery was all too eager to view him with the suspicion and distrust that was only fitting for a scoundrel, and "the cripple" was listened to with disdain. Burney too had taken an instant dislike to him when they first met at Juniper Hall. However, the extent to which she moved from this view was evident in her diary entries and, Fenella suspected, was also testament to Talleyrand's ability to wield another indispensable political tool, charm.

It is inconceivable what a convert M. de Talleyrand has made of me;

I think him now one of the first members, and one of the most charming, of this exquisite set:... His powers of entertainment are astonishing, both in information and in raillery.

By the time Fanny Burney had met him, the French National Convention had abolished the monarchy ahead of Louis XIV's execution in January 1793, and Talleyrand, accused as "disposed to serve the king", had had his name placed on a list of undesirables, or emigres. However, true to form, he had spotted this coming and manoeuvred to ensure he was granted a passport by Danton, the Minister of Justice, that notionally appeared to charge him with "a mission" to Britain, rather than having simply run out to save his head. That the prime minister, Pitt, issued an expulsion order on him in March 1794, forcing him to leave for the United States, only helped maintain his protestations that he was a loyal citizen of the revolution, enemy of France's enemy, and all too ready to serve once this misunderstanding of his attitude towards the monarchy was cleared up.

So, it was the time he had been in England, September 1792 to March 1794, and his associations with Fanny Burney and Watkin Tench, that Fenella was trying to pin down.

Burney's relationship with Queen Charlotte was a puzzle. Second Keeper of the Robes sounded like something grand. However, basically it meant she was the queen's hairdresser. This undoubtedly meant access to more interesting tittle-tattle than your average street corner boutique - Fenella pictured Fanny Burney, chewing gum, bashing the Queen with her bustle, asking, "So, you goin' out this weekend your majesty?", as she pencilled a beauty spot on her face - though it would hardly be something that would feed Fanny's intellectual appetite. Indeed, she had sought, and was granted, release from the position after four years in 1790. However, she remained on close terms with the Queen and princesses for the rest of her life. These hardly seemed relationships that could be sustained in the face of suspicions of her loyalty during a war with France, especially as she had spent over a decade in the country married to a minister of the Napoleonic government who was prosecuting the war. If she was B, either she was involved in a network operating to pass British secrets to the French, that included Francis Austen, and she had somehow managed to cast herself as so loyal to Britain, as to be above suspicion. Or, and this was tantalising to the degree that it would be worthy of a game she wouldn't have minded for herself, or Fanny Burney was playing a long option of double bluff, offering herself as a French spy, whilst acting to pass on disinformation initiated with support of the highest levels. Fanny Burney spymaster and double agent, tasked by the Queen to use her French connections, especially Talleyrand, in British interests.

Even knowing there was no evidence for this, she rolled the

possibilities around her mind. If this were so, did it mean Burney could be playing Watkin Tench as a French agent? That she had turned him? Or that he too, was involved in the long double play, or playing the double play?

There seemed to be mirrors reflecting mirrors, the images becoming more vague and distant. As she considered the alternatives, and placed them in a balance of possibilities, these seemed to slip all the time into probabilities that required a subtler and subtler grasp.

The dance between what seemed and what may have been, was becoming something her mind was struggling to hold all at one go. She would need to get some perspective on this. Let it have some air in a place where her mind wouldn't worry it into abstraction. Let the dark wheels of her unconscious turn it towards something that was not acting as a dangerous attractor, forcing it to fit a view of the way she would like the world to have been. She had to let it form in a manner that was aside from her ambitions.

She left the library and walked out into the grounds of Laudanum Grange, following the path that ran around the front of the house and crossing the lush lawn, towards an area of woodland and a narrow worn path through the trees. A red squirrel skittered among the leaves in front of her carrying a nut in its mouth. The path wound down through the woodland to emerge beside a small stream. She paused, shading her eyes against the low Autumn sunlight towards the East. What was a letter from Watkin Tench to Fanny Burney doing with Francis Austen's documents? Had Francis and Burney met at some point?

She followed the stream reflecting the glimmer of the sun, passed over a style and walked out to the unbounded moors. There were sheep dotted amongst the low heather and gorse bushes. The path turned Northerly and started to steepen heading up towards a rocky outcrop on the skyline. When she reached the summit the prospect of the moorland ran out to the higher Pennine peaks on the horizon. The view took her mind to the high, wide open Wyoming plains. Though the scale was different the aspect brought her to the same appreciation of her place within a landscape; with the light behind her shoulders, the warmth spreading across her back, like the opening of an aura and a sense of herself extending out toward all the probable and possible paths of what would endure to become this reality and the next.

As she emerged from the woodland Fenella Morningstar could see Pamela Larrup on the lower level of the Grimalkin museum. She watched her walk one way, pause, turn and walk back the other, then, taking a ninety degree turn, she walked away from the atrium into the recesses of the museum, only to return to the hand rail again and look out. In the middle of the lawn, Fenella felt her gaze fall upon her like an exposed deer in the cross hairs. She quickened her pace as Pamela disappeared from view.

Entering the library she sat down with Harvey Premnas in the reading room.

'I've just seen Pamela upstairs. She looked a bit unstrung. Any idea why?'

'What makes you think I'd have any idea about that?' he smiled. 'The plan is afoot, as they say here.'

Fenella grinned and flashed her eyebrows. 'Aw come one, we're gonna have to get you and her in a place where you can talk. I've got to see that.'

'Let's leave it up to her.'

'Oh, I don't know if I can. No, but you're right,' said Fenella, her gaze drifting off before she returned to the books in front of her.

The more she read, the more convinced she was that what Fanny presented to the world, was at odds with her motives. Deliberately creating a somewhat naive persona; put upon, frustrated, pressured and controlled, and that this was intended to present a feint for anyone who might be watching. What better mask to assume, playing to the general perception of women at the time, if one were seeking to pass and not draw attention to more nefarious activities?

Having befriended Talleyrand at Juniper Hall, also meeting her future French husband there, she was ideally positioned to pursue his acquaintance when she became isolated in France upon the resumption of hostilities after the failure of The Treaty of Amiens. By this time, Talleyrand had returned from exile in the United States, and moved his pieces in a campaign of position, along the dark passages beneath the corridors of power, as one of the key conspirators involved in the coup d'état that saw the inevitable rise of Napoleon Bonaparte. That Fanny Burney had also published a pamphlet previously, calling for support of the revolutionary French cause, could only have gone further to promote a picture of a somewhat put upon, hapless waif, cut adrift amidst the turmoil of war from England, lucky to be enfolded in the embrace of a country whose ideals she aspired to, with a marriage and friendships that would protect her from any suspicions otherwise. Though, these same relations also happened to leave her in the ideal position to operate behind the scenes. But to do that implied, at some conscious level, a plan, or a hunch about a plan, that would have been hatched with a long, slow fuse. That was what she needed now. Some evidence of the fuse being fashioned, laid and deliberately lit.

'Harvey, could I have a word with you?' Pamela Larrup emerged from some hither to unseen position.

'Sure.'

'I think it would be best in private. There's something I would like you to see.'

He followed Pamela toward the staircase, expecting her to take the flight up to the ground floor. However, she turned and took the door down to the stacks. He looked over his shoulder at Fenella as he passed through it.

As she watched the door close she tried to think of a plausible reason to follow and caught herself with annoyance when she couldn't. She wanted to watch Pamela's body language as she tried to talk to Harvey about something she wasn't supposed to know about. How would she broach it?

She tried to send it out to the wide open plains and get back to the questions around Talleyrand and Burney, however, the prospect of an exquisitely awkward encounter taking place somewhere deep in the bowels of Laudanum Grange, kept the distance at bay.

The stacks in the Grimalkin Library were extensive. They started through the locked door at the base of the staircase in the post-modern extension and extended across the full footprint of the building into what would have been the basement rooms beneath the old house.

The first section is well ordered, modern and systematically arranged. However, the section under the old house had to be retro-fitted into the maze of barrel-roofed store rooms, cellars, narrow stone flagged corridors, and other assorted spaces that had been excavated ad hoc as the house above had grown. Some of these had been fitted with the type of orderly rows of moveable stacks, cranked by roller handles, normally expected in such spaces. However, to make the most efficient use of space, and to fit the stacks in among the switch backs and oddly shaped rooms under the old building, there were places where the stacks opened to act as passage ways through to other rooms and sections of moveable shelving, which in turn rolled open to reveal further mobile doorways and passages giving access to more distant spaces. The area felt as though it had been designed by a malignant archivist inspired by Escher's illusory drawings, determined to frustrate the retrieval of knowledge with the manipulations required to negotiate the architectural planes of a subterranean Rubik's Cube.

Harvey was intrigued. Not least because this was not among the range of responses he had loosely played out as possibilities. He was standing beside her in a small cloistered space whilst she rolled closed the passage they had just walked through. She rolled across two sections of stack at right-angles to this, revealing an open passage beyond, which they went through to another recessed return, where the process was repeated as they headed deeper into the library's basement.

At each turn Harvey became more disorientated, wondering momentarily how he would find his way back should she abandon him. 'How do you keep track of where you are?'

'It does take some time to get used to. There is a floor plan but I don't need it anymore.'

Harvey stooped as they passed through an archway and along a narrow

Cringe

corridor lined with shelves. Ahead of him, Pamela slowed as she started to look more closely at the shelves.

'I think it's around here.' She stopped and scanned the book spines in front of her. 'Ah, here. Have you heard of this?' she said, as she passed a book to Harvey. He took it and angled the spine towards the light. *The Works of Ossian.*

'Nope,' he said, looking towards her curiously.

'It is a collection of epic Scottish poems collected and published by James Macpherson in the 1760s. He uncovered the manuscript written by Ossian and translated them from the Gaelic.'

Harvey Premnas opened the book and turned some of the pages. 'What's it got to do with my work?'

'It's a hoax.'

Harvey stopped turning the pages. 'I,' he paused. 'What do you mean?'

'There was no such person as Ossian. James Macpherson, a poet himself, he made the whole thing up. He wrote the poems. He got away with it for some time. There was some contest over their authenticity during his lifetime, with him defending it, but subsequently, everyone agreed, it was a hoax.'

'Well, that's interesting. I still don't see what it's got to do with my work.'

'I wondered whether you had considered the authenticity of the manuscripts. Not necessarily all of them. Just, whether you had considered it?'

Harvey looked intently at the book as he turned a couple of pages. 'What makes you think they might not be authentic?'

'Nothing in particular. I have not looked at them of course. But as you are the first to do so, from an academic perspective, I thought that you might want to have this in mind.'

Harvey turned a few more pages.

Pamela continued. 'The conservator's report suggests nothing untoward, but that simply means the paper is consistent with the age and stocks of paper around at the time.'

'I see.'

'Do you still have your suspicions of espionage?'

Harvey Premnas nodded. 'Yes I do. In fact, more so.'

'It would be a very radical challenge to the accepted historical record. If, or when, you published, you could expect lot of flak. It will almost certainly cause more experienced scholars to look at them very closely. I just thought you would want to be careful and might want to keep this in mind.' She paused. 'I could help you if you like.'

Harvey Premnas stopped turning, placed his finger on a page and ran it along a line of poetry. 'I got the impression previously that you thought I was on the wrong track,' he said, without looking up.

'Really? No, no. I was just drawing your attention to the possibility, just to encourage you to be thorough and rigorous. If there was anything that you were unsure about I would be happy to take a look? You know anything at all that seemed questionable.'

Harvey's finger came to a stop. He lowered the book to reveal Pamela's enquiring face. He let the moment sit. 'There was something,' he said, eventually.

'Oh yes, what would that be?'

'Yeah, something that I came across the other day.'

'Yes?'

Harvey looked away from Pamela's gaze taking in the books on the shelf behind her.

'Though, I'm not sure.'

'Not sure?' she said.

Harvey continued to stare at the books behind her, considering. As he closed *The Works of Ossian*, dropping the hand holding the book to his side, scratching at his bottom lip with the other.

'No, there was something the other day, but I'm not really sure enough in my own thoughts about it yet. You know, when you've almost got the sense of something, a thought, an interpretation, and can't quite put it into words. I need to get the right words for it first. It'll come.'

'Perhaps I could help?'

'How do you think you could do that?'

'Well, my doctorate was in the analysis of eighteenth century punctuation styles and sentence construction. Jane Austen's in particular. I can apply the techniques to any documents you have questions about. Check them for consistency and compare them to already verified samples of prose and handwriting.'

'Aw yeah, see what you mean. It's a thought. Let's see how I go.'

'Well I will leave the offer with you. Let me know how you get on. If you find anything more that is interesting or radical you will let me know, won't you?'

CHAPTER TWENTY-NINE

Ahh yees, that's the ticket. He clicked on the send button and a satisfying swoosh sound moved across the room. How does it do that? He looked at the computer screen as the picture of an envelope flew across it. That was his work done for the day. Or was it? There was something else that he had meant to do. He looked at the clock on the screen. 11.15. It would come to him. He settled back into his chair and spun to look out of the window. The email would have arrived by now. Sitting in the in-box on a computer in Billy Crouchmoor's office. He would open it and that would be the beginning of the end of his relationship with them, and his commission for this lot would be enough to cover the short fall for now. It would only be a matter of time before those investments started to turn and he would actually start making more than he had borrowed from the contingency fund. He wasn't exactly sure how much it was, but it was bound to be more than enough. Bound to be.

A ping sound came out of the computer. He swivelled back from the window and clicked on the message. Could he meet Billy at the golf club, just outside Bradford on the A58, to pass on the items later today? His Chinese colleague was eager to have them as his client was becoming awkward, making sounds about offering less for them, or not buying them at all unless he had them soon. Tomorrow at the latest? Don't like the sound of that. Better make it today. Rick typed a reply, clicked send and the satisfying swoosh noise crossed the office again. He looked behind the computer screen. Did something actually move inside? They must have gone to a lot of trouble to make that happen when they could just have made it make a beep beep sound. It was so much more satisfying to have it move though, made you feel as though you were actually responsible for it flying through the ether. Clever Johnnies these computer boffs.

He'd suggested they meet at 2.30 that afternoon and, whilst there was something else that he was sure he was supposed to be doing, he couldn't for the life of him recall what it was, so he had time. He would leave now and have lunch in the club house before meeting with Billy.

He had taken up golf at the suggestion of Billy and Henry Crouchmoor shortly after he had first met them. It was, they said, a sport that was essential to the standing of all aspiring executives. His rising status amongst the North Yorkshire business fraternity may be questioned if he were not seen out at the tee. If he wasn't seen to be able to play on the greens, in the company of other directors and executives, why, then they may think that he wasn't able to play at all. Later on, the golf bag had also become essential in smuggling the larger stolen maps out of the building.

He went down to his car, took the golf bag out of the boot, slung it over his shoulder and took it up to his office. On his way back out he stopped at reception to let the office ladies know he would be out for the rest of the day.

'Bonjour Rick, Qué tal?'

'We, Qué tal?

'Spanish and French today?' said Rick. 'That's unusual ladies.'

'We are stepping out,' said the sister in the tortoiseshell glasses.

'Stepping out. Testing ourselves. Broadening our horizons.'

'It does not do to be too set in your ways. You can become lazy you know.'

'Ah, yees. Lazy, know what you mean, won't catch me being lazy. Just off to meet some other directors and chief execs, make some business deals and get some exercise at the same time. Two stones with one bird.' He slapped the golf bag.

'Qué bueno.' said the sister in the full red rimmed glasses.

'Must be off then. You two have a very excellent day, eh, excellent day.'

They watched him leave the office.

'Do you think he understands birds and stones?'

'His speech is green, like the language of birds and he is after all, a "Chief". But do they understand him?'

'The birds may. They have always been circling. But the stones?

'The stones and the Chief? Chief from the Latin caput, meaning head. With his head, stones wouldn't even understand.'

'They have been bested?'

'Yes, better even than that. Though he is also "Executive". To plan, to carry out.'

'To execute?'

'Yes, that too. To execute. And his head, caput.'

'And an "Officer". The official position, conferred with authority?'

'Conferred, but not in command.

'But a gentleman?'

'Of the lowest rank. Though he does aspire.'

'Breathes?'

'For the moment, breathes for the moment. But that too will cease.'

'He can hold on to it of course. Try to still the moment. But yes, it will come to cease. Caput.' said the sister in the tortoiseshell, half-moon glasses, running her finger across her neck above the pearl choker.

They both turned and looked out of the window as Rick Callow walked down the drive to his car.

Major Duncan Sinclair signed in at the golf club, ordered a drink at the bar and sat down with a newspaper in an alcove overlooking the car park and the eighteenth green. Since he had retired he divided his time between golf, attending socials at The Royal Antediluvian Order of Buffalos and working as a volunteer at Laudanum Grange. Of the three, it was the latter that gave him greatest satisfaction. It was this that had prompted him to join the 1813 Society. Not because he was any great fan of Jane Austen, he preferred Bernard Cornwell, but because it provided him with more opportunities to play witness to the Buffalos motto; *"No man is at all times wise."* Though if it were Laudanum Grange's motto, one of the words would have to be left out, and was perhaps more properly fitting for the individual he had just spotted signing in through the screen of rubber plants atop the alcove's partition. For without him, the bizarre, fabulous and incredulously ludicrous events he had enjoyed at Laudanum Grange could hardly have eventuated.

He watched Rick Callow go into the restaurant next door and returned to his crossword: shrink from phone in church. Anagram? He wrote out the letters on the edge of the paper and played around with them. Palindrome? Or maybe container. He couldn't get it, so moved on to the next clue. He looked through the foliage in front of him and could make out Rick tucking into lunch. Something fishy by the look of it. What would it be like to play a round of golf with the man? My god it would be worth watching. Like a Jacques Tati film, *Mr. Hulot's Holiday*, with a golf scene. The major smiled. Only you might just want to watch from a distance. Playing with him might make one a protagonist, prey to hapless golf swings, insufferable boasting and nonchalant slap stick.

He turned to reading some of the articles in the paper. The Tour De France starting off in Yorkshire next year. That'll scare the sheep. When was the last time the French tried to invade Yorkshire? There was that ship, wrecked off Hartlepool during the Napoleonic wars. The only survivor to struggle ashore was a monkey. Not having seen a Frenchman nor a monkey before, the locals, putting prudence before virtue, hanged the poor blighter on suspicion of being a spy. Though perhaps virtue had played some role, at least the thing was given a trial on the beach. He couldn't recall another occasion.

He looked up as he heard Rick Callow talking on his mobile phone on the way out of the club house, pulling on a sheep skin coat. 'Yes, yes. I can see you now,' raising his hand to somebody outside.

That man was good value. The number of times he'd been at some event where Rick Callow had exceeded his expectations of the man's ineptitude, very much worth the money. Last time with that Professor chap. No such thing as a decent female writer. The Major smirked, how did he get it so wrong? Marvellous stuff, bloody marvellous.

Major Sinclair looked out the window to the car park and watched Rick Callow walk towards an old black Jaguar XJ6. A large, simian looking man was standing beside it, tucking something away in his inside jacket pocket. He waved towards Rick, beckoning him over. Rick pointed towards a mustard yellow Smart Car which they walked towards. He didn't recognise the man, but he looked unusual for the company Rick Callow normally associated with. The supporting cast of academics, professors, authors, and librarians at Laudanum Grange, contrived to give Rick a little of the gravitas he thought himself born to. However, the man he was currently with looked as though he'd be more at home in a boxing ring, his features suggesting pugilism as something he deliberately sought, with Rick perhaps playing Stan Laurel stalked by this oversized bruiser from The Bowery.

The man was standing close to Rick, staring down at him, talking slowly in short, deliberate, threatening surges. The colour had drained from Rick's face. Avoiding the man's gaze, he appeared to start to speak from time to time, only to be cut off by another studied pulse of quiet abuse.

Though the Major would not have gone out of his way to stop Rick making a fool of himself, he did not wish harm upon him. It was with some concern that he continued to try to interpret the situation in the car park. He took a mobile phone out of his pocket. He had not seen Rick looking this fearful before, if something did happen he wanted to make sure he had evidence. He started to film the scene. The man continued to swat down Rick's attempts to interject for a few moments more before Rick opened the boot of his car, removed his golf bag and extracted two large rolls of paper. The man unrolled what appeared to be a couple of large maps, with Rick looking anxiously around. Then Rick reached further into the golf bag, took out two books and gave them to the man who looked at them and cracked a grin revealing crooked teeth. He nodded at Rick who responded with such a wide, fixed grimace, it brought to mind the slot of a post box. There were more exchanges, with Rick Callow again being cut off, the man pointing a finger towards his face, which Rick rolled back from, before the man took the maps and the books and lurched off to the XJ6, leaving Rick pallid and shaken, standing by the yellow Smart Car. The Major focused his phone on the number plate on the XJ6 as it pulled out of the car park, placed it on the table and steepled his fingers, his elbows resting on the table. Rick Callow got into his car and drove off. Somebody had scared the sheep.

CHAPTER THIRTY

They had felt like naughty children sneaking out of the gate at Laudanum Grange earlier that morning. Quietly closing it so as not to attract attention. For their mission was one of disarray, setting out to unsettle the conventions of an event at the centre of the academic social calendar at Northrop University - the annual Regency Masquerade Ball of the university's Eighteenth Century Studies Conference, held at Laudanum Grange. Now, with the event in the offing, they were executing a plan that had been conceived in hardly suppressed laughter and fits of giggles.

The ball is planned and run by the Yorkshire Society of Regency Ballroom Dancers and is re-enacted along the strict and very correct guidelines set out by Thomas Wilson's *Etiquette of the Ball-Room*, 1815. This includes such edicts as:

"Gentlemen must not enter the Ball room in whole or half boots or with sticks or canes."

"Snapping the fingers in Country Dancing and Reels, and the sudden howl or yell too frequently practised, ought particularly to be avoided, as partaking too much of the customs of barbarous nations; the character and effect by such means given to the Dance, being adapted only to the stage, and by no means suited to the Ball Room."

"No person must, during a Country Dance, hiss, clap or make any other noise to disturb the company."

Fenella Morningstar and Harvey Premnas had been briefed about these and other niceties contained in the small booklet that Pamela Larrup, a leading light of the Yorkshire Society of Regency Ballroom Dancers, had presented to them a couple of days previously.

She had been standing beside the long table in the common room and had just completed the formal part of her instructions guiding them through the small booklet.

'As you are here during the ball you are entitled to come. However, you will have to pay for the hire of your own costume as we do not have enough to lend out,' Pamela Larrup said, going on to give detailed instructions about precisely the type of costume they should seek from the hire shop in Leeds. 'For the women, you will need a full length Regency ball gown, puffed sleeves, an empire waist, possibly a gathered bodice,' she paused, 'you might want to take notes,' the intonation of her voice rising.

Harvey and Fenella dutifully pulled note pads and pens out from about their person and started to write.

'I'll give you pictures to help, we must make sure we get the details right, so we all look as authentic as possible. You will need your hair dressed too, close to the head with curls and twists on top and down the sides of your face. I can help you with that on the day.' She turned to Harvey Premnas. 'And you, you will need a drop sleeve shirt with a high collar and ruffles at the throat and cuffs. You need a waistcoat, it can be colourful if you like, and a white neck cloth for a tie.'

Harvey made a show of making detailed notes.

Pamela continued. 'You need a tailcoat, double breasted with wide lapels and a high collar, and knee breeches, high waist, baggy seat and tight legs, and white stockings held up by garters.'

'And how should I do my hair?' asked Harvey.

Pamela regarded him with a slight look of resignation.

'Yes, that is a little disappointing. Ideally you should have it longer, curly, but I suppose you could just brush it forward. It's just long enough to be a Caesar cut. Pity you don't have long sideburns,'

'I could cut some out of fake fur and stick them on with glue,' Harvey said seriously. Pamela Larrup looked at him for a moment, pursing her lips.

'Noo, I do not think that would work, it would look too artificial. Nice thought though.'

Harvey and Fenella sat opposite one another in the almost empty train carriage, quietly reading and occasionally dozing on the journey from Hebden Bridge to Whitby, changing trains twice. As they approached their destination they both became more alert, looking out the window at the passing scenery.

Fenella Morningstar turned from contemplating the view. 'How did you find this place?'

'I heard about it from a friend in Sydney. He's into the whole scene and went to the annual festival here last year. It's big in the town, people come from all over for it.'

'Whitby. That's in Dracula right?'

'Yeah, it's where he comes ashore.'

'I suppose that's what attracts them.'

'Partially. Taking to Andy, he said that the whole town has a certain air to it, some kind of spookiness.'

The train was running close alongside the River Esk. They had just passed under a road bridge as the town came into view. It was late morning and sun shone across the river as a northerly breeze drifted low white cloud above its mouth. They could see the masts of boats and yachts moored along the bank. Fenella leant forward and stretched up to get a better view. She could see the houses of the old town, all red-roofed, and they seemed to be piled up, one over the other, stacked along the opposite bank. Then above them, up the hill looking down on the small port, the ruin of Whitby Abbey.

The train pulled into the station and they walked out into a high blue sky, the breeze having moved the clouds down the coast. Harvey Premnas was looking down at the map on his mobile, trying to identify the route to their destination. He looked up and around.

'Well I'll be stuffed,' he said, 'I had no idea.'

'No idea of what?'

'Of course, I should have realised. Just forgot I guess.'

'Forgot what?'

'Captain Cook, this is where Captain Cook started his sailing career. There's a museum just around the corner,' he said, pointing across the river.

Fenella Morningstar looked blank.

'First recorded European to encounter Australia. Well he commanded the expedition anyhow. We're all taught about him in school. I'd just not put it together. You come all this way and there he is, well holey doley' said Harvey. 'OK,' he said, collecting himself, 'we need to go over the bridge. This way.'

They walked over the swing bridge and turned right down Grape Lane on to Church Street. They paused outside the Captain Cook Memorial Museum, looking through the glass doors, quickly deciding not to go inside, giving favour to their enthusiasm to reach their destination in The Strand shopping arcade off Church Street. A Victorian affair with fluted, Doric pillars and laced wrought iron arches. The glass domed roof gave a light airy feel to the second floor which belied the contents of the shop they were looking for.

Harvey and Fenella approached a sign along a narrow galleried walkway: "The Gallery Serpentine: An Antidote to the Mundane." They stopped, looking in at the window display.

'Geez, this'll do it,' said Fenella Morningstar, raising her eyebrows.

There were two tall male mannequins dressed in high drama Steam Punk and Goth clothing, wearing top hats and gas masks. Around them, placed on stools of varying heights, were the headless upper torsos of female mannequins, clad in corsets, bustiers, corselettes and PVC fetish clothing, whilst the lower parts of their bodies were inter-placed between these clad in a variety of stockings, and suspender belts. Nothing here bore any resemblance to the eighteenth century Regency pictures that Pamela Larrup had left with them.

They went into the shop and were greeted with a breezy smile by the woman dressed in black, sat behind the counter by the door. She had a pale complexion, china blue eyes, long, slightly wavy Titian red hair and Alizarin crimson lip stick.

'Good morning, can I help you?'

'We want to hire some stuff. Can we just look around a bit first?'

'Sure, no problem,' she said easily.

Fenella Morningstar and Harvey Premnas were not quite sure where to start. The shop was split into two sections. The front half contained an array of rails, stands and displays, packed with over blown and sensational Cyber Goth and Steam Punk clothing. The rear part was approached through what seemed to be a stage set, defined by ornate, draped, golden velvet curtains and a tasselled pelmet. The sense of the theatrical was heightened further by the male mannequin sat on a chair just in front of the curtain, wearing a corset, long trousers and top hat, and poised to present a very haughty gaze. Behind this there were rails, racks and displays of corsets, lingerie, bloomers, suspender belts and fetish knickers. The intimacy of this boudoir was brought closer by the half dozen white parasols, edged in red lace, hung upside down from the ceiling. The shop was an emporium of decadence and display.

Harvey Premnas loved it. He started to browse around, taking in the range and variety of clothing and feeling the quality of the fabrics. What was the largest excess baggage fee he could afford? There were Gentlemen Assassin Tailcoats, Steam Lieutenant Jackets, Dirty Gold Pirate Shirts and Batboy Vests. A Dante Cravat Shirt with frilled cuffs looked particularly appealing, but he dismissed it as too close to the type of authenticity that would have pleased Pamela Larrup. There was a Matrix Priest Coat, a vest with studs and skull buttons, a high collar frock coat and a Stanton top hat. Harvey picked it up and tried it on.

'Wha'dya think?'

'Cool,' said Fenella Morningstar, tilting her head sideways, nodding and smiling slightly. She had a black Obsidian Dress in one hand and a short figure hugging Blood Amaryllis Dress in the other, holding them at arm's length, considering, before placing them back on the rail and fingering the pointed spikes on an Enforcer Choker. She picked up a Scrolls mask and held it over her eyes. It was cut from black leather, in an asymmetrical design, falling from her forehead across and down the left-hand side of her fine boned face, in a sensuous, lacy filigree.

She looked in the mirror. 'I think I'll have this,' she said out loud to herself. She took it with her as she moved into the back of the shop. There were French Lolly Bloomers in Broderie, Pixie Bloomers, a Pirouette Movement Corset and Pin Up fetish knickers with suspenders. She spotted a Vixen Warrior black feather bolero and took it off the stand, looking at the label. "For those who dare," she read aloud. The bolero was rubber, cut from tyre inner-tubes. Placing it round her shoulders and looking at her neckline in the mirror, it lent her a sense of elegant fetish with an industrial edge. I like this. It was also just the sort of thing that would guarantee apoplexy amongst the authenticity sought by the hard core Janeites of the Yorkshire Society of Regency Ballroom Dancers and Pamela Larrup in particular. She smiled.

Harvey Premnas was considering footwear. He was holding a red suede leopard print brothel creeper in one hand, comparing it with a red tartan brothel creeper studded with spikes around the front of the shoe. Now, which would be most offensive to authentic tastes? Don't really suppose it makes much difference. It would have been at least a hundred odd years until anybody started wearing things like this anyhow, and even then, they were hardly associated with the refined sensibilities of upper class Regency England.

'What'cha got there?'

He held out the shoes. 'Which do you think would be best?'

'I think this is more you,' said Fenella, picking up a Demonia Steam Plate Boot.

Harvey Premnas took the heavy leather, knee high boot. It was shiny black, with a thick, heavy treaded soul and distressed brass plates running up the front, attached to straps that ran around to cog buckles down the outside of the leg. ' "No whole length boots", good call,' he said, nodding.

'How's it going?' said the shop owner, walking out from behind the counter.

'I'm just advising on footwear,' said Fenella Morningstar, 'What do you think?'

'I definitely think you should go with the boots,' she said, 'they would play to your height and make a great statement. How tall are you?'

'Six, four'

'So, you'd be around six six in these, and you could really carry off something like this,' said the owner, taking a three-quarter length frocked coat from the rail.

Harvey Premnas took the gold brocaded coat, slipped off his jacket and put it on. It was deep red with a high collar, two black velveteen pleats down the back, large leather braid trimmed cuffs and pockets.

Looking in the mirror, Harvey Premnas preened. 'It does have something,' he said.

'With that coat and those boots you would be channelling Buccaneer, Chevalier and Modern Romantic, but with some Steam Punk edge,' said the shop owner.

'Mmmmm,' said Harvey Premnas, nodding.

After they had paid and had their costumes packaged, the shop owner had agreed they could leave them with her whilst they looked around the town. They retraced their steps down Church Street, walking parallel to the river in the direction of the coast. As the street swung west, taking the cars across the swing bridge, they continued straight on, the tarmac giving way to a narrower, cobbled road where only pedestrians were allowed. They street looked as though it had changed little since the 1700s, with cottagey shop fronts, low doorways, which Harvey would have had to do a double stoop to enter, and narrow yards running down to alleys on one side, and the river on the other. They walked past The White Horse pub which had a sign over the yard entrance, 'Good Stabling'. Then a few yards further they passed The Black Horse.

'The good and the bad, where's the pub for the other guy?' said Harvey.

They continued on to the Town Hall set in the market square. Harvey Premnas read the plaque. "Erected 1788 by Nathaniel Cholmley."

Fenella Morningstar noticed that each of the yards, really just narrow alleys, was named. "Lees Yard", "Sanders Yard leading to Fish Burn Yard where Captain Cook's ship The Endeavour was built in 1764." She stopped Harvey, who was looking up across the street away from her. 'Look.'

'Just keeps comin' doesn't it.'

The street curved south and started to double back on itself before it ended in a dramatic run of steps up the steep hill to the Church of St. Mary. A sign stated that there were one-hundred and ninety-nine of them. They started up. Harvey Premnas counted under his breath. When they got to the top he turned.

'Yep, one hundred and ninety-nine.'

'Oh good, I was worried,' said Fenella Morningstar, catching her breath.

They turned to the view. The sun was at its zenith and they looked down to the harbour, with the sandstone piers reaching out into the deep, steel-blue North Sea which flexed, slow muscled, under the surface. The West pier was much longer and behind it, in the distance, a spit of cliffs topped with copses of reddening and orange flamed trees reached out further. The wind had picked up a little and the Michelangelo clouds rippled faster across the view.

'It's hard to feel dark and Gothic about this place from up here,' said Fenella Morningstar.

'Ah, that's because we need a little mood music,' said Harvey Premnas, mischievously. 'Imagine the scene. It's been a beautiful Saturday afternoon, people have been out tripping all day. Tired and happy they return to a fine evening sun set. The view is as idle as a painted ship upon a painted ocean. However, those sea folk who know say there's somethin' a brewin'.

As the evening darkens, stillness settles. Suddenly, there is a boom out to sea. The wind grows, thick and fast, the light darkens further, and the storm heads gather. Nature convulses. There are peals of thunder. The sea runs mountainous and great shifts of damp fog soak to the bone. Then, amongst the turmoil, a vessel, The Demeter, full sailed, is driven into the harbour's mouth, and runs aground,'

Harvey Premnas led Fenella Morningstar's gaze, with a lazy sweep of his arm, through the view of the harbour up to the shingle beach below them. 'And the people see the captain, his hands tied to the wheel, a crucifix knotted in his grasp. Dead. No other soul on board. As they watch, a large black dog jumps from the ship and runs up the cliff.' Harvey swept his arm and hand up to where they were standing.

Fenella Morningstar had been smiling through his arch Gothic oration.

'Then,' said Harvey, turning, 'it disappears amongst the grave stones,' pointing to the grave yard behind them.

'And then what?'

'Then old Drac hangs about a bit, has a bite or two, then heads off to Carfax Abbey.'

'Speaking of which, I'm hungry. Should we get something to eat?'

Harvey nodded.

They walked through the ruins of the abbey, stopping briefly for him to check out the facts. Built in 657 AD, sacked by the Vikings in 867 AD, abandoned until 1078 AD, when it was used again until that old goat, Henry VIII, dissolved the monasteries and destroyed it in 1540, in turn breaking away from Papal authority and the Catholic church, creating the Protestant Church of England. Which later, England feeling threatened by invasion between an allied Catholic France to the East and Catholic Ireland to the West, invades Ireland, suppresses and outlaws Catholicism for a few hundred years, causing his Catholic forbears to be transported to Australia as criminals for trying to stick up for themselves. A bit simple, but about the basics of how he had come to be here now, walking down from Whitby Abbey to find some fish and chips.

CHAPTER THIRTY-ONE

The lady in the half-moon tortoiseshell glasses paused in her typing. She looked up from her screen, raised her nose and sniffed.

'Can you smell it?'

Her sister in the full red glasses look across and inhaled deeply. 'Bitter almond?'

'I think, though with something else. Something musky, dirty.'

'Like frankincense mixed with earth?'

'Oak moss, and cinnamon?'

'Cinnamon.' The other sister agreed. 'They are the smells of a tired age.'

'The age that has come to be.'

'To be, and to pass again, to become. It might be disturbed.'

'He disturbed me.'

'Which one?'

'This one,' said the sister with the full red glasses, pressing a couple keys on her computer and clicking the mouse.

Her sibling waited, looking at her computer screen. 'Not the most flattering of pictures but you can tell who it is. He hasn't begun to fulfil his potential, at least not yet.'

'I have hope.'

'Hope?'

'Yes, hope. A feeling it will happen.'

'I know hope. I had it once, remember? But hope about what happening?'

'That he will do this, or do that.'

'But didn't he do it already? We have the evidence,' said the sister with the tortoiseshell glasses, nodding toward her computer screen.

'Yes, but I wasn't sure whether that was this or that.'

'This or that, no matter which, he will regret both I think.'

The sister with the red glasses looked out the window at a flight of swallows gathering and turning into a pitched dive toward the small pond in front of the woodland at the far end of the lawn, scattering above the water before pulling up and reforming. 'The swallows are after the dragon flies,' she said, pointing toward the window.

Her sibling looked out through the lead mullioned panes. 'I can't decide which is which. They'll be leaving soon anyhow.'

'Which, the swallows or the dragon flies?'

'Both, you can't have dragon flies without swallows. This without that.'

'And both still to be regretted?'

'Once hope has gone, all that is left is regret.'

They looked at each other without smiling and let their gaze hold a moment. The sister with the tortoiseshell glasses was the first to crack, the edges of her mouth started to twitch and she lowered her head tittering into a handkerchief she produced from the sleeve of her cardigan. 'It's no good, you know we won't regret it,' she said, between breathes of laughter.

'Oh I was hoping we wouldn't. This or that?'

'We've established it makes no difference.'

'True. Should I?'

'Oh, could I?'

'Sois mon invite.'

The sister with the tortoiseshell glasses attached the footage her sibling had previously sent her to an e-mail addressed from the generic Laudanum Grange account and pressed send. A satisfying swoosh crossed the room.

Harvey had finished early at the library and was heading back to The Terrace in the late afternoon of the last day of an Indian summer. He felt the buzz of an email arriving on the phone in his pocket. He took it out. Checked the message, which was empty, and clicked on the attachment.

'You little ripper,' he said out loud to himself, as he looked about the landscape for some evidence of the message's source, before checking again, and feeling as though the universe had just formed in an especially fortuitous manner, continued on his way.

'Ear, dad. We've got an invite.'

'What's that then?'

' "Northrop University cordially invite Henry Crouchmoor and William Crouchmoor to the fifth annual Regency Masquerade Ball of the Department of Eighteenth Century Studies." What the fuck is that all about?' said Billy Crouchmoor.

'Well well, looks like we're going up in the world my son.'

Henry Crouchmoor took the card from Billy and placing his pince-nez on his nose inspected the invitation. 'We're going to have to get dressed up for this Billy.'

'Wot suited and booted?'
'Eighteenth-century style my son.'
'What's that then?'
'Hmmmm. It seems were going to have dress like girls. Stockings and blousy shirts.'
'Fuck that for a game of soldiers. Can't we just rent a tux?'
'Hang on a moment. You're OK. We can play at soldiers. We can rent military dress uniform. That's more like it.'
'What's that look like then?'
'You've seen Sharpe on the telly, you know, Sean Bean.'
'Oh, yeah.'
'Yeah, like that. That's not so bad is it.'
'Naw, that's alright that is. Do yu reckon we could take the shooters too? Put the shits up old Callow.'
'Now, now Billy.'

He was trying not to think about it.

Having busied himself with things that didn't need to be done, and so ensuring things would need to be undone in the future, Giles Skeffington had resigned himself to getting ready for the ball.

He had not received an invitation, though he wished he had, as this would have provided him with the opportunity to decline. As it was, he knew that he was obliged to be present. Dressed in ill-fitting breeches and mothy tailcoat, the thought of this was causing him as much discomfort as he knew the clothes would.

At times like this he envied librarians at less exotic institutions. Don't expect they have to do this at the British library. It's not as though it was part of the job description; once a year dress up in badly tailored replicas of eighteenth century dress, wear a silly mask, try to pretend you're enjoying yourself as you fail to follow the over-zealous torture inflicted by the Yorkshire Society of Regency Dancers, laughing at you from behind their frilly cuffs as you stumble through the baroque complexity of a stupid dance that nobody does anymore, all the while engaging in simpering conversation with the hoi polloi of eighteenth century studies and local notables, some of whom you wouldn't mind talking to, but can't recognise, because they're all wearing masks. Giles Skeffington sighed. He'd rather be a home reading a book in front of the fire.

With an attention to detail that slowed her pulse Pamela Larrup removed the curling tong from her hair and arranged a curl so it fell towards her cheek. She turned the left side of her face toward the mirror and stepping back, straightened the empire-waist of her dress and tied on her modest mask. Satisfied, she checked her watch before taking it off. She was just in time.

She left the large lady's room on the ground floor of Laudanum Grange. Looking along the corridor, through the porch, she could see vehicles pulling up, disgorging knots of anachronistic passengers, women dressed in unassuming ball gowns, and men wearing breeches, tri-corn hats, and tail coats. She approved. It was nice to see that people took this seriously. After all, if one was to have an eighteenth century ball it should be an affair that could be easily recognised as such.

The scene that greeted her when she entered the great hall was even more pleasing. The music provided by the Regency Players wafted amidst a growing crowd of masked guests and ball gowns, suitably demure, nothing too showy, gentlemen bowing from the waist, breeches ending below the knee, showing fashionable, well-shaped calves clad in silk stockings. There were a scattering of military types wearing very smart dress uniform, high buttoned tunics, a mixture of rifleman green and naval blue, with black trim and dress swords. Jane would have been pleased. But could she now be trusted? Harvey's failure to bite when she'd offered her service, and his reticence to reveal his knowledge of a letter which was ground shaking in its implications, could only mean one thing. He wanted to keep it for himself.

A raffish knot in his cravat, brightly shone buckles on his shoes and wearing a half-mask with a long nose, Rick Callow was shimmying through the crowd, flamboyantly bowing low with an out-stretched arm at every second female he passed. Ahh yees. This was a place where Callow was in his element, the natural habitat for a man with the elegance of a Nureyev, the wit of a Wilde, and the charisma of a Clinton. The scene was set for great deeds, new contacts to be impressed, new business opportunities to be set, and old alliances to be re-positioned. But first things first. He must fill up his dance card.

The music for the cotillion came to an end and the groups of four couples bowed towards one another.

'There will be a twenty minute break before the next dance,' said the announcer, as the dancers broke up and began to circulate towards the bar, buffet and mingle back towards people they recognised. Major Sinclair moved through the crowd, determined to seek out a foil he could use to enliven the proceedings.

'I say Giles, you look very dapper old boy.'

'Is that you Major?'

'Yes. What do you think?'

'I should have guessed. Which regiment is it?'

'Eleventh Hussars, Major General's dress uniform. Charge of the light brigade and all that,' said Major Duncan Sinclair.

'Into the valley of death,' said Giles. 'A bit more nineteenth than eighteenth century. Better watch out for Pamela.'

'I can't be fussed with that too much. Good turnout. Expecting any fireworks?'

'There are some. Due to be set off at ten I think.'

'Real ones? No I meant, is Rick going to get up to his usual? Is he going to give a speech?'

'Oh Lord. I hope not. I don't think so.'

'Shame. Damn Shame. Is he here yet?'

'I expect so, though I'm not sure where.'

The major looked about. 'I'll track him down.'

'Don't suggest a speech major.'

'I wouldn't do that old boy. There he is. I'd recognise the back of that hair cut anywhere. Rick is that you?'

'Why hello,' said Rick turning, 'that can of course only be you major, in that uniform. What a stunner. You know I was thinking of donning a bit of the military attire myself. A few epaulettes here and there, always thought I had the shoulders for them. Ah yees, military blood in my family major, but then I thought the sword might get in the way of my moves. Wouldn't want that eh? Let the blade get in the way of these twinkling toes. Enjoying yourself Giles? Haven't seen you dancing yet.'

'No. Unfortunately that pleasure is still to come.'

'Do you want me to set you up? I could get a few fillies on your card. Meredith,' Rick waved and shouted over Giles' shoulder. 'Meredith.'

'No no. Really Rick, I'm fine,' said Giles.

A large woman in a bonnet turned and broached the confines of the three men. Meredith Ferryweather, an investment banker whose appetites and interests had tilted more than once at a beguiling Rick Callow.

'Meredith, do you have a dance free?' said Rick.

'Why yes I have, thank you very much.'

'No, not me. Giles here. He's a bit stuffed for partners.'

Meredith looked at Giles with a face that diminished his enthusiasm. 'Oh, alright then.' She handed him her card and he pencilled in his name.

'Are you going to give a speech Rick?' asked the major.

Giles' eyes widened in entreaty.

'A speech eh. You know me major. Always up for that, but alas I think, what with the old dances, I think it's a bit of a tight schedule. Though I do get to announce a special guest a bit later,' Rick said, with a pleased nod.

Giles knew he was referring to Percy, the vaguely obese gardener, who was annually plied with brandy in order persuade and add verisimilitude to his portrayal of the Prince Regent.

'Shame. Damn shame. I always enjoy your speeches. Saw you at the golf club the other day, how's your game?'

'Weeel, a bit below par. But you know me, bit more practice and I'll be swinging with the best of them,' said Rick, miming a swing.

'Can't say I liked the look of your partner. Sore loser is he?'

'Sorry?'

'In the car park, looked like your partner was a bit angry with you. Is he a sore loser?'

'Oh that. No, he wasn't my partner. Just a misunderstanding. He thought.... he thought I'd blocked him in, but it was someone else's car, that's all. Anyway, good to see you major. Got to get off and circulate, you know, the burden of leadership. Everyone wants to meet the boss. See you later.'

Rick moved off leaving the major staring at his back.

'Didn't look like that to me,' said the major, half to himself.

'What's that?' asked Giles.

'In the car park. Look here, I filmed it.'

The major pulled out his mobile and showed the footage to Giles.

'Can you send me a copy of that major?'

Rick Callow had just danced a Scottish reel, finishing off with a deep bow before the dancers applauded. Having excelled himself he was particularly enthusiastic in his applause and nodded at the rest of the dancers. They clearly appreciated the finer elements of his pointed toes and careful pivots. He looked around the great hall. A fine evening. Plenty of intricate dancing to be had, fine company, and having already introduced himself to more new contacts than he cared to shake a stick at, he was trying to identify more of the opportune amongst the sea of masks.

He bounded across the clearing dance floor and eased his way through groups of people, trying to spot someone who was yet to be acquainted with the favours that could accrue from a chance meeting, and which he could engineer towards such mutual benefit, they would be in no doubt that they had indeed had a lucky encounter.

He spotted Giles craning his neck around the crowd and quickly ducked out of his view. Having already set him up with one dance, to do so again would only be to the embarrassment of ladies who knew that librarians don't dance. Checking over his shoulder, Rick turned through the doorway into the entrance hall to be met by a bluff wall of deep green cloth and silver military buttons. He looked up into the leering, warped grimace of a particularly grotesque mask.

'Ear, watch where you're going there matey.'

The piggy eyes behind the mask met his briefly as he muttered sorry and turned back quickly into the hall. Billy Crouchmoor. He was sure of it. Though he should have known to expect them he hadn't thought about the possibility until now. He'd have to make sure he wasn't in a place where his conversation might identify him. Hadn't seen them on the dance floor though. That should be safe. Tough guys don't dance. Tough guys and librarians. That both had come into his life through books made it seem as though there was something about a book that meant an inevitable meeting was due. Something like the front and back covers coming together, closing in on the meaning between the pages, closing in on him. He shook off the feeling. Nothing like this should really intrude upon the quest at hand. The quest for the last dance partner of the evening.

Looking around the crowd in the great hall he spotted a neatly trim young lady who looked as though she would benefit from an expert twirling her around the floor and made towards her. He was about to speak when she was joined by someone he knew to be Pamela by the mask she always wore. She looked straight through his to somewhere over his head.

'I would have thought you could have at least made an effort.'

Rick turned and gave Harvey a quick glance up and down, as he made a sidelong glide away from their convergence. He'd rather not become entwined in an imbroglio about Harvey's failure to turn up in correct dress. Though quite how he'd expected to get away with jeans and T-shirt, with Pamela's marshalled eye, was courting the wrath of a harpy whose stony breathe could freeze even Harvey's antipodean blood.

'I tried Pamela, but there was nothing in the hire shop that would fit. Seems I'm a little outsized,' said Harvey.

'Didn't you pack anything for a special occasion?'

He thought of the RAAF jacket and accompanying apparel. 'Nothing that I think you would've approved of. I've been thinking about our conversation in the stacks the other day,' Harvey said.

Pamela Larrup's attention switched out Harvey's clothing, her mind now attuned toward the definitive moment to come. 'Yes? You think there may be something that's problematic?'

'Not exactly what you might have been expecting. But yes, there is a problem. Here.' To her surprise he pulled out his mobile phone. 'Take a look at this.'

As she watched, something writhed in the pit of her stomach, sending nervy tingles down her arms and legs. The music that the quartet were playing seemed to become muted and distant, a space that became filled by an anxious gasp of self-consciousness.

'Those are my papers he's going through,' said Harvey.

'Ow we gonna spot the little Berk?'

Rick Callow knew that the Berkshire Hunt in question was not one that was led by a pack of dogs, though he could see their snarl approaching.

After leaving Harvey to Pamela's attention, he had continued to hunt down an appropriate partner to complete his dance card. The little filly he'd seen previously had slipped his view which was annoying. Scanning around the multitude of masks, he wanted to be sure that the last name on his card was one that was worthy of his attentions, not just any old bint, when the Crouchmoors had once again loomed in his direction.

Not one to be intimidated, he decided to seek refuge in a place where solace was assured by the locking of a cubicle door. He dropped his breeches and settled himself in the lavatory furthest from the entrance. Ahh yeees. He felt his gut relax. The door to the gents banged open followed by the jangle of regimental medals, swords and spurs. He tensed. With his trousers round his ankles, he felt unduly exposed and more than a little impotent, and since to pull them up might attract expectations of his emergence, there was nothing to be done but sit and endure; trying to be silent and yet present enough to be known as a witness within the chamber. The air whiffled at his extremities as Billy and Henry's thick draughts of piss hit the porcelain releasing the pungent smell of urinal cake.

'I heard someone say he's gonna be givin' a speech later. Introducing some local nob. We'll get him then if not before,' said Henry.

'You reckon he'll go for it?'

'Wot option 'as he got. He's too far in now to get out. We'll tell him this is definitely the last time.'

'We did that before. You don't think he'll pull the plug on us?'

'Nah, we'll take him outside an' show him your sword.' Henry laughed. 'Nah, listen, if we get The Shakespeare Portfolio and the Lavater we'll be set for life. It really will be the last time. So we can turn the screw. Tell him we've got nothing to lose if he doesn't come through 'cos were leaving the country - which we are anyhow. Tell him we'll go to the cops and tell them about him trying to sell us stolen goods. You still got those last things?'

'Yeah'

'Any funny business from him, we tell 'im that we'll tell the fuzz how we thought he was a genuine dealer. Only now we've realised this stuff is stolen. So, like good citizens, we're gonna take that last lot along to the boys in blue an' say as how we want nothing to do with the likes of him. They'll have him bang to rights. An' there's nothing that connects us with the other stuff he's taken. Once the police start investigating all they'll find is a load of stuff missing, with us having pointed the finger. An' it don't matter if he can convince them about us, 'cos by then we'll be gone. He's got nowhere to move my son, nowhere.'

Rick listened to the buttoning of flies amidst a clatter of military regalia, stifling waves of panic, before the door closed. The Lavater and the Shakespeare Portfolio. It couldn't be done. They would be missed immediately. After posting a blog about the Lavater Giles had received several bookings, including the local news, who wanted to come along and do a piece to be broadcast on Halloween. He'd been looking forward to that. And the Shakespeare was so high profile.

Rick cast his mind around its furtive crevices. There must surely be some way, some means, some angle that he could manipulate to create opportunity from the cold certainty seeping into his bones. It could not come to this. He would not let it come to this. For it to have come to this would mean that somehow all those plans, visions and grand projects, why they would not come to fruition. But then there would be others. Perhaps others somewhere else? If he weren't here, and he were elsewhere, then elsewhere would be a place where this was not. Not to be here. That was the thing. Not to be here right now. Tell them he was going. They would be sad, but it was necessary. He didn't want himself to become the story when it should be about the successes of Laudanum Grange. He would resign. Now. Immediately. Explain he'd been a victim of blackmail. Blackmail. The dark letter sent in the middle of the night to lure him. Indeed it could have been any man. Sent to disgrace him in the interests of something that seemed to have an honourable end at the time, only for the Crouchmoors to have manipulated it and exploited his good nature. Ahh, yees. Resign now, leave immediately, quietly, so as not to make a show. Avoid the Crouchmoors' clutches this evening. Having not threatened him yet they wouldn't know he was forewarned. Then go to the police tomorrow. Confess as the put upon victim. Then leave to start another day. Ah yees. That's the ticket. Now to go and tell someone. Set the plan afoot. He wiped his arse and pulled up his trousers.

Having expected an admission of the existence of Jane's letter to Frances, Pamela was not at all ready for Harvey's revelation. Having braced her face for an expression of incredulous scepticism, declining to a generous suspension of disbelief, it became a numb palimpsest, uncertainty and fear writhing with the need to compose some appropriate response. How had he got hold of that CCTV footage?

She pulled Harvey away from the flood of guests converging on the buffet laid in the wide corridor beyond the entrance hall, took the phone from him and played the footage of Gustav rifling through Harvey's papers again, and a third time. Steadying herself, she began to compute. Own up? Come clean and let her numbed look set the stage for her part in the affair. Denial? An open mouthed parade of righteous shock and awe at a clearly outrageous deed. Dissemble? Wryly acknowledge an uncertain act done for higher purposes, which were also in Harvey's interest.

She looked around for inspiration to delay any immediate decision.

'Have you seen Gustav this evening?'

'No I haven't.'

'Clearly I will have to speak to him about this. I think it would be better if it were done in an official capacity, don't you? In my office tomorrow, with yourself present.'

'Well alright, but if I see him I'm gonna have to say something.'

'How did you get this footage?'

'Somebody sent it to me earlier today. I don't know who, the address was just Laudanum Grange.'

'I do not think it wise to say anything before tomorrow. Forewarned is forearmed.'

'I see what you mean. We wouldn't want to give anyone time to plan excuses would we?' said Harvey.

Pamela regarded Harvey slowly, an awkward misgiving chasing a host of unformed doubts across her mind. 'No, you are right.'

'But you see, I would really like to know what he was looking for, and whether he's told anyone else about anything he has found,' said Harvey.

'Couldn't it wait until tomorrow?'

'Mmmm. I've found some pretty ground shaking stuff in the last couple of days. If anyone else knows about it....well, let's just say, it would set Twatter alight.'

'What have you found then?'

'Oh, I reckon you know Pamela.'

The doubts raced amidst an anxious need to prolong a masquerade she was no longer sure was veiled. She placed her mask to her face. 'What? Confirmation of Frances' espionage?'

'Definitely confirmation of some very underhand activities.'

'I see. Very well, I will seek out Gustav now.'

'I'll come with you.'

'Harvey. I really do not think that will be necessary. He is my research assistant after all. If this is as serious as it looks then it could be a sacking offence.'

'Okay. But when, if, you find him. You will let me know if he's told anyone about anything?'

'I will do my best Harvey. And I will see you both in my office tomorrow, alright?'

'Alright.'

'And you will leave this to me. Not say anything if you see him?'

'Alright.'

'Until tomorrow?'

'Alright.'

Giles Skeffington was urgently craning his head around and above the crowd of masks, gowns and tailcoats, trying to discern the presence of Rick Callow. To see him approaching, waving toward him, in a rather ruffled, urgent manner wasn't what he'd expected, but then neither was the thought that Rick would be responsible for stealing from the collections.

The stupidity of the man beggared belief. However, stupidity could be forgiven as an unfortunate trait that ran somewhat beyond one's control. No one set out to be stupid. However, what he suspected Rick to be guilty of went further than stupidity. Though coupled with it, perhaps explained the mendacity of an act beyond reason; worse than dereliction of duty and abuse of trust, which Rick's position ought to have held as inconceivable. No, what he appeared to have done spoke of such a degree of disrespect for himself, Laudanum Grange and the scholarly community, Giles found himself in a state of highly agitated disbelief; faced with something that at once made no sense, yet seemed to be entirely self-explanatory.

The announcement of the final dance was made. As Giles and Rick were closing on one another, Meredith Ferryweather stepped into Giles' path. 'It's our dance Giles'.

'Not now. I have more important things to do,' he said, trying to bursh past her towards Rick.

'Well I...' She bustled after Giles, a clutch bag swinging from her hand.

'Giles, good,' said Rick, as they met, 'I need to speak to you urgently. Very urgently,'

Meredith Ferryweather imposed her stout frame between Rick and Giles, who stumbled back a couple of paces. 'Rick. Giles has just been very rude,' she said.

'Wha.?' said Rick.

'You asked me to dance with Giles and now he's refusing,' her face flushing red.

'Not now, Meredith, I'll dance later,' said Giles, his head peering around her shoulder towards Rick.

'But this is the last one. I put him down especially as a favour for you Rick.'

'Look I'm sorry Meredith, I can't do this now,' said Giles, trying again to push past the broad pillar of Meredith Ferryweather to get closer to Rick as the tide of expectant dancers eddied around her, carrying him further away and on to the dance floor.

'He's right Meredith, there is an emergency,' said Rick.

'Emergency. I see no emergency, other than I have no dance partner.'

The quartet struck up the introductory music as the crowd formed into two long lines of couples, paired off with one another. A pair of burly hands grabbed Giles from behind by the shoulders and turning him, positioned him roughly in the line of male dancers. He turned to see one of the Yorkshire Society of Regency Dancers grinning squarely at him.

'I'm not dancing you bloody fool,' said Giles, his voice rising as he pushed back towards Rick, Meredith once again blocking him off.

'Look you bloody woman I have to talk to Rick now.'

Meredith Ferryweather turned and brought her bag down smartly on

Giles' head who raised his hands to fend her off. 'I_have_ never_ been_ so_ insulted,' shouted Meredith, punctuating each word with a swipe at Giles' head. The lines of dancers became distracted, half turning away from their steps and watching the fracas.

'Meredith stop', Giles shouted, trying to dodge the blows, 'I have to talk to Rick. He has things to explain.'

The dancers came to a stop with the musicians squeaking to a fractured halt.

'Why you insulted me being one of them I presume,' a flustered Meredith Ferryweather blurted out.

'No, it is not. He has been stealing from the collections,' shouted Giles.

'Are you ready?'

'I'm ready.'

A loud burst of dirty, pumping gay disco blared through the great hall. Meredith Ferryweather along with the rest of the crowd cowered at the volume. The sound came from behind the closed doors to the hall. A deep blue light throbbed with the electronic bass against the doors. A detonation of baroque electronica burst forth as the doors opened releasing billowing waves of dry ice. The rolling tide of smoke ran around the fashionable calves and ladies hems. The crowd gasped. Screams of ripped white noise jagged across the hall as an anthemic surge welled out of the doorway. Two figures appeared. Silhouettes against the singeing light of the strobe, they paraded out of the mist into the carnelian red light.

One, an impossibly tall figure wearing a black devil's mask, clad in gothic steam punk, ruby red, western bridal wear; multiple layers of chiffon, lace, and silk spilling widely over his hips, his waist cinched tightly in a matching corset, spreading up to a heaving bosom that any madam would be proud of. His head was crowned with a tall top hat. Over seven feet of wild west, malevolent whore.

The second, was dressed as a gentleman's assassin. A tailcoat over a corset, with an industrial punk bolero of feathered rubber around her shoulders, high heeled, long spiked, daemon boots, stockings, suspenders, and a bowler hat tipped on her head. Her mask cut from black leather, an asymmetrical cascade angled across her face, in a sensuous, lacy filigree. A perverted Moriarty voguing a Rococo Phantom.

EPILOGUE

Press Release.

Laudanum Grange in association with Oxford University Press is pleased to announce the publication of *The Morocco Manuscripts* by Dr. Harvey Dominic Premnas and Fenella Morningstar.

The first investigation into these recently discovered documents has provided a startling reassessment of the role of Jane Austen's brother, Francis Austen, before, during and after, The Battle of Trafalgar.

This first part of an on-going project led by Dr. Premnas, whose PhD was awarded on the basis of this, *The Morocco Manuscripts* takes us into the newly opened heart of a debate about who was doing what, and to what ends, during the wars between Britain and Napoleonic France. Featuring a cast of historical figures, including; Fanny Burney, The Austen Family, Talleyrand, Warren Hastings and Pitt The Younger, the work is an analytical, historical and bibliographic study of *The Morocco Manuscripts*, which suggests a major re-interpretation of the motivations and actions of many of these figures is now required. Not least being those of Francis Austen, later to become Admiral of the Fleet, whom, the documents suggest, was involved with an international spy network set upon betraying Britain and furthering the prospects for a victorious Napoleon.

Newly appointed CEO of Laudanum Grange, Dr. Pamela Larrup said:

"The work of Dr. Premnas has been exemplary. Without him the revelations that have been suggested by the manuscripts would have been nowhere as near well formulated, nor would we have acquired the funding for further research. It has been a challenging time for Laudanum Grange financially, but now, with the international attention attracted by his research, and so ably assisted by Dr. Gustav Crumb and Ms. Morningstar, we have very substantial international donations, with ongoing commitments, which will see both this project and the future of Laudanum Grange secured for years to come. It is a substantial achievement."

After the death of Nelson, Captain Francis Austen faced a dilemma. Burning the documents would be one answer, however, to do so would mean he would have no evidence of his part in the British victory. No memory for the future.

Having followed the admiral's orders and sailed the Canopus, along with five other ships to Gibraltar, ostensibly to re-supply the fleet, he had missed the battle. This was expected and something he'd been instructed to do, presenting a frustrated and annoyed face to the other officers – missing out on the prestige, honours and prizes that such a victory conferred was a loss to them all. Not that this caused him as much annoyance as he liked to pretend. Any losses would be more than made up by the garlands bestowed as part of the expedition to Gibraltar. Or, at least, that had been the idea. He was now supposed to be savouring the fruits of a longer game he had introduced to the admiral and which they had planned together to ensure the victory. With the admiral's death, however, the only account of this was now contained in the letters and manuscripts now sitting in the leather satchel in front of him on the desk of his ready room. Which he'd written despite the admiral's orders.

The admiral had insisted there be no record, that all his instructions be memorised, and should Austen be caught by the British, he would have to deny all knowledge of his actions. To do otherwise would have compromised the other agents in the network in France. He would have to be seen to be punished to maintain their cover.

Having brought the plan to Nelson this was not something he had expected. It had arisen out of conversations with his sister, Jane. She had speculated on the way his associations with the exiled French emigres at Juniper Hall could be used to nurture contacts in Napoleon's regime; that should he appear sympathetic to the French cause it may cast him as a favourable source; and if he could earn their trust he could pass on information that could be used to mislead them, aiding British interests. At the time he had thought this a little fanciful, the type of thing that she might contrive for one of the characters in her stories. Though he'd told himself he had continued to make favourable relations with the émigrés just as any gentleman might have, this later became part of a grander scheme he imagined for himself once the fortunes of those same émigrés changed with the rise of Napoleon, and the emergence of Fanny Burney from the shadows. He'd used this as a gambit to oust competition for Nelson's favour among his fellow officers. That this worked, naturally, pleased him.

However, the notion that he may become a sacrificial scapegoat, dishonouring his family, losing the position and favour he had so lately garnered, meant that keeping a written account seemed more than prudent, and potentially beneficial financially, regardless of the admiral's orders.

Of course, what neither of them had conceived, was that the admiral himself should have lost his life. Once complete victory over the French was assured, on land as well as sea, Nelson was supposed to inform all and sundry of Francis' part in their defeat; of his meeting with a Spanish go between in Gibraltar; how he'd risked his life and honour to misinform him of the strength, armament, preparedness and morale of the British fleet; how this had been relayed to Villeneuve, the commander of a weakened, disgruntled fleet moored in Cadiz; and how this was crucial in persuading him to sail for battle despite light winds. That Nelson was currently laid out on the table in his cabin on The Victory was really most annoying.

Now all he had were the documents. If he were to publicise them he may appear boastful. Without the admiral's corroboration it might be construed by his peers as a vainglorious attempt to enhance his reputation. He'd seen their jealous looks. It would have been so much more convenient if Nelson were alive. However, if he weren't to alert the admiralty, history would record that it was Nelson's genius that had won the day, and with him dying in battle, immortalised as the saviour of the nation. Though undoubtedly a talented admiral, to deny his own part in the victory would see the future only recalled him as a captain. It was Jane's fault. If she hadn't planted the idea he wouldn't be facing this predicament. Those fictions she wasted her time on had fed an imagination that left him the victim of one of her whimsies.

He looked towards the satchel on the table. Discretion would be the better part of honour. Probably what a gentleman should do. However, to have missed the battle and the promised rewards for his subterfuge, why, it would test the manners of any man. He sighed as he lit a taper from the oil lamp on his table. He contemplated it momentarily before blowing it out. He took the satchel from the table, levered up a loose floorboard with his sword and dropped it into the hollow. That would do for now.

***

The leaving cake had not been in the shape of a heart but it was this that he had decided to follow after resigning from Laudanum Grange. Rick Callow had always suspected that service was his forte. It was, after all, the purist form of motives. Whereas in ordinary employment once you'd got a job, well that was it. There was little need to continue to justify one's actions with efforts beyond the perfunctory. Simply required to tick along and tick the boxes. Especially when you were the boss. He realised that this had been the problem at Laudanum. People hadn't expected enough of him. He had simply not been required to rise to the expectations that he'd normally have set for himself and, as he'd always sought to please, so he'd simply lived down to their presumptions. In the end he had been let down and now Laudanum Grange had to get along without him. However, this had provided him with the opportunity that he'd always suspected would be his. Now, with the freedom bestowed by his decision to resign, that apparently some people believed had been required, he could give free range to his true calling. To serve. He knew he had always been destined to do so. Not simply just to lead, the calling of ordinary mortals, but to serve. To know that each day he was required to continually renew his commitment to the faith that people placed in him. To struggle for their needs and aspirations. What purer form of occupation could there be? And one that he knew had been born to but which had only formed its opportune nature amidst his departure from Laudanum Grange.

Having been invited to do so by Nigel Fromage, a friend from university and leader of the recently formed Coalition Against The National Imposition of Parliaments or CATNIP, he was going to enter politics.

ABOUT THE AUTHOR

Bruce Sinclair worked as a musician, gardener and a teacher before returning to university in his forties to complete a masters in Security Studies at University College London. He currently lives in the North East of England. *Cringe* is his first novel.

Printed in Great Britain
by Amazon

17386233R00122